DEATH IN AMBUSH

DEATH IN AMBUSH

A Lost Christmas Murder Mystery

SUSAN GILRUTH

with an introduction by
MARTIN EDWARDS

BRITISH LIBRARY

This edition first published in 2025 by
The British Library
96 Euston Road
London NW1 2DB
bl.uk

1 3 5 7 9 10 8 6 4 2

Death in Ambush was first published in 1952
by Robert Hale Ltd, London.

Represented in the EU by Authorised Rep Compliance
Ltd., Ground Floor, 71 Lower Baggot Street, Dublin,
D02 P593, Ireland. arccompliance.com

Cataloguing in Publication Data
A catalogue record for this publication is
available from the British Library

ISBN 978 0 7123 5588 9
e-ISBN 978 0 7123 6889 6

Original cover illustration by Gwen White,
© Medici/Mary Evans Picture Library.
Text design and typesetting by Tetragon, London
Printed in England by CPI Group (UK) Ltd, Croydon, CR0 4YY

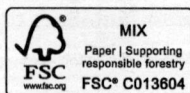

MIX
Paper | Supporting
responsible forestry
FSC® C013604

CONTENTS

INTRODUCTION

Death in Ambush is a witty whodunit set in the Christmas season and narrated by the likeable if impulsive Liane "Lee" Craufurd. If she'd been the sort of person who believed in evil omens, Lee says, she'd never have accepted an invitation to spend a few weeks at Christmas with her friend Betty Sandys and her family. But as she adds, in rather characteristic fashion, "we all disliked the victim so heartily that nobody could screw up much actual grief on that score; but all the same it was an upsetting thing to happen…"

Betty and her husband Howard, a doctor, live in Staple Green, a quintessential English village in the south of England. It is a truth universally acknowledged that a quintessential English village will prove to be a hotbed of murder, mystery, and intrigue, and Staple Green certainly doesn't disappoint in these respects. A major consolation for Lee is that when murder is done, Scotland Yard are called in, and she gets a chance to renew her acquaintance with Detective-Inspector Hugh Gordon. Their flirtatious relationship is a pleasing if unorthodox (given that Lee is married and her husband Bill is expected to arrive on Christmas Day) ingredient of the story. Lee acts, in effect, as an unofficial Dr. Watson to Hugh's Sherlock Holmes, although he indulges her curiosity to a degree that in a less forgiving environment would surely call for disciplinary action.

The victim's wife is lured away from home by a bogus telephone call, a familiar trope in detective fiction. One of Susan Gilruth's in-jokes is to give two characters in her story the surname

Qualtrough. This was the unusual alias adopted by the phone call hoaxer in the real-life Wallace murder in Liverpool in 1931; sure enough, the original case is directly referenced in the penultimate chapter of the book.

Although this was only her second novel, she shifts suspicion around from one character to another with a practised ease. The characters are nicely drawn and the plot sound. Overall, the quality of *Death in Ambush* (also the title of a novel by John Bude, published seven years before this book) is such that it is a shame that both novel and author have for so long languished in obscurity.

Susan Gilruth produced seven detective novels over the course of thirteen years, but during her lifetime none appear to have been published in the United States, although there were at least a couple of translations. As a result, the books soon went out of print and for many years most of them have been hard to find. At the time of writing this introduction, no copy of *Death in Ambush* was available for sale online anywhere in the world. So it is a particular pleasure to resurrect this novel.

Information about Susan Gilruth is hard to come by. Her books have been almost universally ignored in reference works about the genre, with the notable exception of the first volume of Colleen Barnett's *Mystery Women: An Encyclopedia of Leading Women Characters in Mystery Fiction*; I've consulted the third edition, from 2006. I'm also indebted to Barry Pike, a long-time enthusiast for her books, and Jamie Sturgeon, for filling the gaps in my knowledge.

She was born Susannah Margaret Hornsby-Wright in Rochester in 1911, the only child of Lionel Bache and Margaret Eveline Hornsby-Wright. Her father was a popular science master at Sherborne School; in his obituary in 1953, the school magazine described him as a "vivid, vital and original personality", particularly remembered for "his whimsical sense of humour, which never failed to come bubbling up, even in what sometimes appeared to be the most adverse circumstances." Susan Gilruth's lively writing suggests that she inherited his sense of fun.

It is interesting to note that Sherborne was the school where Anthony Berkeley Cox, better known to fans of the British Library's Crime Classics as Anthony Berkeley and Francis Iles, was educated. He kept in touch with the school in later years and, although he was not taught by Susan Gilruth's father, it is possible that the two men knew each other. Whether Berkeley was acquainted with Susan Gilruth is unknown, but there is one fascinating coincidence. Sharp-eyed readers of the Crime Classics edition of Berkeley's *Not to Be Taken* will have spotted that, in March 1938, she was (as Mrs. S. M. Gilruth) the joint winner of the first prize offered for solving the mystery when the story was serialised in *John o'London's Weekly* magazine. So, by that time, she was clearly a fan of detective fiction and also accomplished at unravelling ingenious puzzles. *Not to Be Taken* is, like *Death in Ambush*, a mystery about a poisoning in an English village, although the storylines are quite different.

Susan was educated at Sherborne School for Girls and Saint Felix School, Southwold, and took a degree at University College London. In 1937 she married a Scottish doctor, James Gordon Anderson Gilruth, and during the Second World War she was employed in the War Office and later by a firm of publicity agents in London. At one point she lived at 7 Reston Place, Hyde Park Gate, which she described as a mews cottage with an attractive garden; her third novel *Postscript to Penelope* (1954) was set in a West London mews.

She and her husband drifted apart, and were divorced some time before 1948, when James Gilruth married Laetitia Russell Spry Lillico (now there is a name that deserves to belong to a character in a Crime Classic mystery…). Susan herself remarried in 1971. Her second husband was Major Maurice Godley, a former Queen's Diplomatic Service Messenger. She wrote some light verse and a few short stories, but her main literary focus was the detective novel.

Her first book, *Sweet Revenge*, set in Cornwall, was published by Robert Hale in 1951. Hale had an eye for talent, although, because they aimed mainly at the library market, copies of older editions in pleasing condition are often hard, if not impossible to find. In this novel, Lee meets Hugh Gordon for the first time and a mutual attraction soon develops between them. Lee, to some extent a self-portrait, had, like her creator, worked in the War Office during the war. Whether the fictional romance with Hugh Gordon was inspired by developments in Susan's own life is a matter for conjecture.

Her accomplishment as a writer led to her being picked up by Hodder, who published her next four novels, starting with *A Corpse for Charybdis* (1956). This book, incidentally, received praise from Berkeley when, writing as Francis Iles, he reviewed it for *The Times*, saying: "Susan Gilruth has a pleasant, light touch." In 1968, the story was adapted for broadcast as a five-part serial on BBC radio, with a cast led by Frederick Treves.

Never a prolific author, Susan Gilruth said that her special interests, besides music, poetry and gardening, included lying in the sun, "preferably beside the Mediterranean or Adriatic", adding that her ambition was to own a villa in southern Italy. Lee shared her creator's enthusiasm for warmer climes. *Drown Her Remembrance* (1961) saw her holidaying in Majorca, while *The Snake Is Living Yet* (1963) is set in Tangier and was adapted for BBC radio in 1964. By this time, Lee and her husband Bill have separated, and conveniently Hugh has taken a job with Interpol, which allows him to come to Tangier to investigate the murder of an undercover agent.

And with that, Susan Gilruth's career as a crime writer came to an end. Perhaps she was frustrated by lack of literary success; perhaps she felt written out; perhaps she simply preferred to lie in the sun. Not even the satisfaction of having *A Corpse for Charybdis* adapted for radio seems to have been enough to tempt her out of literary retirement. She is a good example of an author who produced enjoyable mysteries that disappeared from public view all too soon, but which do not deserve oblivion. I much enjoyed reading *Death in Ambush* and I hope that Crime Classics fans will find it a delightful Christmas treat.

MARTIN EDWARDS

www.martinedwardsbooks.com

A NOTE FROM THE PUBLISHER

The original novels and short stories reprinted in the British Library Crime Classics series were written and published in a period ranging, for the most part, from the 1890s to the 1960s. There are many elements of these stories which continue to entertain modern readers; however, in some cases there are also uses of language, instances of stereotyping and some attitudes expressed by narrators or characters which may not be endorsed by the publishing standards of today. We acknowledge therefore that some elements in the works selected for reprinting may continue to make uncomfortable reading for some of our audience. With this series British Library Publishing aims to offer a new readership a chance to read some of the rare books of the British Library's collections in an affordable paperback format, to enjoy their merits and to look back into the world of the twentieth century as portrayed by its writers. It is not possible to separate these stories from the history of their writing and therefore the following novel is presented as it was originally published with minor edits only made for consistency of style and sense. We welcome feedback from our readers, which can be sent to the following address:

British Library Publishing
The British Library
96 Euston Road
London, NW1 2DB
United Kingdom

Some fell by laudanum, and some by steel;
And death in ambush lay in every pill.

SIR SAMUEL GARTH—*The Dispensary*

People in the Story

Howard Sandys, M.R.C.S., L.R.C.P, *of Tithe Barn, Staple Green.*
Betty Sandys, *his wife.*
Sara Sandys, *his daughter.*
Robin Sandys, *his son.*
Liane Craufurd, *a guest.*

Sir Henry Metcalfe, *a retired Judge, of Oakhurst Place, Staple Green.*
Diana Metcalfe, *his wife.*
Michael Metcalfe, *his son.*

John Wickham, *an agent, of The Lodge, Oakhurst Place.*

Lewis Qualtrough, *an art dealer, of Little Hodges, Staple Green.*
Ann Qualtrough, *his daughter.*

Sonia Phillips, *a widow, of Holly Tree Cottage, Lower Bunnet.*

Mrs. Prendergast, *of The Vicarage, Staple Green.*

Norah Wright, *a dispenser, of Bankside, Staple Green.*

Mr. Willis, *landlord of The Blue Boar, Staple Green.*

Dick Henderson, *a solicitor, of Birling Road, Tunbridge Wells.*
Sheila Henderson, *his wife.*

Detective-Inspector Hugh Gordon, C.I.D.
Sergeant Spragg, C.I.D.

I

MRS. DOSE THE DOCTOR'S WIFE

If I'd been the sort of person who believes in presentiments and evil omens and all that sort of thing, I suppose I'd never have accepted Betty Sandys' invitation to spend a few weeks at Christmas in their house at Staple Green—and would thus have escaped becoming involved in a lot of subsequent unpleasantness. As far as the murder went, we all disliked the victim so heartily that nobody could screw up much actual grief on that score; but all the same it was an upsetting thing to happen and caused a good deal of distress one way and another in the village.

The day Betty's letter arrived was Friday the 13th of November, and I remember the coincidence particularly because it was the day the old gilt convex mirror in the hall of our flat fell off the wall for no apparent reason and broke into thousands of pieces. Very strange, we said, sweeping up the bits—you might almost call it sinister; and if we'd been the sort of people who were worried by superstition we'd have felt quite nervous. It never occurred to anyone to regard Betty's letter as the Third Omen on that fateful day. I simply showed it to Bill, my husband, and we agreed it was very nice of Betty and Howard to ask us down for Christmas and we'd go. And that was that.

Two days before we had arranged to travel to Kent I upset the contents of a salt cellar all over the dining room carpet and on my way to fetch the Hoover to clear it up I met Bill holding a telegram which had just arrived. It was from the War Office ordering him to report back to his Battalion H.Q. the following afternoon.

"Oh, God," I said, my heart sinking like lead. "I'm sure that means Korea."

Bill put the telegram down on the hall table and pulled his pipe out of his pocket. He didn't answer at once, and by the time he had refilled the pipe and was fumbling for the matches I was a widow. I'd been through it all and had just reached the point of deciding that I should have to take a job because I wouldn't be able to live on my pension, income tax being what it is, when Bill said casually through a puff of smoke: "Oh, I shouldn't think so. Much more likely some damn silly course at the Staff College."

And so, of course, it ultimately turned out to be. I dismissed the salt episode from my mind and as there seemed a good prospect of Bill being able to get down to Staple Green at least by Christmas Day, I telephoned to Betty to say I would come as planned and Bill would follow when he could.

"Good," Betty said. "Howard's in the middle of a 'flu epidemic and I've hardly set eyes on him for a week, so I've practically got to the stage of talking to myself in the evenings, after the children are in bed. I'm terribly disappointed about Bill, but we'll just have to hope for the best—that he can get away for Christmas."

Howard Sandys was a doctor and he and Betty lived in an attractive old house called the Tithe Barn. I'd seen photographs of it, but for some reason fate had prevented every plan I had made to stay with them since the beginning of the war, so I had never been to Staple Green and hadn't seen Sara, the elder child, since she was a baby, or Robin, now aged six, at all. That is partly what I mean about the omens. They'd always been against my going to Staple Green—and maybe they were right.

There were two more incidents of the salt-cellar kind the day I went down to Kent. Bill went off to Camberley in the morning and I later rang up for a taxi. When it arrived I noticed idly that the driver had the most appalling squint. Even then I never thought of holding my thumbs or whatever it is one is supposed to do when a cross-eyed stranger darkens one's path. All I said was: "Charing Cross, please—and as quickly as you can, because I'm rather late for my train."

As I subsided breathlessly into the corner of a half empty carriage, I caught sight of a large black suitcase on the rack above the vacant seat opposite. It had a label which said: "DEATH—Passenger to Tunbridge Wells." Somehow that did shake me slightly, but I pulled myself together and thought "So what?" Lots of people are called Death—only they usually spell it De'Ath and pronounce it in two syllables. I resolutely absorbed myself in an evening paper and gave the thing no further thought.

That night after dinner we were sitting in front of a cheerful log blaze in the big open fireplace of the Sandys' drawing-room, and I was thinking what a charming house they had and how glad I was I'd come, when Betty suddenly put down her coffee cup and remarked to her husband: "By the way, I did tell you, didn't I, that I've asked the Metcalfes in for a drink tomorrow evening?"

She said it in the defensive tone of one who knows she has done nothing of the kind, and Howard looked up at once with a slight frown of annoyance.

"You certainly didn't," he grumbled. "You know I can't bear the sight of that man—and I thought you couldn't either. Why on earth—?"

"Diana's one of my greatest friends," Betty interrupted indignantly. "And I couldn't ask her without Sir Henry. I've asked them in to meet that new woman who's just come to live at Lower

Bunnet. You know, the attractive widow who's taken Holly Tree Cottage."

"Oh," said Howard noncommittally. "Well, I expect I shall be in surgery."

Betty shot him a look of reproach. "I *had* to do something about her. She's been here for over a month and she hardly knows anybody. I think she must be very lonely, so when I met her in the village this morning I asked her to come round for a drink."

"Why the Metcalfes?"

"I gather she's met Michael somewhere—and after all they are neighbours. I wanted her to know Diana."

Howard flung down *The Times* crossword puzzle with a grunt of dissatisfaction. "The clue is 'Sic transit mundi'," he announced gloomily. "And the answer is a word of seven letters begining with 'i'—the third letter 'h'."

"It can't be," I said, picking it up. "It's impossible. Anyway, it ought to be 'Sic transit *gloria* mundi'. Why have they left out 'gloria'?"

Howard grabbed the paper back out of my hand.

"Bless you, Lee," he said. "I can quite understand why you are such an invaluable asset to Scotland Yard. Of course that's it! The answer is 'Ichabod'—'and the glory is departed'."

"Oh," I said weakly. The crack about Scotland Yard was a little unkind, I felt, just because I had once acted as an amateur Watson where my rôle had been to supply fragmentary clues that I couldn't see the answer to, and then to watch somebody else unravelling the thing from my unwitting information.

"Anyway," Betty said returning to her attack on Howard, "I'm relying on you to get through surgery as quickly as you can and help me with Sir Henry. The only things in the world he's interested in are market gardening and oriental china and I don't know the first thing about either of them."

"And the law," Howard reminded her. "You might get up a cosy discussion on the Hargreaves case. Wasn't he responsible for hanging that unfortunate woman?"

"Oh," I exclaimed, enlightened. "Are you talking about Mr. Justice Metcalfe? The judge?"

"Yes, but he's retired now on health grounds. Not that there's anything much the matter with him, except chronic bad temper. He's our local squire—or likes to think he is. They live in the big house with the impressive lodge gates on the green—oh, I forgot, you haven't been up to the village yet, have you, Lee?"

"No," I answered. "But of course I've seen his name in the papers. Was he supposed to be a good judge?"

"About as good as Judge Jefferies I should imagine." Howard said. "And in many ways very like him. A thoroughly unattractive character, Lee. I'm sorry Betty's thrusting him on you the second evening of your visit—I should have thought we could have raised somebody a bit less poisonous than old Metcalfe."

"Well, I'm sorry," Betty said. "I admit I really wasn't thinking of Lee at all. But you'll like Diana, Lee—you couldn't help it. She's one of the sweetest people I know."

"And why she ever married Sir Henry is an unsolved mystery," Howard put in, returning to his crossword.

"She's his second wife," Betty explained to me. "The first wife died when the two children were quite small and Diana married him about fifteen years ago. She's been the most wonderful stepmother to Sheila and Michael and they both adore her. In fact I don't know how they'd have survived without her, because there's no doubt Howard's right—he *is* a horrible old man, and he's been beastly to both his children. Diana's always stood up for them and fought their battles for them. There's a major fuss going on at the moment because Michael, who's twenty-three, is terribly keen to go on the stage and Sir Henry doesn't approve of the idea. And there was another fearful row when Sheila got married about five years ago. Of course she was only twenty, but her husband's a very pleasant young man—nothing wrong with him, except that he hasn't got much money. He's a struggling junior partner in a firm of solicitors over in Tunbridge Wells. They live in a little house in Birling Road and have two babies—Diana says they're very happy but perennially broke. Sir Henry refuses to do anything to help them and even went so far as to forbid Diana to do anything either."

"I bet Diana does, all the same," Howard said. "I can't see anyone appealing to her in vain. But I think old Metcalfe takes a sadistic delight in bullying people—especially his own family."

"I can't understand an attitude like that," Betty said. "It's inconceivable to me how any man can behave in the way Sir Henry does to his own children. He's got nothing against Dick Henderson—that's Sheila's husband—and he could perfectly well afford to help them with a little money. But just because Dick's family aren't rich and titled he considered Sheila threw herself away and he's washed his hands of the whole thing. And now he's going to do exactly the same with Michael and Ann."

"Who's Ann?" I asked.

"Ann Qualtrough—Michael's fiancée. She and her father live in the village. He's an art dealer—or he was. They haven't got any money either, and Ann is studying at the R.A.D.A. I think that's really why Michael wants to go on the stage. Sir Henry's dead against it and he blames Ann for influencing Michael. He'll break that up too, you'll see, if he gets half a chance."

Howard rose and threw a couple of logs on to the fire. "One of these days," he remarked with a yawn, "Diana will reach the end of her tether and she'll run away with John Wickham, and I for one shan't blame her."

"Howard," Betty said sharply, "you mustn't say things like that! You know there's absolutely *nothing* to—"

At that moment the front door bell rang.

"Hell," muttered Howard, picking up his paper and making for the door. "Betty, if that's a patient—unless it's something really urgent—you're sorry but I'm out on a case." He escaped towards the study.

"I'd better go," Betty said with a sigh. "I expect Mrs. Padgett's gone to bed. I don't think Howard's expecting a baby or anything, but you never know—"

In the hall I heard a young man's voice raised in apology. "I'm sorry to disturb you," he was saying, "but I really just looked in to see if Ann was here."

"No, Michael, she isn't," Betty said. "Why, have you been along to the Qualtroughs?"

"Yes, and the old man said she was out. He didn't know where she'd gone, so I thought she might have popped in on you."

"Perhaps she's round at the Prendergasts," Betty suggested. "Come in, Michael. Lee, this is Michael Metcalfe—Mrs. Craufurd."

A good looking young man with dark hair and restless hazel eyes came into the room. He was of medium height, slim, and very carefully dressed. The general impression was that he was just a bit too pleased with himself. He spoke in a clear rather high-pitched voice and was apt to wave his hands about when he talked. I found myself thinking that if and when he ever went on the stage he would have to learn how to move less jerkily.

He refused Betty's offer of a drink and proceeded to prowl aimlessly round the room.

"I didn't know you had anyone staying," he said rather resentfully, "or I wouldn't have barged in."

"That's all right, Michael. What's the trouble?"

"Oh, nothing more than usual," the young man mumbled. "You know my delightful parent. There was another of the famous family bickers at lunch today, so I simply couldn't face the idea of a tête-à-tête evening alone with him, and I thought I'd run Ann over to the cinema in Tunbridge Wells."

"Isn't Diana at home?" Betty asked casually.

"Monday," explained Michael briefly. "It's her Women's Institute night. There are evenings when one could wish Diana wasn't quite so assiduous in her good works about the village. The only time Oakhurst is bearable is when she's there."

"Oh, of course, I'd forgotten it was Monday. Would you like some coffee, Michael? I can easily heat it up again."

"No, thanks very much," Michael said. He continued to stand fidgeting by the window, and I wondered if he wanted to unburden himself to Betty about the family fracas. I was about to murmur some tactful excuse and leave them to it, when he swung round abruptly from the window and ran his hand through his dark curly hair.

"It's really getting altogether beyond a joke," he burst out suddenly. "Do forgive me, Mrs. Craufurd, but I'm a bit on edge. Betty, Ann came to lunch today and my father was so rude to her that in the end she simply walked out of the house. Well, I mean—honestly! That's a nice state of affairs isn't it."

He uttered a forced laugh. "It was all so *silly* really. It started over father's boring china collection. He will go *on* about it so, and nobody else is in the least interested whether this beastly jar he was showing Ann was Ch'ing or whatever it's supposed to be—and still less in long lectures on under-glazes and graded washes and so forth. It was a very ordinary looking blue-and-white thing with a lid—you know, he's got several of them and I don't think they're particularly rare or valuable. Anyway, Ann bore it for a long time and then she said how very interesting, and added that her father had a jar just like it at home. The old man got quite excited when he heard that and started asking about the date and so on, and then Ann said: 'Oh, about 1950, I should think. We got it from Mr. Perkins' shop last Christmas full of stem ginger.' Well, of course I laughed; but the old man was absolutely furious and said the most unforgivable things to Ann—called her an impertinent play-acting schoolgirl, and said she'd insulted him and that remarks of that kind weren't funny, they were just plain bad taste; and in the end if it hadn't been for Diana I think we'd practically have had a stand-up fight. After Ann had gone, I went back and told my father I thought it was a pretty poor show talking to my fiancée like that and I considered he ought to apologise to her; and he simply laughed in that sneering beastly way he has and said he certainly didn't propose at his time of life to go round apologising to ignorant impertinent little girls with no manners, and if Ann didn't like his opinion of her she'd better keep out of his house. I said she wasn't likely to want to come into it again after being spoken to like that, and he said that suited him. So there it is. And now you can see why I wasn't very keen to spend the evening alone with my dear papa."

"Oh, Michael, I expect it will soon blow over," Betty said soothingly. "After all your father is a collector of some experience and it was a bit naughty of Ann to tease him like that."

"Well, I suppose it was silly of her," Michael admitted. "She is apt to be a shade tactless with him—I've often asked her not to go out of her way to rile him. But you know how outspoken Ann is."

Betty nodded.

"It's all so wearing," Michael complained. "Oh, well, I'm sorry to have bored you with our domestic squabbles. As Ann isn't here I may as well look in at the Prendergasts and if I can't find her I shall go back. Diana will be in about ten, and with any luck the old man will have incarcerated himself in the study by now and I shan't have to see him again."

He moved towards the door.

"Goodnight, Michael," Betty said. "Oh, by the way, we'll be seeing you tomorrow evening if not before. I asked your father and Diana in for a drink to meet a new neighbour. I think you know her, don't you—Mrs. Phillips from Holly Tree Cottage?"

Michael stood with his hand on the doorknob.

"Mrs. Phillips?" he echoed rather stupidly.

"Yes. She told me she'd met you at some party. Do you know her well? I thought she seemed charming."

"I hardly know her at all," Michael said formally. "But I agree she looks very attractive."

The conversation languished again and a few minutes later Michael Metcalfe left.

Howard returned from his study.

"Was that Michael?" he asked. "If I'd known that, I wouldn't have bothered to go to ground. Lee, have a drink?"

"No, thank you," I replied. "As a matter of fact I'm awfully tired and I'd like to go to bed quite soon."

Betty came upstairs with me.

"I'm beginning to see what you mean about Sir Henry," I remarked as Betty turned on the light of my room.

"Nasty old brute," Betty said with unwonted viciousness. "The best thing that could happen to him would be death."

"And who would you cast for the part of the first murderer?" I asked lightly. "There'd be a good selection of suspects."

"Oh," Betty said, a little taken aback, "I didn't mean anything quite as stringent as murder. I was thinking of a nice convenient apoplectic fit or something. Lee, have you got everything you want?"

I assured her that I had.

"I'll just close this window a bit," Betty said, going over and pulling back the curtains. "It's freezing hard outside. Oh look, Lee—the new moon! Isn't it pretty?"

I stood beside her regarding the thin shining crescent through the glass pane of the window. Suddenly I felt myself shivering.

"Lee, you're cold! I'm so sorry—I should have put the fire on earlier," Betty exclaimed in compunction.

"No," I said slowly. "It isn't cold. It was just a goose walking over my grave. Goodnight, Betty—sleep well."

II

ROUND THE BINS

WHEN I WOKE UP THE NEXT MORNING AND LOOKED OUT of the window I thought for a moment that it must have been snowing during the night. Then I saw that it was really a thick frost which had had the effect of turning the lawn into a glittering white arena which, with the bare tree-trunks behind silhouetted sharply against the pale sky, would have made an extremely suitable back-cloth for a ballet setting of the "Snow Queen." The garden looked still and silent and bitterly cold.

After breakfast Betty said she had various things to do in the village and asked me if I would like to go with her.

We muffled ourselves in several layers of cardigans and overcoats, put on fur-lined boots and set out. Howard had taken the Daimler on his rounds and Betty's little Morris was being greased at the garage, so we walked.

It was only a short distance to the village green, and we strolled up the lane admiring the wonderful patterns of filigree lace made by the spiders' webs which hung festooned all over the high hedges, sparkling in the chilly sunshine, and the way each blade of grass on the verge stood out stiff and encrusted with thick frost.

The lane opened out into a wide green triangle with the church on one side and cottages all round. A few of these had been converted into shops, the main one being a kind of general store-cum-post-office with a shiny red public telephone box outside.

On the corner of the green next to the church stood two impressive stone pillars with ancient carved eagles on top enclosing a pair of fine old iron gates. There was a small lodge just inside the gates, and a winding drive lined with rhododendron bushes led up to the house which was out of sight, hidden among a clump of trees.

"That's Oakhurst Place, where the Metcalfes live," Betty remarked. "John Wickham has the lodge—he's their sort of agent. Sir Henry took up market gardening some time ago as a hobby but he didn't know very much about fruit trees, so they imported John Wickham to look after the orchards. He spent several years farming in British Columbia and Diana says it's wonderful what a difference he's made to the place in the last two years."

"Oh, yes," I said, remembering. "He's the person Diana Metcalfe's going to run away with when Sir Henry gets too insufferable. Would Howard have any grounds for saying that?"

The same look of annoyance came over Betty's face as I had noticed the previous night.

"Of course not," she said crossly. "I wish Howard wouldn't say such stupid things. Of course it doesn't matter with you, Lee, but you know how silly people in villages are about gossip. John Wickham's always been devoted to Diana—well, why shouldn't he be? She's a charming woman and I'm very fond of her myself. Everybody here loves her. But—oh well, it's true what Howard was saying about Sir Henry—he's a sour old thing, and John—quite naturally—resents his manner to Diana. He's sometimes awfully rude to her in public and John's a bit apt to try to interfere. It's a difficult position, you see. John's an employee of Sir Henry's and although it's very awkward and embarrassing to have to listen to him speaking as he does to Diana, it's hardly John's business to take offence. It's tactless of him, that's all. People notice it, so of course the next thing is that some village gossip starts a scandal—and, well, although it's all very well meant on John's part it doesn't help Diana."

"Is he in love with her?" I asked bluntly.

"No, of course not," Betty said uncomfortably. "At least certainly not in the accepted sense. There's nothing *wrong* in it at all. Diana simply isn't that kind of person."

We passed the turning which led to the station and Betty pointed out a picturesque old cottage covered with the bare branches of wisteria and roses which was standing a little way back from the green with a small trim garden in front. It was colour-washed pale pink and had a reed thatched roof. The name on the gate was "Little Hodges."

"What a perfectly sweet house!" I exclaimed.

"It's the Qualtroughs'," she said. "Oh, there is Mr. Qualtrough now, coming out of the door. Good morning, Mr. Qualtrough! This is Mrs. Craufurd, who was just admiring your house. You ought to see it in the summer, Lee. Mr. Qualtrough has the most beautiful garden which is the envy of the whole village. His roses are four times the size of anybody else's and you can smell his stocks right across to the other side of the green."

Mr. Qualtrough smiled deprecatingly, but is was easy to see he was delighted with the compliment. He was a little stooping dried-up pippin of a man, who looked a lot more than his age. I afterwards discovered that he was about fifty-five, but he deliberately cultivated the appearance and mannerisms of a much older man. He affected a knickerbocker suit of archaic cut and a deerstalker cap of the variety associated with the early pictures of Sherlock Holmes. The effect of these sartorial eccentricities was heightened by the fact that he wore a neat little grizzled Imperial. We shook hands formally.

"Dear ladies, you flatter me," he said. His high fluting voice was precise and scholarly. "As you say, this is no time of the year for showing off one's garden. However, even in this inclement season I am not entirely without flowers. Betty, my dear, if you can spare the time, it would give me great pleasure to conduct Mrs. Craufurd round to the iris bed."

"Iris bed?" I echoed, surprised. I mightn't be much of a gardening expert, but I did at least know that irises came out in June and this was the middle of December.

"These are winter irises," Betty explained as we followed our host through the gate and along the narrow brick path which led round to the south wall of the cottage. "I don't know what Mr. Qualtrough does to them—he's a magician, of course. I have some at the bottom of my vegetable garden and they never come out before the end of January no matter what I do—and then they're mostly leaves. But these seem to flower all through December."

"Starvation," said Mr. Qualtrough, happily launched on his favourite hobby. "The secret of the cultivation of *iris stylosa*—or as some people prefer to call them *iris unguicularis*—lies entirely in the cultivation of the soil. Poverty is essential. All they require is a light gritty compost composed largely of lime rubble. And they must have a south wall. Your vegetable garden, while producing delicious ingredients for the *pot-au-feu*, is much too rich in phosphates for the meagre requirements of the humble winter iris. And it isn't properly sheltered."

We turned the corner and stopped abruptly. The narrow border which ran between two french windows at the back of the house was literally smothered in blossom—lovely china blue, white and purple flowers, which looked as incongruous among their frost-bound surroundings as a jaguar at the North Pole.

Mr. Qualtrough delved in to the capacious pocket of his tweed jacket and produced an ancient pruning knife.

"Allow me," he murmured stooping down.

"Oh, but you mustn't cut them!" I exclaimed involuntarily. "They look so lovely growing there against the house. It would be a shame."

"Another secret of successful cultivation," Mr. Qualtrough grunted, busy with the knife. "They should be cut every day. It is the only way to keep them in flower over a long period."

Betty refused the old man's pressing invitation to stay and have a glass of claret and a biscuit, protesting that she must get on as she had a lot to do.

"You will no doubt encounter my daughter in the village," Mr. Qualtrough observed. "She is engaged in an occupation which she describes unattractively as 'going round the bins in search of food'."

"An unattractive description of an unattractive job," Betty sighed. "Well, we must be getting on too, or the bins will all be empty. Thank you so much for the lovely flowers, Mr. Qualtrough. Goodbye."

"Does Mr. Qualtrough do anything besides garden?" I enquired as we walked across the green to the general stores.

"Oh, yes," Betty said. "He's an art dealer. Well I suppose he's more or less retired now. Before the war he used to have a small gallery off Bond Street and I believe they were quite well off. And then all sorts of awful things happened. Ann's mother died in a terrible way—she went off her head, poor woman, and committed suicide. And they lost all their money somehow. I don't really know the full story, because naturally it's not a thing one would talk to them about. Mr. Qualtrough opened an antique furniture shop in Tunbridge Wells where they sell a few pictures and some old china and glass. He's still got it, but I don't think he makes much money out of it. Ever since his wife died he just hasn't bothered about anything very much except music—which he's mad about—and his garden. The shop is run by a manager and Mr. Qualtrough goes over there two or three times a week to supervise. He goes round to sales and buys a few things from time to time. But his heart isn't in it."

"What about Ann?" I asked. "I suppose he's interested in her."

"Oh yes, of course he is," Betty agreed. "Ann's very good to him when she's here. But she spends most of her time in London now, you see. She only comes down during the vacations from the R.A.D.A. and soon I suppose she'll be finished with that and going off on tour and all that sort of thing."

"Well," I said, "if they haven't got any money she'd have to have a job of some kind."

"Yes—though Ann would still have gone on the stage if they'd been millionaires. It's her whole life. All I meant was that it seems a bit pathetic that the old man has to be left alone so much. He has a woman in for the cleaning about twice a week, but all the rest of the time when Ann's in London he does everything for himself. He's very proud of his cooking, which is extremely good. But I'm always sorry for these poor elderly widowers who have to fend for themselves. It seems somehow unnatural."

"He seems happy enough in his cottage with the garden to occupy most of his time," I observed.

"Yes, I know. If he ever lost that it certainly would be a tragedy. As a matter of fact, now I come to think of it, there was some fuss over the cottage with Sir Henry Metcalfe. It belongs to him—most of the property round here does, and there was a rumour that he wanted to turn Mr. Qualtrough out and sell it. I know Ann was a bit worried about it."

"But surely Sir Henry wouldn't sell the place over a tenant's head?" I asked. "He would be bound to give the present occupant the first refusal."

"You'd have thought so," Betty said vaguely. "Mind that bicycle, Lee—the way those children tear round the green simply isn't safe! Sara's been agitating for a bicycle for months and at last Howard's agreed to give her one for Christmas, but I must confess I hate the idea. Oh, about the cottage—actually, I suppose, there must be a bit more to it than that. I only know what Ann told me. Maybe Sir Henry thinks he can get more money from somebody else. I really don't know. But I wouldn't care to have him for a landlord myself, mean old Pig!"

We entered the general stores. It was simply a little whitewashed cottage converted into a shop. A bow window had been built out on to the pavement some time during the early part of the last century. We were greeted by a friendly smell of coffee, with a faint undercurrent of bacon and cheese.

A girl was standing by the counter with her back to the door. She was *petite,* not more than five feet tall, very slim and neatly built, hatless, and wearing navy blue slacks and a duffle coat. What made me notice her particularly was her hair, which was a pale silvery blonde colour, cut with a fringe and falling perfectly straight round her head like a medieval page boy. She turned as we came in and smiled at Betty. She had a small pointed face, rather like a kitten's, which could not possibly be described as pretty, but the general impression was attractive in a gaminesque sort of way.

"Hullo, Ann," Betty said. "I thought we might meet you in here." She performed introductions.

Ann Qualtrough shook back her fair curtain of hair and held out a small hand in a very large fur glove. Even if I hadn't known that she was destined for the stage, I should have guessed it from this gesture and the dramatic tilt of her chin. I found myself instinctively classing her as a rather affected little minx.

"Darling!" she exclaimed to Betty in a clear ringing voice. "You've come just in time to save me! For God's sake lend me twopence—I'm broke!"

"Of course," Betty said opening her bag. "Here you are. We've just been to call on your father. Look at these lovely irises he gave me."

"Oh, Dad loves to show off with his *stylosas,*" Ann said. "Poor sweet. It's his one little relaxation really. I honestly think he'd be capable of murdering anyone who got between him and his garden. Darling, talking of murder—have you seen my young man anywhere about this morning?"

"I don't quite follow the connection," Betty replied. "But no, I haven't. Are you proposing to murder Michael?"

"I've got a bone to pick with him," Ann said darkly. "More I could tell, but more I dare not say; the text is old, the orator too green!"

She struck a burlesque attitude and Betty became engrossed at the counter. I wandered round the shop thinking how odd it was that there seemed to be an infinitely wider choice in the way of tinned food in this tiny village store than I ever found in the lordly emporia of the West End, where I was accustomed to doing my own scavenging.

"My!" Ann remarked, lingering to see what Betty was buying. "Olives *and* salted almonds! I believe you're having a party on the sly and you haven't asked me. I'm *bitterly* hurt."

"It's not exactly what you'd call a party," Betty explained a trifle sheepishly. "It's just that I felt I ought to do something about that new woman who's taken Holly Tree Cottage, so I asked the Metcalfes in tonight to meet her. You don't want to come, do you?"

"The mysterious widow?" Ann asked, opening her eyes very wide. "But, *darling,* she's so sinister! She's either a beautiful spy or else she's fleeing from justice. What other reason could a person who looks like that possibly have for burying herself in a remote hamlet like Lower Bunnet? I fancy she's a bit predatory too. Do you really think you're being quite wise in introducing her to Howard?"

"I don't see why not," Betty replied shortly. Mr. Perkins had disappeared into the back regions of his establishment to search for an under-the-counter tin of very special cocktail biscuits. "I should think she's probably rather lonely, poor thing, and it seemed a civil gesture to ask her in for a drink."

"But of course I want to come!" Ann said. "I'm *madly* intrigued about that woman. You've only got to look at her to see at once that she's got the most *malign* past. And such technique! All cool and aloof on the surface and underneath a seething man-trap."

"What on earth d'you mean, Ann?" Betty asked sharply. "I thought you didn't know her?"

"Darling, I don't. But I do happen to know that she met my intended the other day at some deadly party over at Cranbrook. Michael was the only man there under eighty and I gather from my spies that the widow made a bee-line for him. Michael was awfully gallant about it, of course, and defended the reputation of the little woman against all aspersions. But even in the expurgated edition of his adventures which I dragged from his unwilling lips it was perfectly obvious to me that he only just managed to get away with his virtue intact."

"Ann, do stop talking nonsense," Betty said frowning, Mr. Perkins had reappeared from the back room and was stacking a selection of tins on the counter. She turned with evident relief to the discussion of biscuits.

"D'you know this fascinator?" Ann asked me, and when I shook my head she went on: "She has a Duse-like quality of stillness and Russian ballet hair. You know, all smooth and sleek and oh, so simple! I bet it takes her hours every morning."

We emerged on to the pavement.

"Goodness," Ann cried, "I must fly! Darling, I'm so looking forward to this evening—oh, am I to bring the aged parent?"

"Of course, if he'd like to come," Betty said. "But I warn you it will be very dull. I'd have said before bring him, only I thought cocktails weren't much in his line."

"They aren't," Ann said cheerfully. "But he hates being left out of things, and I really believe he gets a sort of morbid thrill out of Sir Henry—you know, a macabre kind of *frisson* that anyone *can* be so awful! He's a masochist, of course—my parent, I mean. It's funny how many people are—when they're not sadists like Sir Henry. Well, good-morning again—and thank you for letting us come to your party!"

We watched her small figure speeding across the green, tossing back her hair as she ran. She turned at the gate to wave and disappeared in to Little Hodges.

"This little drink gathering of yours looks like turning into quite a party after all," I remarked to Bettty as we walked down the road.

"I know. Howard will be furious. But what could I do? I wonder why that child is so anxious to meet Mrs. Phillips. I've known Ann since she was eleven and I can assure you she's nothing like so wide-eyed and ingenuous as she sometimes appears."

Half-way back across the green Betty was struck by a sudden doubt about the Tithe Barn gin supply.

"I think I'd better get another bottle—I know we've got one in the cupboard, but it's a nuisance to run out. That means we shall have to go to the pub. Mr. Perkins hasn't got a spirit licence. It's a rotten pub kept by a very rude and dirty old man called Willis who's one of Howard's most unfavourite patients. But it's the only place here where one can raise the odd bottle."

Once more we retraced our steps. I could see what Betty meant about the pub. The Blue Boar was not at all a prepossessing looking hostelry. We walked into the door marked "Off Licence" and were served in an atmosphere of deep suspicion by the sour-faced landlord.

"Good morning, Mr. Willis," Betty said with forced brightness. "May I have a bottle of gin, please. And how's Mrs. Willis's asthma getting on?"

"Middling," grumbled the old man ungraciously. "That medicine doctor sent round for her don't seem to do her no good at all. Coloured water, that's all it is if you ask me my opinion."

Betty bore the reproach to Howard's professional ability with unruffled calm. This, it seemed, was typical of Mr. Willis. He took an inordinately long time shuffling things about in a dark cupboard before producing the required bottle of gin, and all the time a stream of complaints poured from his lips. Complaints about the weather, the political situation, and finally the hard life of a publican who couldn't even make his little bit of profit in the bar but was compelled, so his manner implied, to sell his customers their liquor at a controlled price in order that they might carry it away to sozzle in the privacy of their own homes.

"What a revolting old man," I said to Betty as we made our escape at last.

"Oh, he's always like that. Nobody takes any notice of him any more. He'd die if he hadn't got something to grumble about. Oh, dear, there's Mr. Qualtrough waving to us again. And I've got so many things to do at home before lunch."

Lewis Qualtrough was leaning over his gate holding an untidy spray of small mauve flowers almost hidden amongst thick evergreen leaves. His eyes were gleaming with pleasure.

"*Lardizabala biternata,*" he announced with pride. "I thought this frost would have finished it off, but it hasn't." He began delicately pulling off a few of the tougher leaves. "You ought to grow it yourself," he said. "That arch of yours at the far end of the tennis court would be just the place for it—sheltered from the north and east. An ideal spot. And once it's naturalised it's no trouble at all. Interesting climber—comes from Chile. Tell you what I'll do. I'll pot up some cuttings for you next summer. You remind me."

Betty made suitable acknowledgements and again refused the offer of a glass of claret.

"But we'll be seeing you tonight, won't we?" she added. "Did Ann tell you—"

"Cocktails!" Mr. Qualtrough said, pursing his lips in disapproval. "A glass of sherry perhaps, my dear, since you are so good as to invite me to your house. I understand we are to meet a lady called Mrs. Phillips. I know her by sight." For a moment his beady little eyes held the awakened spark of interest which he usually reserved for rare plants. "At half-past six? That will be most agreeable."

"This Mrs. Phillips seems to have got something," I remarked as we turned down the lane to the Tithe Barn. "Maybe Ann wasn't so far wrong—she certainly seems to have caused something of a flutter among the male population."

"Ann's a silly little ass," Betty said firmly. "She talks too much. One of these days one of her little cracks will catch up with her, and she'll have quite a time explaining she didn't mean a thing."

I nodded. But I was remembering the way a shutter had come down over Howard's face at the mention of Mrs. Phillips' name, and the exceedingly stiff manner in which Michael Metcalfe had said: "I hardly know her at all."

I couldn't help admitting privately that I was getting quite intrigued myself at the idea of meeting the mysterious widow.

III

PRELUDE

At a quarter-past six I tore myself reluctantly away from the drawing-room fire and went up to my bedroom to change my dress. Sounds from the other end of the passage indicated that supper was in progress in the nursery.

Robin called out: "Auntie Lee! Auntie Lee! Sara and me have got cocktails too!"

I went along and poked my head in at the door. Robin and Sara in their dressing-gowns were sitting at the table. In front of them was a jug of what I took to be orangeade and two small glasses.

"Cockatails!" Robin repeated happily. "Cheeri-cheeri-oh!"

Sara was inclined to be superior and injured.

"They're not *real* cocktails, silly," she said. "Real ones have stuff in them we aren't allowed to drink. Auntie Lee, don't you think it's mean of Mummy not to let me stay down? I've handed round before, but she said not tonight. And I *never* go to bed before seven."

"Oh, rubbish, you do," I said. "Nanny usually fetches you at half-past six. Besides it isn't a party tonight—not a proper one. It's only a few people."

"Well, I wanted to stay down and see that lady again."

"What lady?"

"The one with black hair done up in a bun. I heard Mummy telling Norah she was coming. I wanted to see her. She was nice."

Norah Wright was Howard's dispenser, a quiet competent girl who lived with her widowed mother in the village. I was a little bewildered by Sara's remarks and, although I had now left myself no time to have a bath as I'd intended before I came upstairs, I was determined to get to the bottom of them. "Do you mean Mrs. Phillips?" I asked curiously.

"Yes—that's right. Do you know her too?"

"No," I said slowly. "And I didn't realise you did. Where did you meet her before, Sara?"

"Here, of course," Sara said impatiently. "When she came to see Daddy. Daddy wasn't in, so I talked to her in the waiting-room. She was nice. Auntie Lee, will you ask Mummy if I could come down—just for five minutes—in my dressing-gown to say goodnight?"

At this moment Nanny came bustling in.

"Now, Sara," she said briskly. "No wheedling! Mummy's busy. You just finish up your cornflakes like a good girl, and then Mummy will come and say goodnight to you when you're in bed."

"Can I read?"

"Yes, if you're quick now."

"How long can I read?"

"You can read until seven. Robin—you've finished with that orange now—you don't want that bit of peel any more. Come along!"

Robin allowed himself to be led away without further protest; and I became suddenly aware that if I didn't start changing pretty rapidly I wouldn't be ready by the time Betty's guests arrived.

While I was brushing my hair I pondered a little over Sara's remark. I had no idea the mysterious Mrs. Phillips was a patient of Howard's—nor, I was sure, had Betty. Not that there was the smallest reason why she shouldn't be, but it just seemed slightly odd that Howard hadn't mentioned last night that he knew her, even in a professional capacity. I remembered again the look on his face.

Oh well, I thought, why should he talk about her? A good doctor doesn't chatter about his patients—even to his wife. And he had never said he *didn't* know her. He had simply risen above the whole discussion.

The bell rang in the hall downstairs and I heard the front door open as I slid hurriedly into my dress and paused at the dressing table to see that I looked all right. As I was applying a final touch of lipstick the front door banged again. I heard voices in the hall and footsteps and then a low murmur of conversation coming up from the drawing-room which was immediately under my room. I snatched up my bag and hurried downstairs.

Betty was in the drawing-room talking to Michael Metcalfe and Ann Qualtrough, who seemed so far to be the only arrivals.

"What a relief," I said. "I kept hearing the front door bang and I thought I must be the last person."

"No, what you probably heard was Howard going out," Betty said with an edge of annoyance in her voice. "It's particularly maddening—and always happens when I've asked him to get through surgery quickly. It isn't his fault, of course. But there's old Mrs. Gibbs and the Cheeseman boy still waiting, and now he's had to dash round to the Vicarage because their maid's scalded herself with some boiling fat. It's only a step away, but it's a nuisance all the same."

She handed a drink to Ann, who took it and perched herself on the arm of one of the big chintz covered armchairs. She made a charming picture in her straight red frock with the shining cap of smooth blonde hair outlined against the oak beams of the fireplace; and I found myself reflecting rather uncharitably that she was well aware of this, and with her unerring sense of theatre had placed herself on purpose in just that position. When she turned her head to look at Michael and found him staring across towards the other side of the room, evidently wrapped in some brown study of his own, a faint frown of disappointment passed over her piquant face and it was as clear as if she had spoken aloud that she was sorry Michael had failed to appreciate her little tableau.

"I can't wait," Ann said in her clear high voice, "to meet the glamorous widow."

Michael swung round. "What widow?" he demanded.

"Darling, there's only one mysterious widow in these parts, glamorous or otherwise," Ann said. "If she is a widow, that is to say—which personally I rather doubt."

"Are you referring to Mrs. Phillips?" Michael enquired with elaborate detachment. "From the little I've seen of her, I thought she seemed charming."

"That's because she made such a pass at you, darling," Ann said. "Your vanity was flattered. I think she's quite madly sinister and I'm certain she's a sort of female Bluebeard who goes round marrying credulous young men for their money and then bumping them off with arsenic."

"That's a terribly silly thing to say, Ann," Michael snapped coldly. "You know nothing whatever about her—none of us do. Anyone listening to you would think you were jealous just because she happens to be exceptionally good looking."

Ann made no reply, but I watched her hand clenching and uncurling itself against the back of the chair. She picked up her cocktail from the table beside her and sipped it slowly.

A diversion was luckily caused at this moment by the sound of steps in the hall and a woman's voice calling: "Betty! We found the front door open so we walked straight in."

Betty rose as the drawing-room door opened. A tall woman in a dark blue dress with a fur coat flung over her shoulders came in. She was smiling and I was at once struck by the serenity of her face and the candid beauty of her wide blue eyes. She wasn't otherwise remarkable, but I received an instant impression that this was a very nice person whom I would like to know better. Her voice was warm and friendly and she carried an air of dignity which was at the same time simple and unassuming. She was followed by a man a good deal older, who would have been handsome in a cold craggy way if it had not been for the hard line of his mouth and the steely glint of his bleak grey eyes.

This, I gathered without difficulty, was Lady Metcalfe and her husband, the retired hanging judge.

Lady Metcalfe sat down by the fire and Sir Henry stood beside her. There was an immediate atmosphere of constraint. Michael walked over to the other side of the room and began examining the titles of the books on a shelf in front of him. He made no attempt to greet his father. Ann Qualtrough turned her back on Sir Henry with studied deliberation and I watched her darting veiled glances at Michael from under lowered eyelashes.

Betty was explaining to Diana Metcalfe about Mrs. Phillips. "Have you met her?" she added.

"I think I know her by sight," Diana replied. "Rather a striking-looking person, isn't she? She reminds me of one of those Laura Knight pictures—only less muscular and beefy. I suppose really it's the way she does her hair. Do you know the girl I mean, Henry? She's often about in the village."

Sir Henry shook his head. "Phillips?" he repeated. "No, it conveys nothing to me. As you know, my dear, I have other things to occupy my day besides loafing about the village green."

There was a slightly uncomfortable pause, which Betty filled by remarking conversationally that Sir Henry sounded as if he had a nasty cold. He was immediately diverted and launched into a vigorous diatribe against the English climate, especially in December.

"It gets much worse in January and February," Michael put in. He had not spoken since his father had entered the room. "I can't imagine why you stay in it. Why don't you take Diana out to the South of France for a couple of months? It would do you both good."

"I find your solicitude most touching," Sir Henry replied sarcastically. "Unfortunately it is not as simple as you appear to assume. There are such matters as currency restrictions to be considered, for one thing; and for another I am not, as you seem to think, made of money. Furthermore, there are mercifully a few people left in this country who continue to feel a slight degree of responsibility for their duties as citizens, and who are not constantly on the look out for opportunities to shirk them."

I could see Michael biting his lip. He flushed and turned away and muttered something to Ann Qualtrough under his breath. It was an uneasy moment for everybody in the room.

"Michael was only thinking of your health, dear," Diana Metcalfe said quickly. "And if it weren't for the garden and all the village things I can't leave, I must say I should love to get right away for a change and see some sunshine. Think of it," she went on wistfully. "Instead of shivering round in this biting cold, we'd be seeing the blue sea and all the lovely mimosa. And you know, Henry, John Wickham's been so clever with the fruit trees that I'm quite sure we could perfectly well leave the orchards in his hands for a little—"

Sir Henry Metcalfe gave a short unpleasant laugh.

"Really, Diana," he said. "I seem to be the only member of the family with any degree of practical sanity left. Here is Michael talking of idling his time away at some dramatic establishment in London, while you propose—regardless of expense—to go gallivanting off to the South of France to do nothing but gaze at a lot of mimosa bushes—in my opinion a most overrated form of vegetation, neither beautiful nor even particularly profitable. I simply don't know what's come over people nowadays. No wonder the Empire's going to the dogs when people of our standing—the very ones who should know better and set an example to the working classes—behave like a set of hedonistic escapists. I am surprised that you—"

"I think I hear my father outside," Ann said clearly. "Shall I go and let him in?"

"Yes—will you please, Ann?" Betty said with relief in her voice. "Lee, your glass is almost empty. Bring it over here. I can't think what's keeping Howard so long—you'd think he'd have had time to see to fifty scalded cooks."

Ann returned with Lewis Qualtrough in tow. His beady little eyes with their sudden flashes of acute observation travelled slowly round the room. He glowered with intense dislike in the direction of Sir Henry Metcalfe and said in his piping querulous voice: "This is most exceedingly jolly."

He accepted a cigarette from Betty and seated himself on the extreme edge of an armchair by the fire.

Diana Metcalfe joined him and began to talk in her easy friendly way about gardens. Sir Henry leaned against one of the oak beams by the fireplace and regarded everybody in the room with a baleful glare of disapproval. Michael and Ann retired into respective shells of silence. I intercepted a despairing glance of appeal from Betty and determined to pull myself together.

"I hear you have a wonderful collection of oriental china," I said brightly to Sir Henry. "What a very interesting hobby that must be."

Sir Henry turned his cold grey eyes upon me as though I were something that had not previously been brought to his notice and about which he was fairly unenthralled now that it had.

"You are interested in eastern porcelain?" he demanded austerely. His expression conveyed little hope that I would be intelligent on the subject.

"Er—yes," I replied weakly, confirming his original low opinion of my charms. "That is—of course I don't know very much about it, but—" I floundered dismally and hoped that I was not about to be cross-examined on a subject on which I probably knew rather less than Sara and Robin upstairs, now peacefully ensconced in the night nursery. I attempted to assume an expression of wide-eyed you-tell-me eagerness.

Betty glanced gratefully at me, and a nightmare vision of a hideous green dragon with blood-bespattered jaws rose before my troubled eyes. It belonged to Bill's Aunt Adelaide and was said to be extremely valuable—Ming, I rather fancied she supposed it to be.

"I happened to make a very remarkable purchase a few days ago," Sir Henry was saying, "which, if you have made anything of a study on the subject of the enamelled porcelain of the Yung-Cheng period, would interest you. You are, of course, familiar with the ordinary *famille rose* ware which was exported in large quantities during the middle years of the eighteenth century; but I fancy I am correct in stating that comparatively few specimens of the genuine early Imperial *famille rose,* such as are to be seen in their true glory in the Summer Palace collection, ever arrived in Europe."

"Yes," I said judiciously nodding my head. "I'm sure you are quite correct about that."

Ann Qualtrough rose from the arm of the chair on which she had been sitting and moved to the glass-fronted bookcase behind Sir Henry. She had been watching me sardonically, and suddenly she grinned and contorted her small features into the most hideous grimace aimed at Sir Henry's back. I looked away hurriedly.

"I alighted on this particular bowl," Sir Henry continued, "at the very back of a shelf where it had been misleadingly hidden behind an indifferent collection of later Ch'ien-Lung ware. As soon as I saw it, of course, I recognised it instantly for authentic early Imperial *famille rose*—it has a peach-spray design, with a sitting bird beside it. It should be arriving from London in the course of the next day or two, and as you are so interested in Chinese porcelain, it will give me great pleasure to show it to you one day at my house."

"Thank you," I said. "I shall look forward to that."

"I have a considerable collection of the ruby-back egg-shell china," Sir Henry told me remorselessly, "including a very fine plate with *mille fleurs* panels. This is not, as you know, a very rare type of porcelain, but among the Canton artists as a whole—"

The door burst open.

"I'm sorry to be so late," Howard Sandys exclaimed as he came in unwinding a thick woollen scarf and shuffling out of his motoring gloves. "Hullo, Diana—good evening, sir. I got held up on a case. My God, it's cold outside. I shouldn't wonder if we had snow tonight. Darling, pour me out a small drink—I'll be with you in a second. Yes, Norah—what is it?"

Norah Wright, efficient in a white overall, was hovering by the door.

"The medicine for Mrs. Potter, Ambleside," she said. "Her little boy's come round for it. Same as before?"

"Yes—no—what were we giving her?"

"Mist, bismuth, sed."

"Try her with hyoscyamine sulphate—an eightieth twice daily. Tell the kid I'll be round in the morning to see the old girl."

"I'm pretty sure we're out of hyoscyamine sulphate. It isn't a thing you prescribe much, and I remember we used the last of it on old McGregor of Selsey Farm. You didn't tell me to order any more."

"Oh, damn," said Howard irritably. "Sorry, Diana—excuse all this. Hi—Norah, I've just remembered. I think there's a tube of hyoscyamine sulphate in the top right hand compartment of my bag on the surgery table. Go and see, like a good girl, and if it isn't there let me know, and we'll think again."

Norah Wright departed. Sir Henry broke off from his discourse on oriental ceramics to sneeze loudly and repeatedly.

"That's a nasty cold you've got, sir," Howard said, handing round the cigarette box. "You'd better let Norah make you up something for that while you're here—it won't take her a minute."

"Well, I don't know—" Sir Henry began doubtfully.

"Yes, you'd better have something, Henry," Diana agreed. "You know you said this morning that you thought you'd ask Howard to prescribe some medicine for you. I know it's an awful breach, Howard, to bother you with professional things on a purely social visit, but I do really think as we're here—and if Norah isn't too busy—"

"Of course," Howard said automatically. He scribbled a line of hieroglyphics on a pad which he drew from his pocket. "I'll take this along to her straight away."

As he left the room Betty drifted back. "I can't imagine what's happened to Mrs. Phillips," she remarked. "Of course she hasn't been here before and perhaps she's lost her way. It's dark now and it isn't easy to find this house if you don't know the place. But you'd think if she got lost she'd telephone or something, wouldn't she?"

"If she'd lost her way she couldn't very well telephone from the middle of a dark lane with no call boxes," Diana Metcalfe pointed out. "Still, she must know her way as far as the village—and having got that far, anyone would be able to tell her. She has a car, I imagine?"

"Oh yes—I've seen her getting into it in the village. A little Ford Eight."

There was a sudden yowl of pain from Ann Qualtrough who was standing by the window, lighting a cigarette. Michael Metcalfe stepped quickly to her side and I saw him take her hand in his and examine it.

"What happened, Ann?" Betty asked. "Are you all right?"

"The beastly match exploded," Ann exclaimed, dragging her hand away from Michael and sucking her finger ruefully. "It's burnt me like hell."

"Take it into the surgery and get Howard to put on a dressing," Betty said practically. "Here—come along!"

"Poor Howard. A doctor has no peace, even in his own house," Michael said. "Don't bother, Betty—I'll take her."

He linked his arm through Ann's and drew her out of the door. I glanced round, and noticed that Diana Metcalfe was talking to her husband at the other side of the room. I saw no reason for putting my head into that particular lion's den again. I felt I'd done my stuff with Sir Henry, and it was now up to somebody else to keep the ball rolling. Then I remembered Mr. Qualtrough and was somewhat surprised to observe that he wasn't there at all. This was odd, because I knew he had been there a few seconds before—I had subconsciously registered him sitting rather unhappily in a wing chair, sipping a glass of sherry and regarding Sir Henry Metcalfe with acute dislike. He must have left the room under cover of the fuss created over Ann's burnt finger. I couldn't think why he should have done so, but since he could hardly be hiding behind the curtains or under the sofa there was no other explanation. I was mildly curious, because whatever Mr. Qualtrough might or might not be he certainly hadn't struck me as rude, and to sneak off without even bothering to say good night to Betty seemed distinctly impolite.

Ann and Michael were out of the room for quite a long time. There was still no sign of Mrs. Phillips. Betty was now talking local politics with Sir Henry, and his wife came over and sat down beside me on the wide chintz sofa.

There was a tattoo on the front door knocker and almost simultaneously the sound of footsteps in the hall. Betty started to her feet, but, just as she reached the drawing-room door it opened to disclose the figure of a lanky young man in corduroy trousers and an ancient British warm. He paused in the doorway in obvious embarrassment at finding the room full of people.

"Hullo, John—come in," Betty said. She introduced the young man to me as Mr. Wickham. His uneasy eyes travelled rapidly round the room and alighted on Sir Henry Metcalfe. He went through a slight motion of shuffling his feet.

"I'm frightfully sorry," John Wickham said to Betty. "I'd no idea you'd got people. I went round to the surgery door just now and there was nobody there. I wanted to catch Howard for a moment. Is he in?"

"Yes," Betty replied "I thought he was in the surgery. He took Ann and Michael in there a few minutes ago—Ann burnt her finger on a match. I wonder where they've all got to."

As she spoke, Ann Qualtrough appeared at the door, her right hand decorated with a piece of pink sticking-plaster.

"Hullo, John," she said. "Behold the wounded warrior. To Carthage then I came—burning—burning—burning—burning.

You've no conception how it hurts! Oh, Betty—Howard's gone up to say goodnight to Robin. He was yelling. And Michael's gone to put the lights on in his car because he left it in the lane. Still no sign of the merry widow?"

Betty said vaguely: "She's probably got lost or else forgotten all about coming. John, have a drink. Howard will be down in a minute. Sir Henry, let me give you a little more sherry."

John Wickham said: "I didn't really come in for a drink, you know. It was only to tell Howard that Pewsey's wife has got a touch of 'flu and they'd be grateful if he'd call round some time tomorrow. No hurry about it at all."

"Oh dear, I'm sorry to hear that," Diana Metcalfe said. She added to me: "Pewsey's one of our gardeners. I'll look in on the way home, John, and see if there's anything I can do."

"I fail to see the slightest necessity for you doing anything of the kind," Sir Henry put in tartly. "The Pewseys' cottage is right over on the other side of the village. And in any case, what on earth do you imagine you could do?"

"I only thought Pewsey might like it," Diana said, colouring a little. "Just to make sure they're all right and that there's somebody to see to the supper and putting the children to bed and all that sort of thing."

"My wife can never stop picturing herself as Lady Bountiful," Sir Henry remarked waspishly to me. "She makes a fetish of cosseting the labouring classes, who don't appreciate her attentions in the least, and would infinitely rather be left to themselves—"

"I can assure you, sir, that is not so," John Wickham interrupted violently. "Everybody in the village appreciates what Lady Metcalfe does for them. If you knew what store people like the Pewseys set on her kindness, you wouldn't say things like that—" He broke off, embarrassed.

The sardonic expression on Ann Qualtrough's face deepened. She raised one eyebrow and gazed quizzically at the ceiling. I avoided Betty's agonised eye.

Sir Henry stared unpleasantly at John Wickham over the top of his steel-rimmed spectacles.

"Indeed!" he said softly. "Lady Bountiful has a knight errant. Very charming. And in the meantime, while Diana is interfering in the domestic arrangements of the Pewseys, who are perfectly capable of looking after themselves, I am to be kept shivering outside in the motor car waiting for her; or alternatively I am to return alone to anticipate the preparation of a meal which will be indefinitely postponed. That indeed shows true consideration."

For an appalling moment I really thought John Wickham was going to strike Sir Henry. I rather think Ann thought so too. A gleam of malicious excitement came into her eyes. Then Diana turned away and fumbled blindly in her bag for a handkerchief. The muscles of John Wickham's clenched fists relaxed gradually and he rose slowly to his feet.

"I think I won't wait to see Howard now, Betty," he said quietly. "If you'd just be good enough to give him the message"

"Of course," Betty replied mechanically. She accompanied him to the door. There was complete silence in the drawing-room.

It was a relief to everybody a few seconds later when we heard a great stamping of feet in the hall and Michael Metcalfe's voice upraised to speak to Howard who was coming down the stairs.

"Something wrong with the rear light," Michael was saying. "I had to keep kicking it and even then it wouldn't stay on till I'd wedged it with a bit of stick. Must have it seen to. Was that John Wickham who went out just now?"

"Yes," said Betty hurrying to the door and scooping them both inside with determination. "Come in, Michael—you must be frozen. John came with a message for Howard."

She glanced round the room and a puzzled frown settled on her face. "What's happened to Mr. Qualtrough?" she asked. "Has he gone, Ann?"

"I expect he's snooping," Ann said casually. "He always does, you know. I've tried hard to train him, but he's an impossible parent socially. My three guesses are that he's in Howard's study cosily reading a book. I admit it's eccentric but you know what Dad is."

"Well," said Betty doubtfully. "As long as he's enjoying himself—"

"I expect he's doing that all right," Ann assured her. "I wouldn't worry about him if I were you."

"Perhaps he'd like a drink," Betty suggested, glancing in a slightly distrait manner round the room. She seemed aware that as a cocktail party the present gathering lacked bonhomie. "Lee, d'you think—would you mind just taking him along a glass of something? What does he like, Ann? I know he doesn't drink gin. Would he like whisky or sherry?"

"I expect he'd adore some sherry," Ann said. "But really you know, darling, I shouldn't bother. He's probably perfectly happy as he is."

I got up and poured out a glass of sherry. I was beginning to feel the strain a bit myself, and it seemed to me that Mr. Qualtrough had chosen the better part. It must be a lot cosier reading a book in Howard's study than standing about in here listening to lectures on Chinese porcelain or suffering from the general atmosphere of uneasiness due to Sir Henry Metcalfe's uncomfortable presence. Struck by this thought I poured out a second glass of sherry for myself and carried them carefully out into the hall.

The door to the surgery was open and the light was still on. I glanced inside, but there was nobody there. Norah's white overall hung tidily on the peg inside the door and I presumed she had gone home for the night. There was also a light under the door of Howard's study.

Ann was perfectly right. Mr. Qualtrough was sitting hunched up like a little gnome on the edge of the leather chair, completely immersed in a book. He hardly raised his head when I opened the door and became instantly absorbed again.

"I brought you a drink," I explained, putting down the glass of sherry on the table beside him and sitting down in the other arm chair. He grunted some perfunctory acknowledgement and went on reading steadily.

After a few minutes I ventured another remark.

"Is that an interesting book?" I asked him. I really wanted to know.

"*Gascoyne, The Sandalwood Trader*," he replied without looking up. "Ballantyne. Haven't read any of them since I was a boy, and they were out of date then. Great stuff, Ballantyne. Fascinating!"

He unglued his attention long enough to take an appreciative sip of sherry, after which he sighed gustily and said: "Ah!" He then returned avidly to his adventure story.

I gave it up. I stayed there a few minutes longer, drinking my own glass of sherry, and then got up. As I reached the door, he suddenly became aware of me. He put down his book reluctantly and regarded me with an owlish expression of guilt.

"H'm," he said. "Yes. Party—bad manners. My daughter will be annoyed with me. Have those people in the other room gone yet?"

I told him that the Metcalfes were still there as far as I knew, and that Mrs. Phillips had not yet arrived.

"Come back and sit down," he invited me, waving his hand in the direction of the arm chair I had just vacated. "Your friend Betty is a charming young woman. But she has lured me to her house under false pretences. I was to meet a pretty widow who has failed to materialise. Instead, I have been compelled to spend several minutes in the same room with Sir Henry Metcalfe, an imposition which I cannot lightly forgive. Diana Metcalfe has my most sincere sympathy, but presumably she brought it upon herself. I mean, she was not abducted or otherwise forcibly constrained to throw in her lot with one of the most *farouche* characters it has ever been my ill fortune to meet. Tell me, what do you think of the son, Michael?"

"He seems all right," I said lamely. "I've hardly spoken to him for more than five minutes."

"He wants to marry Ann," Mr. Qualtrough said sombrely. "I know that the days when parents had any say in the matter of their children's matrimonial arrangements are long passed, and perhaps that is as well. I myself ran away with my wife in the teeth of her family's opposition when she was eighteen years old and I was thirty-two. I think I can truthfully say that neither of us regretted it for one moment." His eyes were cloudy. I said nothing.

"So I have stated no opinion. Had I done so, it would have been ignored. Ann is as headstrong as I was myself at her age. However, the young couple are not without the blessing of parental disapproval. Sir Henry Metcalfe has set his face against the match."

"Oh," I said. It wasn't one of my brightest shafts of repartee, but it was just about all I could manage at that moment. It occurred to me that this was about the oddest cocktail party I had ever attended.

"He has the impertinence," Mr. Qualtrough went on with a quiver of genuine anger in his reedy high-pitched voice, "to consider that in marrying my daughter, Michael would be contracting a misalliance."

"That seems silly," I observed feebly.

"It is not only silly," Mr. Qualtrough retorted with energy, "it is preposterous nonsense. Ann is a very talented actress. She is—though I say it as her parent—an artist. The stage is not the career I should myself have selected for my only child, had the choice been a matter for my judgment. But things did not fall out in such a manner that I could have interfered. It was a question of inevitability. Acting is Ann's *métier*—her vocation—one might almost say her whole life. She has a clarity of vision to which I bow. What she must do she must do. Young Michael Metcalfe also has ideas about acting. I do not say they are entirely unfounded—I am no authority on the drama—and I understand that he attracted favourable notices from a number of reputable critics when he was at Oxford. That might mean anything or nothing. An actor's equipment has to include a great deal more than a voice and histrionic ability. There's the psychological make-up as well—he requires courage, determination, ambition, ruthlessness and a refusal to accept defeat. Michael Metcalfe may possess these qualities, but frankly I doubt it. We shall, however, never be in a position to prove our hypothesis, since I understand that it has been decided by his unmentionable father that he shall follow the path of law. For my own part, I should not break my heart if the marriage did not take place. But that is entirely Ann's affair. If she wants it and is prepared to accept the integral risk involved, I shall abide by her decision and say nothing."

The malicious gleam returned to his eyes. "But," he added softly, "if there is one factor calculated to make me press this match by every means within my power, it is the fact that the unspeakable Sir Henry Metcalfe has expressed opposition to his son's alliance with my daughter."

"Yes," I agreed thoughtfully. "I quite see that."

Mr. Qualtrough uttered a noise between a snort and a giggle. He cast a crafty glance towards the study door. "However," he said. "I remain civil. Whatever my personal views on the subject,

I subdue them in the presence of my landlord. Sir Henry Metcalfe happens unfortunately to own the house in which I live. You will recollect the familiar precept of Cicero—'*Cave ne quid stulte, ne quid temere, dicas aut facias contra potentes*'."

I tried to look as if I recollected it.

Mr. Qualtrough sat sipping his sherry. There was the sound of footsteps in the hall. Somebody went into the surgery opposite. I heard the click of high heels and the door shut softly. I wondered incuriously if Norah Wright had come back for something she had forgotten, and then I remembered that Norah never wore high heels. She was essentially the sensible brogue type. It could not be Norah.

I stood up, holding my empty sherry glass. What Betty must be thinking of this eccentric behaviour simply didn't bear contemplation.

"I must go back to the others," I said. "They'll be thinking me awfully rude. Are you coming? I'm sure Howard would love to lend you *Gascoyne, The Sandalwood Trader* to take home and read."

Mr. Qualtrough sighed deeply.

"I suppose you are right," he said sadly. "I can't remember when I have enjoyed a party so much. Still, I shouldn't like our friends, Betty and Howard, to consider me unsociable. We will return and mingle with our neighbours. I shall do my utmost in a tactful manner to outstay Sir Henry Metcalfe and to make him as uncomfortable as possible in the process."

He grinned impishly, screwing up his ridiculous face into a pout like a naughty child, and we went into the hall. The surgery light was still on, but the door was shut.

I tried to slide back into the drawing-room as unobtrusively as possible; and for a moment I had the welcome impression that the Metcalfes had gone home. Then I saw Sir Henry standing by the far window talking to Betty. Michael and Ann sat together on the sofa and Howard was on his hands and knees doing something to the fire. Diana Metcalfe was not in the room. The atmosphere of constraint still lingered.

I manoeuvred Mr. Qualtrough into an arm chair by the fire and sent a wordless S.O.S. to Howard for a replenishment of my sherry glass. I felt I needed it.

Howard muttered something about fetching some more logs and left the room. He returned a few minutes later with the logs and Diana Metcalfe, and I remember wondering vaguely where she had been while I was in the study talking to Mr. Qualtrough.

She sat down on the sofa and Howard busied himself with drinks. I thought he seemed a little put out over something. Diana was very quiet too.

The clock on the chimney piece ticked noisily. Nobody was talking and the uneasy silence reminded me rather of the atmosphere of a darkened theatre just before the curtain was due to rise. It felt as though we were all waiting for something—or rather, as though we ourselves were the actors, sitting carefully grouped on the stage, waiting for the cue to speak our first lines.

There was a slight stir in the hall and the sound of voices. The door opened and Mrs. Padgett, Betty's cook, appeared looking rather flustered. She was wiping her hands, to which remnants of flour still adhered, on a corner of her apron and her expression indicated that announcing visitors in the middle of getting the dinner ready was no part of her duties.

"Mrs. Phillips," she said flatly and withdrew.

"I'm so sorry," said an attractive husky voice with a distinct foreign accent, "to be so dreadfully late..."

IV

CAPRICCIO

SONIA PHILLIPS STOOD IN THE OPEN DOORWAY, THE LIGHT from the hall lamp shining behind her, silhouetting her slim figure as she paused on the threshold, one hand clutching her bag against the folds of her fur coat, and the other arrested in a tentative gesture of greeting. For a minute nobody moved, and then Betty turned quickly from the window and went across the room to meet her. But during that pause, the eyes of everyone in the room were riveted with the most shameless curiosity on the new arrival.

There was no getting away from it she was remarkably decorative. She had, as Ann had said, a quality of poise and remoteness which made all the rest of us look slightly gauche and unfinished. She was of medium height, beautifully proportioned, and her plain black dress accentuated the whiteness of her skin and the darkness of her wide slanting eyes. High, smooth cheek-bones indicated some distant Slav origin, and her thick black hair was parted in the middle and fastened in a heavy knot on the slender nape of her neck. Diana Metcalfe had been right, too. She did remind one of a ballet dancer. You could imagine her standing poised in the wings of the theatre, just as she was standing now, waiting for those first liquid notes of a Chopin mazurka which would be her cue. Then she would sweep into movement—movement as liquid and graceful as the music—and float across the stage almost without seeming to touch the ground with her feet.

I recalled myself with a start from this pretty fantasy as Betty began introducing her to people.

Mrs. Phillips said: "I am sorry to be so late. It was stupid of me. I lost my way. And then I could not find your front door in the dark."

"How did you get in, then?" Betty asked smiling. She led the way back to the fire.

"I came in through the side door—it would, I think, be Dr. Sandys' surgery. There were bottles on the shelves and a big desk. And then I met your maid and she showed me the way."

Behind me I heard a sudden sharp intake of breath, and turned to see Michael Metcalfe standing at my elbow. His eyes were fixed on Mrs. Phillips and he was clearly oblivious of the fact that there was anybody else in the room at all. At the same moment I caught sight of Ann Qualtrough's face in the round mirror on the opposite wall. She was biting her lip and looking not at Mrs. Phillips but at her fiancé, and it was a most naked and revealing look.

Diana Metcalfe said something to Sonia Phillips—nothing important, just the usual polite chatter which one addresses to strangers at a party—and her pleasant voice broke the spell. She made room for her to sit beside her on the sofa, and Howard hurried forward with a cocktail. Everybody began talking at once. Ann's back was half turned towards the fire and I couldn't see her face. I went over to a small table on the far side of the room to help myself to a cigarette and for some absurd reason found my hand shaking as I picked it up.

Then I noticed that Sir Henry Metcalfe had not come forward with the others to be introduced. He was standing by the window with a peculiar puzzled expression on his face. He moved towards the little group by the fire and said softly: "I beg your pardon, but I don't think I quite caught your name, Mrs—er—"

"Mrs. Phillips," Betty said quickly. "I'm so sorry, Sir Henry. Mrs. Phillips has come to live at Holly Tree Cottage at Lower Bunnet, so she's quite a close neighbour of yours."

"Ah," said Sir Henry bleakly. "How do you do?"

Sonia Phillips looked up from her seat. Her dark eyes widened in sudden wariness and I thought I saw her hand tighten for an instant on the stem of her glass. Whatever was the cause of her momentary surprise, she recovered from it immediately and said coolly: "I am sure that will be very pleasant—for me."

Mr. Qualtrough began monopolising Betty on the subject of a local laundress who could be relied upon not to tear his shirts into ribbons, and Michael leaned against the back of Ann's chair. I noticed that he was still watching Mrs. Phillips and there was a somewhat set expression on Ann's face.

"It must be rather lonely for you all by yourself in that little cottage," Diana was saying sympathetically to Sonia Phillips. "It's so very isolated, isn't it? Do you have a maid or anybody to look after you?"

"I have no one sleeping in the house, but I don't mind being alone. I am used to it," Mrs. Phillips explained. "I have a woman who comes in the mornings to clean. She is called Bolland and she has nine children."

"Oh, dear Mrs. Bolland!" Diana said. "Yes, of course—she's a very old friend of mine. A thoroughly nice woman—I'm sure she'll take care of you all right. We've just taken on the eldest Bolland boy to help in our orchards and he's doing very well. They're good lads, and a credit to Mrs. Bolland. She had to bring them all up by herself because she doesn't get much help from her husband—he's one of these amiable old good-for-nothings, I'm afraid—he doesn't like work and spends most of his time in the pub. But Mrs. Bolland won't hear a word against him."

"Bolland is a lazy, worthless, drunken parasite," Sir Henry interrupted. "And it's largely the fault of that silly woman, who encourages him in his idleness, that he's reduced himself to the state he has. If it hadn't been for her foolishness—"

Diana relapsed into silence.

A few minutes later she rose and explained that they must go as it was the servants' night out. "I always see to dinner on Tuesdays," she said, picking up her gloves and bag.

"Ridiculous nonsense," Sir Henry grumbled. "Here we keep a pack of idle over-paid chattering girls—and what happens? Once a week, not to mention Sundays, we are left stranded and servant-less while they frivol away their time and my money in the vulgar and overheated precincts of some neighbouring picture palace."

"They take the bus over to the cinema in Tunbridge Wells," Diana amended hastily. "Well, it's much more fun for them to go together—and anyway, I think it's better. I don't like to think of them wandering round by themselves in the lanes on these dark nights."

"Rubbish," snapped Sir Henry curtly. "The bus goes from the green, which is at the bottom of my drive. There is no earthly need to visualise them wandering in any dark lanes—unless, for their own nefarious purposes, they happen to want to. There is more silly hysterical nonsense talked about the protection of young girls in rural areas than on almost any subject under the sun. If they want to get into trouble, they'll get into it—and no amount of organised junketing and consequent sacrifice of the comfort of their employers will prevent it."

"Well, anyway," Diana repeated faintly, "we must go. Good night, Betty dear—and thank you so much. It's been very nice meeting you, Mrs. Phillips, and I hope you'll come up and have tea with me one day soon. I'll ring you up. Are you on the telephone?"

"There is a telephone, yes," Mrs. Phillips replied. "But I have never used it and I am afraid I am stupid enough to have forgotten the number. But thank you for being so kind."

"Oh well, we're sure to meet in the village. Michael, are you coming back with us?"

"I've got the M.G.," Michael said. "I'll be along in a few minutes."

With the departure of Sir Henry Metcalfe an almost audible sigh of relief went round the room. Betty poured herself a cocktail and sank into a chair, prepared to relax.

Sonia Phillips said tentatively: "It is time I also went home."

"Oh, no, you can't do that," Howard protested. "You've only just come, Michael, stop toying with that miserable dreg at the bottom of the glass and have a proper drink."

"I—er—no, I won't have another, thanks," Michael replied, coming to with a slight jolt. He walked deliberately across the room and sat down on the sofa next to Mrs. Phillips.

Mr. Qualtrough had wandered off to a far corner of the room and was studying one of Howard's prints.

"You ought to hang this in a better light," he observed over his shoulder. "It's a very nice little picture and it's wasted in this pitch dark corner."

"Oh for heaven's sake," Ann said irritably. "It's Howard's picture—surely he can hang it in the lavatory if he wants to."

I glanced up in surprise. Evidently the strain of the evening was telling severely on Ann's nerves.

Michael broke off from what he was saying to Mrs. Phillips to frown at the interruption, and then immediately resumed his conversation as if Ann had not spoken.

Ann jumped explosively to her feet remarking that it seemed to be quite time she took her elderly parent home. She added with a cold glance in the direction of the sofa: "And I have to get the dinner, too—only in our case every night is the staff's night out."

Michael's frown deepened. He made no move to rise, and Ann continued to chivy Mr. Qualtrough into gathering himself together and making towards the door.

"Oh, come on," she repeated impatiently. "You know you said you wanted to listen to that thing on the Third Programme at half-past seven—well, it's twenty past now."

Mr. Qualtrough's rather harassed expression brightened at once.

"Ah, yes," he said. "I am extremely anxious not to miss that. I don't know whether you are interested in music," he continued vaguely to Mrs. Phillips, who had stopped talking to Michael and was sitting smiling up at him from the depths of the sofa, "but there is a most interesting recital this evening for a chest of viols."

"A chest of viols?" Mrs. Phillips echoed doubtfully. "What is that, please?"

"It's not the sort of chest the bride in *The Mistletoe Bough* got locked into," Ann said flippantly. "And not fifteen men on the dead man's. D'you know when I was little I always saw that as fifteen strong men all sitting round on the corpse of one poor little sailor flat on the ground. I couldn't imagine how there could possibly be room for them all on his diaphragm."

Everybody except Michael laughed, and the expression of bewilderment on Mrs. Phillips' face became more marked.

"I am sorry to be so slow," she said simply. "I do not understand your references. You see, I am not English."

Michael ground out his cigarette with unnecessary violence.

"No doubt," he said frigidly, "if you wanted to, you could make us feel silly by referring to things you understand that we don't. It's an easy way to get a cheap laugh. But I'm sure you would have the courtesy not to do it."

Ann's chin rose as if she had been hit and a vivid wave of colour flushed into her cheeks.

Betty said quickly: "I'm quite sure Mrs. Phillips doesn't feel that we were laughing at her at all. And frankly I don't mind telling you that I haven't the faintest idea myself what a chest of viols is. And I'm sure Howard hasn't either."

Sonia Phillips smiled. Then she drew on her gloves and rose to her feet. "It is the night out of my staff also," she remarked, gravely, "like Miss Qualtrough, this is an inconvenience which happens to me every night. Thank you so much, Mrs. Sandys, it has been a most charming party."

She walked gracefully across the room to the door. Lewis Qualtrough, who had been standing there for the last few minutes silently watching his daughter, opened it with a little flourish and bowed as she went out. Ann and Michael followed him into the hall.

"Oh, my goodness!" Betty muttered weakly as the door finally closed behind them. "Have you ever experienced a worse hour? Lee dear, I do apologise for inflicting such an awful evening on you. I can't think what was the matter with everybody—"

She flung herself into a chair in an attitude of exhaustion as Howard came back from seeing the guests out.

"Well, thank God that's over," Howard remarked, warming his hands at the fire. "What on earth was the matter with Ann? I've never seen her so much on edge. And what was biting Michael to make him jump down her throat like that? Have they had a row or something?"

"If they haven't, they soon will," Betty said grimly. "As a matter of fact I think Michael was extremely silly to pick on Ann like that over a perfectly harmless remark. How was she to know Mrs. Phillips had never heard of *The Mistletoe Bough*—and anyway, what did it matter if she hadn't? There was no suggestion of any awkwardness until Michael went off the deep end for no reason whatever—and created an embarrassment out of nothing. That really is carrying chivalry a bit far, don't you agree?"

"Ann was being a shade waspish, though," Howard said. He stooped to throw a couple of fresh logs on to the fire. "Even before *The Mistletoe Bough* episode. Look how she flew at her old man for absolutely no cause at all over that picture." He straightened up and walked over to the decanter. With his finger on the handle of the soda siphon he paused. "You don't really think there's anything in it between Michael and this Mrs. Phillips, do you? I mean, if Ann had thought—"

He broke off as a slight noise in the hall made us all swing round. We turned to regard Ann Qualtrough framed in the doorway.

"Sorry to interrupt," she said steadily. "I left my bag behind. And as to Michael and Mrs. Phillips, I can assure you that there isn't *anything* in it. Not a thing!"

V

POST PRANDIAL

IT WAS AFTER DINNER ONE EVENING A WEEK LATER; AND BETTY, Howard and I were sitting round the drawing-room in various stages of exhaustion, Robin had been having a birthday party, and what with preparations, supervision during the party and clearing away afterwards we were all completely worn out.

"Well," Betty remarked with a stifled yawn. "I don't know about you two—but it's half-past ten and I feel just about ready for bed. And if Robin isn't sick in the night, it will be a miracle. Did you see the number of meringues he ate, Lee? I took my eyes off the awful child for about three minutes to deal out the trifle and when I looked at the meringue plate again it was practically empty. He must have eaten about six. I know it was Robin who took them, because Sara sneaked to me afterwards."

Howard's head was nodding over *The Times.* He had escaped the worst ardours of the party by failing to return from his visiting rounds until it was almost over, but he had assisted in the replacement of the furniture; and to look at him now one would think he had carried off the whole affair single-handed.

"Ann was a great asset," I said. "The children simply loved her farm-yard imitations. I must say she's awfully clever if this afternoon's performance is anything to go by."

"Yes, and Michael's conjuring went with a tremendous swing too. It was sweet of them to come and help—I was sorry Michael had to rush off so early—I hardly even thanked him for all he did."

"He said he was going to London or something, didn't he?" I asked. "To a theatre. I wonder why he didn't take Ann. Oh well, I suppose even an engaged couple want some independence."

"I think the little fracas over Mrs. Phillips has blown over all right," Betty remarked, beginning to fold up her knitting. "At least it seems to have done. I met Diana in the village this morning and she tells me they're in the throes of another family crisis up at Oakhurst. Sir Henry has finally put his foot down about Michael going to the R.A.D.A. and has definitely arranged for him to go into some chambers in the Temple and to start reading for the Bar. Michael is being mutinous and swearing he won't go. He'll have to in the end, of course—he's got no money of his own, so therefore no choice. But I must say I agree with Diana that Sir Henry is being a bit harsh with him. His heart was very much set on the stage."

"Would he really have been any good, d'you think? The stage is a pretty overcrowded profession these days. It isn't as if he had Ann's talent."

"Maybe not. But at any rate you'd have thought his father would have allowed him to have a temporary shot at it. He could always have given it up later if it turned out he wasn't good enough. It isn't as if there were all that necessity for Michael to earn his living quickly. Sir Henry's simply stinking with money. I really think he enjoys thwarting people, you know—he gets some horrible perverted sort of kick out of feeling that they're in his power, and that he's got the upper hand over everybody."

"Megalomania," I suggested sleepily. "Hitler had it."

"I suppose so. Well, anyway, Diana says the atmosphere up at Oakhurst is awful. It's getting her down completely."

"Nobody seems very fond of Sir Henry," I remarked without originality. "Hardly the most popular inhabitant of Staple Green. I was talking to Mr. Qualtrough the other night, at your party. He hates him too—partly, I suppose, because he's another of the power-complex victims over the matter of the cottage, but mainly I think on Ann's account. I gather he's fairly indifferent himself as to whether Ann marries Michael or not; but the very fact that Sir Henry's against it is making him doubly keen to promote it in every way he can."

"I've never understood why Sir Henry should be so much against Ann," Betty said, stirring the logs in the fender. "But it's quite true he doesn't want Michael to marry her. I wouldn't put it past him to have engineered the whole of this business of making him drop the stage and go in for law just to make a breach between them. It's exactly the spiteful sort of thing he would do."

"Not a loveable character," I agreed again. "However, as far as Ann and Michael are concerned, Michael's of age—and I imagine if they want to get married they will—Sir Henry or no Sir Henry."

"There's just the little question of money," Betty reminded me. "Michael's earning nothing, and the Qualtroughs haven't got a bean."

"Then they'll just have to wait for the nasty old man to die," I said yawning openly. "Unless he's bloody-minded enough to cut Michael out of his will, as you tell me he did with the daughter."

"Oh, I didn't say he'd cut Sheila out of his will. I don't think Diana would have let him get away with that. I only said he won't make her any allowance now. And I'm sure Howard's right when he says Diana manages to help her a bit on the side, even if it comes out of her own dress allowance—which it obviously does."

"She seems a nice woman, Betty."

"She's an absolute angel," Betty said simply. "And what she has to put up with is unbelievable. Well, you heard a sample of it the other night. If Diana ever banged Sir Henry over the head with a rolling pin I don't believe there's a jury in the country which wouldn't bring in a verdict of justifiable homicide. Or at least they would if they knew the true facts. You mentioned Sheila just now. Diana told me this morning that Sheila rang up last night and asked her to go over to Tunbridge Wells this evening to see her. I suppose the poor girl's in trouble of some sort again—money or the children or something. Anyway, would you believe it—Diana has had to invent some absurd excuse for Sir Henry's benefit about a W.V.S. meeting, so that he won't find out she's gone to see Sheila. Isn't it fantastic? His own daughter!"

I agreed that it was—utterly fantastic.

At this point Howard woke up with a loud snort and asked why on earth we hadn't gone to bed. Gossiping as usual, he supposed.

"And why not?" Betty demanded truculently. "For all the conversational stimulus I get out of you, I might as well be married to a Trappist. Suppose you regale us with some news. When's old Higgins going to let us have that side of bacon he promised me faithfully for Christmas?"

Howard grunted. "Haven't had time to get along to old Higgins' farm lately," he replied evasively. "Too busy."

"Busy!" Betty echoed. "*Nobody's* too busy for bacon! And that reminds me—where were you this afternoon between surgery and tea-time? There was nobody but Miss Butler of Ley Hill down in the visiting book, and Norah said you'd told her she could wait until tomorrow. You are an old stinker—I hoped that meant you were coming in early to help with Robin's mob."

"I was out on a visit," Howard said shortly. Then a moment later he added much too casually: "There's no mystery about it. I went to see Mrs. Phillips, as a matter of fact."

"Oh?" Betty said. "I didn't know she was ill."

"She isn't—not in the sense of being in bed or anything," Howard replied. "But she sent a message saying she wanted me to go and see her. So naturally I went."

"I see," said Betty in a tone which clearly implied that she didn't see in the least. After a moment she added: "I didn't even know she was a patient of yours. You might have mentioned it before I asked her in the other night."

"She wasn't a patient then. If you must know, I saw her professionally for the first time last Thursday—and I made another call this afternoon. Do you mind?"

"Don't be silly," Betty said sharply. "Of course I don't mind. I only thought it was a little funny that you hadn't mentioned it. I mean, seeing that she's a neighbour—and I suppose I shall be meeting her all over the place—"

"Well, you won't be meeting her much, actually, she's leaving the district. She told me today that she had taken the lease of Holly Tree Cottage for three years, but she is allowed to sub-let if she wants to. She saw the agents last week and said she would be willing to move out directly they found another tenant, and at any rate by the end of the month."

"But she's only just come!" Betty exclaimed in surprise. "It all sounds most odd to me. Did she say why she was leaving?"

"I suppose she's decided she doesn't want to go on living here," Howard said casually. "Perhaps she was put off by the cross-section of local community that we produced for her last Tuesday. Anyway, I've no more idea than you have what her plans are—only that she's going. Lee, have you seen this week's copy of *The Radio*

Times anywhere? No—it doesn't matter. I just thought you might be sitting on it. It's really extraordinary how things manage to disappear in this house."

He was obviously anxious to change the conversation, and I could see Betty torn between a lively curiosity and her training as a good doctor's wife who doesn't ask nosey questions about the private affairs of her husband's patients.

In the end she sighed deeply and rose from her chair and I knew that training had won. "Oh well," she said yawning uncontrollably. "I'm going upstairs. Thank goodness, Howard, it looks as if we were going to get to bed at a reasonable hour for once in our lives. Coming, Lee?"

At that moment the telephone bell rang in the hall.

"You didn't touch wood," Howard grumbled. "Now look what you've done!"

He strode out muttering wrathfully.

"It's perfectly true," Betty said penitently, straightening up the cushions. "It happens every time I say it doesn't look as if there were going to be any night calls. I wonder what it is this time. Mrs. Dyer's little boy has been awfully ill with mumps, but he's much better now and the 'flu patients don't usually ring up at this hour. I expect it's one of Howard's old women with what they call gastric stomachs. They go on quite cheerfully for weeks without thinking of calling in the doctor, and then suddenly at eleven o'clock one night some solicitous relation decides that she 'doesn't like the look of grandma'—and bang goes poor old Howard's night's rest. They're always doing it. I tell you what, Lee—I think I should like a cup of tea to take upstairs, wouldn't you?"

"It would be rather heaven," I admitted. "Look, you go up now and I'll put on a kettle."

"No, I'll go," Betty said. "Perhaps with any luck Howard's call will turn out to be a false alarm and he won't have to go after all—"

Howard put his head round the drawing-room door.

"Betty," he said abruptly. "Don't wait up for me. I may be rather a long time. That was John Wickham ringing up from Oakhurst. It seems that Metcalfe's had a stroke. Diana was out for the evening, and she's just got back and found him collapsed in a chair in his study. She's in a bit of a jitter, and John thinks I ought to have a look at her as well. So expect me when you see me. Where's my bag? Oh yes, here it is. Well, goodnight darling—go to bed and dream what a lovely quiet life you'd have had if you hadn't been silly enough to marry a poor perishing G.P."

He kissed her hastily and hurried out. The front door slammed behind him.

Betty and I stared at each other rather blankly.

"Well!" Betty said, and without further comment made for the kitchen. I followed her.

"I wonder if it's a serious stroke," I said slowly.

"It's always serious to have a stroke when you're Sir Henry's age," Betty replied. "He must be well over sixty. And Diana isn't a person who jitters easily—she's one of the most controlled women I know."

We made the tea and carried the tray up to Betty's bedroom where the electric fire glowed comfortingly.

"I wonder," Betty remarked, sipping reflectively, "why John Wickham rang up—and not Diana herself? You'd have thought—"

"Because she was too upset, I suppose," I suggested, fighting back an enormous yawn. I had suddenly realised how tired I was. "It would have been a nasty shock for anyone to come in and find him like that."

"It all sounds a bit peculiar to me," Betty went on thoughtfully. "I can't see what John was doing up at Oakhurst at all. Diana was over in Tunbridge Wells, I suppose, seeing Sheila—she said this morning she was going tonight. And Michael was at his theatre or whatever it was in London. So Sir Henry must have been alone in the house this evening. Where does John Wickham come in?"

"I can't imagine," I said, beginning to lose interest. "Perhaps he'd gone to see Sir Henry and was there when he was taken ill. Oh no, it couldn't have been like that if Diana came in and found him already collapsed. Really, Betty, does it matter? Maybe one of the servants sent for John Wickham as everybody else was out, and by the time he got there, Diana had returned. Only if that was the case, you'd have thought that any servant with a grain of sense would have telephoned for Howard right away. But they are sometimes apt to lose their heads, you know."

"But that's just it," Betty said. "There can't have been any servants in the house—it's Tuesday, when they all go over to the cinema in Tunbridge Wells. They come back on the last bus which doesn't get in until quarter past eleven."

"Well, I give it up," I said, yawning again. "There's probably some perfectly simple explanation which Howard will tell you as soon as he comes in. Just for the sake of pure idle curiosity you might pass it on to me in the morning. And now I really think—"

The telephone on the bedside table rang sharply.

"Yes?" Betty said, picking it up. "Oh. Yes—yes—all right."

She hung the receiver up slowly.

"That was Howard. He said not to worry if he was late because Sir Henry's in a very bad way and they've sent for the ambulance to take him to St. Margaret's Hospital in Tunbridge Wells. Howard sounded rather rattled, Lee. I'm sure there's something odd about all this."

"How d'you mean, odd?" I asked a shade peevishly. I was half dead with sleepiness, and Betty's determination to smell rats where no rats were was beginning to irritate me slightly.

"Just what I say," Betty persisted obstinately. "You can scoff if you like, Lee, but I know Howard and he sounded definitely fussed. And it *is* odd that Sir Henry should have had this stroke just on the one night when everybody was out—and that John Wickham should happen to be there to ring up about it. It doesn't make sense."

"I quite agree about the stroke part of it not making sense," I said, getting up and feeling about for the shoe I had kicked off. "If Sir Henry'd been found with his skull bashed in with a meat axe I should have been much less surprised. Now, that *would* have been—"

"Lee!" Betty exclaimed, and I was stricken to see that she had gone quite pale. "You don't *really* think—?"

"No, of course I don't," I said soothingly. "It's only my elephantine way of trying to be witty. Actually I have no coherent thoughts beyond the subject of bed. Goodnight, honey. Don't let it worry you."

I went to bed, leaving Betty sitting disconsolately on the floor beside the tea-tray.

VI

FURTHER OUTLOOK UNSETTLED

IN SPITE OF THE SUFFOCATING WEARINESS WITH WHICH I crawled into bed, the small clock on the table beside me said two o'clock before I finally put out my light, and there had still been no sounds of Howard's return. I don't know whether it was just because I was thoroughly over-tired, but I lay for some time even after I had put the light out pondering gloomily over this and that.

However, by the time I woke up again the following morning everything had sunk back into its normal proportion and I decided that Betty had let a somewhat morbid imagination get the better of her.

It had evidently been snowing quite hard during the night and the leaden look of the sky above the bare trees promised a lot more snow in the not too distant future. It was still bitterly cold. I scrambled through my bath, then dressed in the warmest tweed suit I had with me, and went down to breakfast.

Howard was alone in the dining-room. He greeted me rather sombrely and said that Betty was upstairs with Robin, who had amply fulfilled everyone's forebodings after yesterday afternoon's party and was now in the throes of a tremendous bilious attack.

"Who'd be a doctor," he added grimly, helping himself to porridge. "In at three—up again holding Robin's head at five—and now off for the daily grind. Well! I only hope it will teach the little beast a lesson not to be so greedy."

He unfurled *The Times* and relapsed into uninviting silence. I wanted to ask how Sir Henry Metcalfe was, but somehow hadn't the nerve. After all, the health of Howard's patients was nothing to do with me. Howard certainly did look shockingly tired. There were dark circles under his eyes and the lines on his forehead were much more pronounced than usual; but whether this was due to worry or just plain lack of sleep, I didn't know.

After a few minutes Betty came down.

"He's been sick again," she announced. "I don't think those powders are much good, Howard, and he makes such heavy weather about taking them. Don't you think, perhaps—"

"Give him anything you like," Howard interrupted wearily. "Give him a concentrated dose of Fowler's solution—only don't come and ask me again what I advise. Of course the child's been sick again—it's the best thing he can do. He'll go on being sick until he's got rid of about half a pound of meringues and Lord knows what else besides, and then he'll be as right as a cricket. Only for heaven's sake don't *fuss.*"

"I'm sorry," Betty said humbly. "I know you're tired. Have you got to go over to Tunbridge Wells this morning to see Sir Henry?"

"Oh, I'll have to look in. Not that there's anything I can do. They're entirely competent and they've got the whole thing under control; but he's a very sick man. What you could do, Betty, if you've got the time this morning is to pop up to Oakhurst and have a word with Diana. I told her to stay in bed today, though I don't suppose she will. We pushed her off upstairs with a sedative last night and she should be all right this morning—but she's all alone in the house, apart from the servants, and she's pretty upset, poor girl. She might be glad to see you."

"Of course I'll go. But when you say all alone, hasn't Michael come back?"

"Well, he hadn't up till midnight. If he came in at all last night, it must have been jolly late. Anyway, Michael's a bit spineless in the face of an emergency, and I'm sure Diana would be grateful if you'd look in for a few minutes."

"Of course I will," Betty repeated. "Poor Diana, it must have been a beastly shock for her."

Howard returned to *The Times* and Betty poured coffee. I fiddled with a piece of toast and decided that it would be more tactful to wait until Howard had gone before bombarding Betty with questions. He was clearly in a very scratchy mood that morning.

Actually by the time Sara had been dispatched to school, pursued and brought back for some forgotten homework, re-dispatched, and Robin had been attended to at some length, it was nearly eleven o'clock before I had any chance to talk to Betty at all. And when I asked her what had happened the night before, she was most unsatisfactorily vague. It seemed that Howard had come home exhausted and uncommunicative. Betty was sure he was worried about something, but didn't know what. All it boiled down to was that Sir Henry had had a stroke—Betty gathered it was some form of cerebral haemorrhage—and that he had been taken to hospital. He was very ill, and Howard refused to be drawn into any discussion of the symptoms or the probability of his recovery—and that was that. The mystery of John Wickham's presence in the house was easily accounted for by the fact that Diana, driving home from Tunbridge Wells, had happened to overtake him walking along the main road and had picked him up and given him a lift back. She invited him in for a drink, and they had then discovered Sir Henry in the study in a state of collapse. Diana was naturally very shaken, so John had undertaken the job of ringing up Howard. It was all completely simple and straightforward and lacking in excitement of any kind.

After Betty had gone out to confer with Mrs. Padgett in the kitchen, I was standing by the drawing-room window meditatively gazing across the bleak fields to a distant oast-house and wishing it would either make up its mind to snow again and get it over or else brighten up a bit, when I heard the click of the gate and looked round to see Diana Metcalfe walking up the drive. She was wearing a fur coat with a silk scarf tied round her head and she waved her hand when she saw me.

I went back to the hall and called to Betty, who came running out of the kitchen exclaiming: "Oh dear, I ought to have gone round to see her earlier—I'm sure Howard didn't mean her to get up today."

Diana came in and sat by the fire. She was looking very pale and tired, which was scarcely surprising. She made light of Betty's solicitude, protesting that she was perfectly well and had thought a little fresh air would do her good.

"And I felt I wanted to talk to somebody," she added rather pathetically. "I suppose there's no further word from the hospital this morning about Henry?"

Betty explained that Howard was going over to Tunbridge Wells and would probably call in at Oakhurst on his way back. "Anyway, they'd have telephoned you if there had been any change," she said.

"Yes," Diana agreed listlessly. "I suppose they would. Howard said there was no point in my going over there myself because Henry's unconscious, and anyway he's much better left quiet. I'm still feeling a little bewildered by the whole thing. Did Howard tell you what happened?"

"No—hardly anything, except that you'd come home and found him ill. Diana, it must have been awful for you—we are so very sorry." Betty hesitated and then went on: "Has Sir Henry ever had any kind of stroke before, d'you know?"

"I've never heard that he has. I believe his heart isn't awfully strong—Howard's been treating him for that for years, off and on. I don't mean there was anything definitely wrong with him—but, you see, Henry isn't as young as he was. He was over fifty when we were married—and that's fifteen years ago."

There was a long pause. I was sure Betty was picturing, as I was myself, the wide and inexplicable gap in age and outlook and everything else between Sir Henry Metcalfe and his wife. Fifteen years ago Diana must have been a very lovely girl in the middle twenties. What on earth could have induced her to marry a cold grim hatchet-jawed widower old enough to be her father? It seemed utterly incomprehensible to me.

Diana said slowly: "Howard warned me last night that it's very unlikely that Henry will recover."

Betty opened her mouth to utter some impulsive cry of sympathy and then shut it again and swallowed awkwardly. I could feel myself doing the same thing. It was all very well for us to sit there opening and shutting our mouths like goldfish in a tank, but it was obviously in both our minds that if Sir Henry did die it would be the most merciful thing that could happen from Diana's point of view. At the same time, we could hardly say so openly.

"Poor Diana," Betty said at last. "It's all so beastly for you. We *are* sorry. But I suppose in a way it would have been worse if he'd had some long painful illness or something. Anyway," she hurried on, trying to sound cheerful at the idea, "he may recover after all. No doctor's infallible—even Howard. Naturally you felt upset because it happened when you weren't there, but you can't possibly blame yourself for that—"

"That's one of the queerest and most horrible things about the whole business," Diana said. "Almost as if the two things were connected. Getting me out of the house like that with a bogus telephone call—and then this dreadful thing happening to Henry the same night. Of course it's only a coincidence, really—it must be. But I shan't rest until I've found out who played such a cruel practical joke."

"Bogus telephone call? Practical joke?" Betty repeated blankly. "Whatever do you mean, Diana?"

It was Diana's turn to stare.

"Didn't Howard tell you about the telephone call the night before last?"

"No—what telephone call?"

"Well, of course he was so busy last night looking after Henry that I suppose he hardly took in what I was trying to tell him. I was—I was a bit upset with the shock, you know. But that telephone call was the most extraordinary thing. It almost looked as if somebody had done it deliberately to get me out of the house."

"But didn't you tell me you were going to Tunbridge Wells last night to see Sheila?"

"Yes, of course I did. But that was just the point. Sheila never made that call. She didn't know anything about it. And when I got to their house last night, she and Dick were awfully surprised to see me."

"But I thought you said—"

"What actually happened," Diana interrupted, speaking rather fast to cover her nervousness, and picking up a cigarette which she lit with fingers that trembled a little; "was that I went down as usual on Monday night to the Women's Institute. They're having a course of classes on leather work and I always go if I possibly can. Well, anyway, the night before last I was a few minutes late getting to the Hall because, as a matter of fact, there'd been a bit of a flare-up between Henry and Michael at dinner—but that's nothing to do with it. When I got there at about five past eight I met

Mrs. Prendergast from the Vicarage who said Sheila had rung me up a few minutes before and had left a message saying would I go over after dinner the next evening—that is, last night. I wondered a little what had happened—you know, whether one of the children was ill or anything—and I was just going to ring Tunbridge Wells back, when Mrs. Prendergast came panting along and said Sheila had particularly said don't bother to ring again as their telephone was out of order and she was speaking from a friend's house. Mrs. Prendergast said she hadn't gathered that there was any sort of crisis—Sheila had sounded quite normal and had left it that she would expect me anyway, but if for any reason I couldn't manage it not to bother. So of course after that I thought no more about it."

"And then what happened?"

"Well, nothing—except that when I got over to Birling Road last night I found Sheila and Dick playing bridge with the people next door, and they weren't expecting me and Sheila had never telephoned at all. We all thought it was very curious, but since I was there they insisted on my staying and cutting in and I left to come home about half past ten. But you must admit it was disturbing—especially in view of what happened to Henry."

"That can't have been anything but pure coincidence," Betty said. "Nobody could have known in advance that Sir Henry was going to be taken ill—and what would be the point of trying to get you out of the house anyway?"

Diana still looked distressed. "I know it all sounds a complete nonsense," she agreed unhappily. "But I don't like it. *Who* could have wanted to play such a silly practical joke on me—and why?"

We both shook our heads blankly.

"Wasn't it an unusual thing for Sheila to have rung you up at the Parish Hall instead of at home?" I asked. "I mean, there was always the risk that she might miss you—as indeed she did."

"Except," Betty put in, "that it wasn't Sheila who rang at all. Yes, Diana—didn't you wonder why she hadn't rung you direct at Oakhurst?"

Diana smiled rather wryly. "That was the least queer part of the whole business," she said. "Well, Betty—you know Henry. He isn't—he's never been very sympathetic over Sheila's affairs. He'd more or less forbidden me to have anything more to do with her, and he would have raised quite a rumpus if he'd known I was proposing to go over and see her last night. I'm afraid I told him I was going to a W.V.S. meeting. Sheila knew the position—and consequently she never rang me up at Oakhurst if she could possible avoid it. She knows my habits—that I always do go down to the Women's Institute class on Mondays and it was quite natural for her to have rung me there rather than at home where Henry or one of the servants might have answered the telephone."

"How well does Mrs. Prendergast know Sheila's voice?" Betty asked. "They didn't come to Staple Green until after Sheila married Dick, did they?"

"No. I thought of that too. Mrs. Prendergast's only met Sheila about half a dozen times—she hasn't been over here at all lately because of Henry's attitude. It would be quite easy for Mrs. Prendergast to make a mistake. But what I keep asking myself is *why* anyone should have done such a silly thing."

She sat staring sadly out of the window. The roof of the distant oast house was suddenly obscured by a flurry of flying snowflakes. Betty poked the fire vigorously.

"Well, I don't know," she remarked. "I can't make head or tail of it, Diana. It was a horrid thing to happen—but the only thing to do is just not to worry too much about it. I'm sure it can't have had *anything* to do with Sir Henry's illness; though I can quite see that when you came in alone and found him there—"

"I wasn't alone, thank God," Diana said quickly. "I overtook John a little way along the road—just at the bottom of the hill outside Brenchley. So of course I stopped and gave him a lift. I asked him to come up to the house for a drink. It wasn't very late and I thought as Henry'd been alone all the evening he'd be quite glad of some company. John wasn't awfully keen to come. He—he doesn't always see eye to eye with Henry, as you know. But I persuaded him to come in for a minute." She paused and stubbed out her cigarette with nervous fingers. "Thank God I did," she added softly. "I don't know what I'd have done without him."

The silence was tense now. I found myself watching Diana's strained face and wondering why she should think it necessary to invent so many excuses for the simple action of inviting a friend into her own house for a drink. There seemed no reason to stress, as she was doing, John Wickham's unwillingness to come into the house. What did it matter whether he had been there or not? Actually, as I remembered the expression in John Wickham's eyes that evening a week ago in this room when Sir Henry had been baiting his wife with her Lady Bountiful attitude, and John had hurled himself out of the room as if unable to restrain himself another minute, I was a little surprised that in any circumstances he had ever consented to visit Oakhurst again—in anything but a purely professional capacity. It would have required quite some persuasion to make me do a thing like that. There must surely be more to John Wickham's feeling for Diana Metcalfe than Betty's casual diagnosis of a disinterested and friendly admiration. Betty had maintained that Diana had no idea of his devotion. I was less sure.

I collected my thoughts in time to hear Betty saying something about coffee and adding quite untruthfully that she and I always had elevenses at this time. She disappeared towards the kitchen.

Diana lit another cigarette and puffed at it rather desperately. We chatted aimlessly for a few minutes about the weather and commented on the robust health of Betty's potted primulas. It was obvious that Diana was talking automatically and that her mind was miles away.

"I suppose when one's a bit on edge," she said suddenly, *á propos* of nothing we had been discussing, "one finds oneself putting the most sinister interpretations on to the simplest little things."

"Does one?" I asked interested. "What sort of things?"

"Oh nothing I could put my finger on," she replied vaguely. "It's just that—looking back on it now—there seem to have been one or two rather curious little discrepancies about last night. Apart from the telephone call, I mean."

I longed to ask exactly what she meant, but I felt I didn't really know her well enough to press the point unless she continued of her own accord.

Betty, however, returning opportunely with the coffee tray, had no such scruples.

"What's that, Diana?" she asked immediately, putting down the tray. "What about last night?"

"I don't really know," Diana confessed with a deprecating little shrug. "Nothing that actually *happened*. But there were one or two rather unaccountable little details—such as the fact that Henry seemed to have been taken ill while he was sitting in his chair reading a book on border lilies. Well, I mean, there's no reason on earth why he *shouldn't* have been, except that in all the fifteen years I've been married to him I've never known him open a book on flowers. He always said there was nothing in the world so boring as books about horticulture. He was keen enough on the fruit and vegetable side of our gardens, but he just couldn't see any point in flowers. With me, of course, it was just the opposite. I adore the flowers—I'll read about roses and rock gardens far into the night, while I can't summon up a scrap of enthusiasm for big bud or onion fly."

She paused and smiled a little wanly. "It wasn't that he couldn't appreciate beauty," she added, defending him from our unspoken criticism. "He adored his china collection. But I'd rather have a live chrysanthemum any day than a pottery picture of one, however beautifully painted."

It occurred to me that Diana was talking about her husband in the past tense, and I wondered if her mind had already adapted itself to the gloomy forecast put forward by Howard.

"How d'you know what Sir Henry was reading if he was unconscious when you found him?" Betty asked practically.

"It was open on the arm of the chair he was sitting in. He'd evidently been having a drink—there was a tray on the table beside him with a decanter and glass and so on—and I suppose he was reading when he felt this—this stroke coming on. As a matter of fact he'd had rather a bad cold for the last week or so, and I made him a glass of hot whisky myself just before I went out. He must have got up and fetched himself another one later. But the thing about the book was that when Howard and John lifted him out of the chair to put him on the stretcher, I went over to straighten up the cushions—you know, how one does without thinking—and there was another book which had slipped down beside him and we hadn't noticed at first. It was Honey's book on *Ceramic Art in China*—far more the sort of thing I should have expected to find him reading, especially as he'd obviously been examining his precious new *famille rose* bowl. And that was another catastrophe—though, of course, hardly comparable."

"What was a catastrophe?" Betty asked, refilling my coffee cup.

"The china bowl—it was broken. He simply adored it—it was supposed to be terribly rare and wonderful and he was so proud of having discovered it at the back of a shelf in some junk shop.

Mr. Qualtrough told him it was only a reproduction, but he didn't believe him, and I suppose he'd been comparing the china marks or something; and then when he was taken ill it slipped out of his hand. We found it in fragments on the floor—quite beyond riveting, I'm afraid. He would—that is, if he recovers—he will be awfully upset to hear about it."

"Oh, what a pity," Betty exclaimed warmly and then glanced rather guiltily at me. I'm sure she was thinking, as I was, that she had shown far more distress at the breaking of a china bowl than in the bursting of one of Sir Henry's blood vessels.

I can't say that I regarded the information about the book as very significant. I frequently read two books at once myself, and could easily be picked up moribund with *The Shropshire Lad* on the arm of my chair, *The White Devil* under a cushion, and *Lord Peter Views The Body* on the floor at my feet. Nobody knowing me at all well would find anything in the least odd about that. But of course I wouldn't have the estimable Mr. Honey (whoever he might be) on *Ceramic Art* anywhere within miles of me, because I am simply not interested in ceramic art. So in a way I did see the point about a book on border lilies striking an incongruous note, though I couldn't see that it led to any immediate conclusion.

"Then there was the wireless," Diana said. "It was still on."

"Why was that peculiar?"

"Henry hated it. He had absolutely no ear for music, and he never turned it on for anything except the news—or occasionally a talk on something which interested him. But there weren't any talks that night. When John and I came in it was blaring away playing the Soldiers' Chorus from *Faust*."

"Perhaps he'd simply forgotten to turn it off after the news."

Diana shook her head positively. "He'd never have done that," she said with conviction. "No, the only solution I can think of is that he was taken ill—that this stroke came over him some time while the news was still on, and that he couldn't get out of his chair to turn it off. It's—it's rather awful to think of all this happening to him while he was alone in the house, with nobody within call. That's why I'll never be able to forgive this crazy practical joker for that bogus telephone message. Even though, as you say, it can't really be connected with Henry's illness, if it hadn't been for that incident I would have been there to help him, and to ring up Howard, and he could have been got to the hospital hours sooner. It might have made all the difference."

Betty made vague sympathetic noises, and Diana blew her nose apologetically. She began collecting together her belongings.

"I must go," she said. "Thank you, Betty dear—it's made me feel better having somebody to talk to. It's the waiting for news that's so nerve-racking."

"Couldn't you stay and have some lunch?"

"No, really, thanks awfully. I must get back. They might ring up from the hospital, you see, and it would be a bad show if I wasn't at home to take the call."

Betty walked to the door with her.

"By the way," she said, opening the hall door. "I suppose Michael's back?"

"Oh yes. I don't know what time he got in last night—I'd lost all count of hours by that time, but it must have been pretty late. He went up to London for some theatre and got involved with friends and missed his train or something. Michael's a good lad at heart, Betty, and I know he's really trying to be sympathetic; he's in, the most awful gloom about the whole thing, naturally—but somehow he's not much of a help. D'you understand what I mean?"

"In a way," Betty said. She picked up Diana's silk scarf from the hall chest. "You know," she said tentatively, "if there's *anything* Howard and I can do—"

"Bless you," Diana said quickly. "And do tell Howard how grateful I am—nobody could have done more. Well goodbye, Betty—thank you for the coffee—see you soon."

She walked rapidly down the drive. Betty went with her as far as the gate and I stood watching them from the window. It was snowing quite briskly now and just beginning to lie like white powder on the grass.

I found myself wondering irrelevantly why Michael Metcalfe should have chosen to go to London by train when he possessed a perfectly good car. The obvious reason, of course, would have been that the car was out of order. Well, perhaps it was—though I had a definite impression that he had arrived in it at Betty's children's party that afternoon and had driven away in it afterwards. Anyway, what did it matter?

Betty returned shivering in an exaggerated manner and went over to the fire to warm her hands.

"There's no getting away from the fact that if Sir Henry dies it will be the best thing that could possibly happen," she observed frankly, "though of course one can't expect Diana to see it like that. At any rate not yet."

"I know," I said. "At the moment I think she's genuinely pretty upset about it all."

"Anyway," Betty said, turning round to warm the back of her legs, "he isn't dead yet. And he's such a tough old bird that in spite of what Howard says, I wouldn't put it past him to recover. I must say I've always thought it would take a bit more than a stroke to finish off old Metcalfe."

In which conclusion, as later events proved, she couldn't have been more right.

VII

NO MOURNING

When, by nearly five minutes to two, there was still no message from Howard, Betty decided to start luncheon without him. Sara had come home from school and Robin had recovered to the extent of being allowed out of bed in his dressing-gown and given a cup of Bovril and some dry toast—both of which he resented bitterly.

"Why can't I have corn-beef-hash like Sara?" he demanded peevishly. "What are you having?"

Betty explained with great patience that corn-beef-hash was not a suitable diet for a convalescent, but Robin remained unimpressed by her reasoning.

"It's got gravy," he complained. "And proper potatoes. I *like* gravy things. Where's Daddy?"

"Out. Go on, darling, up to Nanny and have your rest like a good boy. Then maybe you can have something with gravy tomorrow. Run along."

Howard came in about ten minutes to three. Betty and I were in the drawing-room finishing our coffee.

"How's Sir Henry?" Betty asked as Howard, having fidgeted irritably with the papers on the desk, refused coffee, and lit a fresh cigarette with another one already smouldering in the ash-tray, finally came to anchor in a large wing chair.

Howard blew a very careful smoke ring towards the ceiling.

"Dead," he said briefly.

"Dead?" Betty echoed.

"He never had a chance. They did all they could at the hospital—but it was too late by the time we got him there. He never regained consciousness."

Betty put down her cup and looked hard at her husband.

"Does Diana know?" she asked. "She was in here this morning, and she said she was expecting them to ring her from the hospital."

"No point in their doing that," Howard said. "I went straight from the hospital to Oakhurst. I've just told her myself." He ate a lump of sugar from the basin on the coffee tray, and blew another smoke ring with great concentration.

"How did she take it?"

"Well, I'd done my best to prepare her, you know. I told her it was a bad prognosis. She took it very calmly. Well—you know Diana. She doesn't go in for hysterics."

"Do you think I ought to go up and see if she's all right?" Betty asked anxiously. "I suppose Michael's with her?"

"Yes. Very shaken, I thought he seemed—though not exactly stunned with grief. It was a bit of a shock to him, of course, to arrive back last night and hear the old man had been taken off to hospital. All the same, I wouldn't have expected him to go to pieces in the way he did when I told them both the news just now."

"I feel I ought to ring up or do *something*." Betty said rather helplessly. "After all, Diana's one of our closest friends—"

"I wouldn't ring up just yet," Howard replied. "She—she's lying down. Send up a note, if you like. But I wouldn't try to see her today."

Something in his tone made Betty glance up sharply.

"Howard," she said accusingly, "you're holding something back. What is it? You said yourself you didn't expect him to recover."

"Well, nor I did," Howard said defensively. Then he added with great violence: "All the same. I wish to God he *had* recovered. It would have saved the most awful lot of unpleasantness."

"You *are* hiding something," Betty said. "What d'you mean—unpleasantness? Naturally I don't expect you to go into a song-and-dance routine over losing one of your most expensive patients, but after all—have we got to keep up the pretence among ourselves that this is anything but what they call a merciful release? Especially for poor Diana. I can't summon up any feelings of tragedy at all. *Why* are you being so broody and peculiar about it all?"

"Hell," said Howard. He hurled the contents of the smoking ash-tray with an explosive gesture into the fire, and turned to face his wife.

"Listen," he said quietly. "Since it's bound to come out in time, I may as well tell you now. When I saw Metcalfe last night I thought at once that he'd had a pontine haemorrhage. He had all the symptoms—even down to the famous pin-point pupils you read about in the text-books. He hadn't, as far as I could see, developed any lateral paralysis—however, that didn't mean anything much either way. We got him to the hospital and I had a consultation with Harvey. He agreed with my diagnosis, and we treated him accordingly. But it was pretty soon evident that he wasn't going to recover. And then somehow I got thinking a bit about the case, and there were one or two things I didn't like. His temperature, for instance. You'd expect a degree of pyrexia with a cerebral haemorrhage. Metcalfe's temperature was sub-normal and his hands were cold and clammy. The pupils remained contracted and he developed Cheyne-Stokes breathing. I didn't say anything to Harvey last night, because I didn't want to start up a mare's nest. Then this morning Metcalfe died, and I realised that I didn't care for taking the responsibility of writing a certificate.

I had another talk with Harvey. I think he still thinks I'm a little mad. Anyhow, the long and short of it was that he agreed, since I felt that way about it, to ring up old Venables at Pembury—who, as you know, is the Coroner for the district—and told him that we wanted a P.M. Venables said in that case he thought he'd better lay on an inquest. So there you are." Pie walked over to the window. "Now for the love of God, keep that under your hats for the next day or two. The whole thing may turn out to be nothing but a wild goose chase, and one doesn't enjoy making a fool of oneself unnecessarily."

We sat for a few minutes digesting this information in silence.

"But what on earth do you think happened to him?" Betty asked eventually. "I mean, if he *didn't* have a pontine whatever-it-was?"

"Look," Howard said restlessly. "D'you mind awfully if we don't discuss it any more now? I'm pretty fed up with the whole thing, and I'm a long way behind on my sleep quota. The nerves are not at their brightest. By the way, how's Robin?"

"Much better," Betty picked up the coffee tray. "Better and clamouring for food. Have you *got* to go out again this afternoon? Couldn't you possibly go and lie down till tea-time? You look all in."

"I've got a round of visits as long as your arm. This hospital business took up the whole morning. I'll just go and have a look at Robin and then I must push off."

He heaved himself out of the chair with a deep sigh and made for the door. Betty followed with the tray.

"It's all very well," she said to me a few minutes later when the slamming of the front door had indicated Howard's departure on his rounds. "But just what does he mean by 'one or two things he didn't like'? A stroke's a stroke, isn't it—or at least in medical parlance it's a cerebral haemorrhage—but if it wasn't that, what was it?"

"I'm sure I don't know. Perhaps Howard thinks it wasn't a stroke at all."

"Well, what else could it have been? You're surely not suggesting that somebody poisoned him while he was alone in an empty house, are you?"

"N—no," I said hastily. For a moment I had forgotten the empty house and my mind had been speculating wildly about blunt instruments. Then I realised the utter absurdity of such a theory because whatever else they might miss, two qualified doctors could hardly fail to observe the exterior effects of a fatal blow on the back of the head with a poker or something of that kind. Poison was a much more practicable idea.

"There must have been *some* cause," I stated with idiotic obviousness. "And as you said yourself last night, it's all very queer that it should have happened on the one particular night when everybody was out. Especially in view of that telephone call Diana Metcalfe was telling us about."

"I think you and Howard have both gone raving mad," Betty snapped unjustifiably. "I can't think why we can't all regard the thing normally. He was a nasty old man and he's dead. And apart from the fact that he was a good patient, it seems to me there's nothing to get worked up about. Oh *why* does Howard have to start up all this fuss? Why couldn't he have left things alone?"

I forebore to point out that it was she and not I who had been getting worked up the night before. She was the person who had been reiterating the oddness of the situation—and this before Sir Henry had actually died, and long before we had any reason to suppose that there was anything in the least abnormal about his stroke.

"I hate Howard being involved in fusses," she said and burst ridiculously into tears. "Don't you see, Lee, if it turns out that there's something funny about his death they'll blame Howard? Lay people are all the same. They'll say it was neglect or something—that he ought to have found out sooner that it wasn't an ordinary straightforward stroke."

"Don't be silly," I said. "Even doctors are allowed to be human. Howard did all he possibly could, and the minute he had the faintest suspicion that there might be something wrong—which in any case hasn't been proved—he consulted the hospital pathologist and refused to give a certificate. He couldn't have done more. If he'd covered it up as you're suggesting, and *then* it came out later that there'd been some funny business—well, then he *would* be in a mess! As it is he's entirely in the clear."

"You don't know people in a village," Betty said, refusing to be comforted. "This will lose him a lot of patients. And it'll be the paying ones who'll leave him, not the National Health crowd. Oh *why* did this have to happen?"

At this very ill-chosen moment we heard the front door burst open and a clear familiar voice calling from the hall: "Betty! Betty! Are you in?"

"Ann Qualtrough," Betty whispered to me unnecessarily.

"Oh, bother! Can't we slip out somehow—"

The drawing-room door opened. Ann stood on the threshold, her eyes sparkling with excitement.

"Have you *heard?*" she demanded breathlessly. "But of course you must have done, if Howard's been back. We got it from Jarvis's boy who'd met young Bolland coming down from Oakhurst where the Greek messenger in the shape of your husband had just been breaking the news to the bereaved widow. Won't dear Diana be thrilled? Now she'll be able to marry John Wickham and live happily ever after. She's wanted to for years."

Betty pulled herself together and blew her nose.

"*Ann*," she said repressively. "I simply won't have you saying things like that. It's outrageous. As well as completely untrue and—and indecent. Here's Sir Henry—"

"Barely cold in his grave!" Ann mimicked glibly. "Not even that, when you come to think of it. Darling, how conventional you are at heart! Don't tell me you're really bowed down about the best bit of news we've had in Staple Green since they put in the main electricity cable? You know as well as I do how devoted and dog-like John Wickham's always been to Diana—"

Betty broke in: "There may be a lot of people who didn't like Sir Henry. I didn't like him myself. But it's disgusting to go round talking like this, Ann, the very day he dies. It's—it's in the worst possible taste. And as for saying that Diana—"

"All right, darling," Ann said, flinging herself down on to the back of the sofa and running her hand through her fair hair. "We'll skip Diana, since you seem to be so touchy on the point. I only thought how nice it must be for her feeling she's got rid of that old horror at last. Let's think of all the other people who'll be pleased instead. There's Dad, of course, and me. We're delighted—naturally. Then there's—"

"Ann, *stop it*!"

"Well," Ann demanded in an aggrieved tone, throwing me a look of appeal which I studiously managed to ignore. "What am I supposed to do about it? Go round beating my bosom and crying 'Oh, weep for dear Sir Henry—he is dead'?"

Betty deliberately turned her back and began tidying some magazines which were lying on the desk. I looked out of the window at the scurrying snowflakes and tried to prevent myself from laughing aloud, because Ann's outrageous parody of grief was really extremely funny.

When I glanced back at her, she had pulled the corners of

her mouth down into a ludicrous expression of dolour, and was blinking rapidly with her eyelids. I was astonished to see large tears brimming up and coursing slowly down her cheeks.

"He's dead," she sobbed brokenly. "Dead and gone! And he never lived to hear me call him Father—"

Betty swung round irritably from the other side of the room. "Ann, do for heaven's sake stop being such a clown! Good Lord, child, you aren't really *crying*—?"

Ann raised her swimming eyes and shot her a brilliant smile. "All done by concentration," she said brightly. "It's one of my *fortes* at the R.A.D.A. Most of the girls have to have a slice of onion up their sleeves to do it convincingly. Actually, it's awfully simple really—I'll tell you the trick if you like, in case you ever want to use it on Howard to make him buy you a new hat or something. You just think terribly hard about something ever so poignant like Tess christening her dying baby, or Black Beauty or Little Nell. It can't fail if you think hard enough. I remember once—"

"You might remember now," Betty pointed out rather coldly, "that it's Michael's father you're making a pantomime about."

"Darling, of course I know that. That's one of the reasons—"

"And that even if you are—as you so frankly put it—delighted about Sir Henry's death, Michael might not think much of such an exhibition of—"

Ann's eyes, fringed with long fair lashes, slid round to Betty's face.

"Michael," she said coolly, "is bearing up with great fortitude. In fact—"

I glanced sharply down at her. She had told us when she came in that she had just heard the news from one of the local village gossips. Michael himself hadn't known until Howard told him at lunchtime. I wondered how Ann could already be aware of Michael's reactions.

"*Naturally*," Ann said, addressing herself for the first time to me instead of to Betty. "*Naturally* I rang Michael up as soon as I heard. Well, it was only civil, wasn't it? To console him in his grievous loss, I mean. I fancy that when time the great healer has done his stuff, Michael will get over it and be a brave little man, like the rest of us."

She fished about in the pocket of her duffle coat and produced a grubby silk handkerchief, which she applied briskly to the tears which still glistened on her cheeks.

"Heigh-ho!" she said with an exaggerated sigh. "By the way, darling, what is all this riveting mystery about Diana being lured out of the house last night with a fake telephone call?"

"What mystery?" Betty asked, obviously playing for time.

"Michael said Diana had told you all about it."

"Oh, that," Betty said, elaborately casual. "Yes, I believe there was some sort of fuss about a telephone call. A practical joke, I should imagine."

"But why should anyone want to play that sort of practical joke? And what had it got to do with the old thing's fit?"

"Nothing whatever," Betty replied firmly.

I wished I could have shared her certainty. To my mind the telephone call was just about the fishiest thing in the whole fishy business. It didn't seem to add up at all. Or, if it did, I didn't much care for the result of my mental arithmetic.

Ann swung herself off the back of the sofa and went over to the cigarette box.

"Well," she said, looking up through a puff of smoke and shaking back her hair, "I agree with Michael that it all sounds very funny. Betty, you don't think there was anything *peculiar* about the old thing's fit or stroke or whatever, do you?"

"No," Betty said promptly. Too promptly.

Ann regarded her through lowered lashes.

"I believe," she said acutely, "that Howard thinks there's something jolly peculiar about the whole set-up—and he's told you not to say anything about it. Otherwise you wouldn't be so cagey and correct about everything. It isn't like you, darling, to be hypocritical. You didn't love the old beast any more than the rest of us—and here you are being all sanctimonious and mealy-mouthed and *nil nisi bonum* about the fact that he's dead."

"Nonsense." Betty shot me a hunted glance which I was sure Ann intercepted.

"I knew it!" Ann crowed triumphantly. "He *was* murdered, wasn't he? Did Howard tell you who did it?"

"Ann, don't be absurd," Betty exclaimed, her temper beginning to fray. "Howard told me nothing. All I've been trying to say is that I think it's extremely silly for you or anyone else to go round the place the very day Sir Henry dies saying how delighted we all are about it. For one thing it's a bit vulgar, and for another it might be misconstrued."

"If he died naturally, I don't see how the misconstruction comes in. All right, darling, I won't torment you any more. I shall just have to throw myself on your mercy and when All is Discovered and it is revealed that Sir Henry died from a poisoned arrow shot from a blow-pipe or an overdose of arsenic in his evening cocoa, I can only beg you not to go into the witness box and testify that I came along this afternoon and said I was glad the old pest was dead."

"I should be hardly likely to do that," Betty said coldly. "You know my views on talking out of turn."

"Darling, are you really trying to keep my head out of the noose? Or is it that I've mentioned one or two other people besides myself who might be just the weeniest shade relieved about it all? Even though they haven't had the bad taste to come and tell you so!"

Betty remained silent.

"Well, in any case," Ann went on lightly, "it's probably just as well I've got an alibi. I haven't been inside Oakhurst Place for over a week—not since the day before we all came here for drinks to meet the fascinating widow. That was the time Michael asked me to lunch and I teased the old thing about his ginger jar. He was livid—and most awfully rude to me. I must say I had to hand it to my intended for outraged gallantry. He took up for me in no uncertain manner, and at one moment I really thought he was going to knock the aged parent for six there and then. Oh dear!" she broke off, covering her mouth and rolling her eyes in mock horror. "I suppose I oughtn't to have said that either, ought I? Now I've gone and given poor Michael a motive as well. What a good thing he happens to have got an alibi too! I took rather a dim view of that theatre party at the time—going off without me the way he did—but perhaps it's just as well as things have turned out. At least he can prove he wasn't prowling round Oakhurst slipping strychnine into the coffee or whatever happened."

Betty made a little helpless gesture with her hands.

"Ann, I wish you'd be sensible and realise that this isn't just a joke. *We* know what a ridiculous amount of rubbish you talk, but—well, please don't go and start a lot of absurd rumours all over the village about—about—"

"I will be as silent as the tomb," Ann promised. "I won't betray anybody's guilty secrets. Don't worry, darling." Her eyes gleamed mischievously. "Anyway," she added softly, "since I've invented the whole of this elaborate little fantasy about the old thing being murdered when you *assure* me that there isn't a shadow of evidence to prove that it was anything but a nice natural straightforward stroke, I don't really see that *anything* I might say could do much harm, do you?"

Betty bit her lip. "You know village people," was all she said. "They don't need facts to start a rumour. I'm just telling you not to be sillier than you can help, that's all."

"O.K. darling," Ann said. "I'll remember. Oh well, I must be going. Thanks for the jolly little wake. All the same," she called back irrepressibly from the doorway, "you mark my words about John Wickham. If he isn't doing a cosy line as Benedict the married man in less than six months I, for one, shall be very surprised. 'Bye, darling—don't bother to come out into the cold. I know my way."

Betty and I returned to the drawing-room.

"The child's incorrigible," Betty sighed. "She'll have it all round the village in half an hour that Sir Henry's been murdered—and that I told her Howard had said so."

This seemed to me so palpably likely that I could find no fair words to reassure her with. We consumed a rather gloomy tea and about half-past six Howard returned looking more harassed and depressed than ever.

"Any developments?" I couldn't help asking him as he flung his bag on the hall table and went into the dining-room to fetch the sherry decanter.

"You could put it like that," he said heavily. "No good hushing the blasted business up any longer. I've spent most of the afternoon closeted with the Chief Constable. Harvey and the police surgeon are doing the P.M. at nine-thirty tonight—I suppose I'll have to go over for that. And the local inspector and his minions are at this moment up at Oakhurst Place interviewing Diana."

VIII

THE ORPHAN BOY

"INTERVIEWING DIANA?" I ECHOED FAINTLY. "WHATEVER FOR? Do you mean that they've established that he—that it was—" I broke off, floundering a little.

"Nothing's established," Howard grunted. "But there's enough mud being stirred up for the Chief Constable to have decided to ask Diana for a statement. After all, she found him. And as there's going to be an inquest they've got to get together all the evidence they can beforehand. Of course if the P.M. turns out to be negative I imagine they'll drop the whole thing—just take the formal evidence of identification and the medical report. But I'm afraid—I'm very much afraid—" He paused and shrugged his shoulders.

"You're afraid it won't be negative?"

"I don't see how it can be. Well, anyway, let's not go into all that again. Betty, are there many people in the surgery?"

Betty shook her head.

"No—just a few of the usual old chronics. Why don't you let Norah deal with them? You know she's perfectly capable of dishing out half a dozen bottles of standard mixture as before."

Howard grinned fleetingly. "Oh, I know," he agreed. "If it comes to that, a lot of them consider she's a much better doctor than I am. 'Miss Wright understands my stomach, doctor'," he mimicked, "and I'm not sure they're so far wrong. She's a good girl, Norah. At least she has the courage of her own diagnoses." He flicked a ball of newspaper irritably across the room towards the waste-paper basket and missed it.

He went off in the direction of the surgery. Betty wandered upstairs to see Nanny and I was left alone.

I had been sitting there for about half an hour reading when I heard the hall door open.

"Anybody at home?" enquired a male voice which I recognised as Michael Metcalfe. A moment later his head appeared round the door.

"Oh, I'm sorry," he said hesitating uncertainly. "I thought Betty was here."

"Come in," I said. "Betty's upstairs with the children. Shall I go and fetch her?"

"No, don't bother, thanks," Michael replied, prowling restlessly round the room. "I expect she'll be down in a minute. As a matter of fact it was Howard I really wanted to see, but I suppose he's doing surgery."

I didn't know quite what to say. I hardly felt I knew Michael Metcalfe well enough to open the subject of his father's death, and yet I felt dimly that some form of condolence was called for.

However he saved me the bother by introducing it himself.

"D'you know," he said, his voice shrill with indignation, "that we've had an Inspector of police up at the house this afternoon? It's perfectly fantastic. Almost as if they thought there was something fishy about my father's death. I thought they only went on like that if it was a case of murder."

I cast about for a suitable reply to this, but Michael gave what can only be described as a hollow laugh, and went on without waiting for me to speak: "They've been badgering my step-mother with all sorts of questions. And then they started on *me!* I suppose they have to get her story—at least I can't really see *why* they have to, but she was the last person to see him before he was taken ill—and of course she found him." His voice rose again. "But why do they have to bother *me?* I wasn't even there! I didn't know a thing about it till I got back about half-past one this morning—dead tired I was, too—and there was Diana in no end of a state telling me they'd taken my father off to hospital at Tunbridge Wells. Well, I said, that's a very bad show and all that, but there was nothing *I* could do about it. And then the next thing I hear is Howard coming up at lunchtime to say he's died without recovering consciousness. So how on earth do they imagine *I* can tell them anything?"

He glared indignantly at me, and I made a few mumbling remarks of condolence which Michael cut short with an impatient wave of the hand.

"Oh, it's a bit of a shock, of course," he said briefly. "But apart from that, I can't really pretend—"

With some relief I heard Betty's footsteps crossing the hall.

"Oh, hullo, Betty," Michael said. "Rotten show all this. What? Will Howard be long, d'you think? I rather wanted a short word with him."

"I expect he'll be through quite soon," Betty said. "There aren't many patients tonight. Michael, I am sorry about this nasty business—it must be beastly for all of you. How's Diana?"

"Well, it seems to me she's in rather an awkward position," Michael said frankly. "That's what I wanted to see Howard for, as a matter of fact—to find out what all the mystery's about. It seems to me that the local police are behaving very strangely—almost as if they thought there was more in it than met the eye, and all that sort of thing. But anyhow, even if there *was*—well, what I mean is that whatever they do or don't ferret out, it was *nothing* to do with Diana. I'd stake my last dollar on that."

"But surely they don't think—" Betty began.

"*I* don't know what they think," Michael returned with a flash of his previous indignation. "But it doesn't take much imagination to see that they're doing their best to hatch up trouble for somebody. And all I'm thinking is that it could be a shade tricky for Diana that it's happened the way it has. I mean, everybody knows she and my father didn't hit it off. My father was a very difficult man, as you know yourself, and there's no doubt that he made life pretty unbearable for Diana."

Betty nodded sympathetically.

"And of course if it comes to that," Michael went on, suddenly remembering something, "I didn't always hit it off particularly well with him myself. As it happens, we had a bit of a dust-up only yesterday morning. Nothing important, you know, but I thought it was just the sort of silly thing one of the servants might go and mention—because the old man was shouting loud enough to have been heard half-way to Brenchley—so I told the Inspector about it."

"I'm sure that was wise of you," Betty remarked drily.

Michael glanced suspiciously at her, but Betty's face was innocently blank.

"Well, it was as much Diana's row as mine," he replied defensively. "That's why I wouldn't have mentioned it if I hadn't been sure that somebody else would. It all began—as most of the rows at home do begin—out of nothing. Father was in a rage because he'd asked old Qualtrough to come up and give him his opinion on that new bit of china he's been making such a fuss about. He's been showing it off to everybody in the village, and it wasn't really an opinion he wanted so much as admiration and people telling him how clever he'd been to find it. Well, anyhow, father's theory was that it was something terribly rare—Imperial *famille rose* or something, which is practically never seen outside a museum in Peking—and although he and old Qualtrough have been at daggers drawn for years, father had to admit he was an expert on old china, and he really asked him up to gloat over him with this wonderful find. Then of course Mr. Qualtrough told him it wasn't genuine Imperial what's-its-name at all, but simply a nineteenth century reproduction made in Paris. Father was furious and practically kicked old Qualtrough down the drive, and he went on raving about his ignorance and impertinence for hours until Diana chipped in and said well, after all, Mr. Qualtrough *was* a dealer, and he ought to know if anyone did. That brought the house down worse than ever. Father went clean off the deep end then, and accused Diana of taking anybody's part against him—and at that point John Wickham came in, you see, which didn't improve matters. John stood glowering in the doorway, sort of muttering under his breath as if he simply couldn't trust himself to speak, and I thought the whole thing had been going on for long enough, so I told father he was being a bit childish—and after all, what did it really matter about the beastly bowl? It was still the same bit of china, and if he'd liked it before I didn't see why anything old Qualtrough said about it should have made it any different. So then father turned on me and was frightfully abusive and said we were a lot of useless ignorant parasites in league with anybody who insulted him, and a lot more besides. John turned on his heel and went out, red in the face, looking as if he was going to burst; and Diana started crying and rushed off upstairs, and I was left in the study with the door open and father roaring his head off."

"Yes, I see," Betty said. "But I don't quite follow what you meant about Diana being in an awkward position. Why should she be?"

"Well, because everybody knows that's the kind of thing which is always happening. And what makes it even worse is that it was John Wickham who was with her when she came in and discovered father'd had this stroke."

"Why should that make things worse?" Betty asked sharply.

Michael shuffled his feet uncomfortably.

"Well, you know how people talk," he mumbled. "And what was John Wickham doing wandering about on the Brenchley road at that hour of the night anyway? You must admit his story sounds pretty thin. He was always having rows with my father—even apart from Diana, who was certainly the chief cause of them—and everybody in the village knew it."

"But—"

"Mind you," Michael went on hurriedly, "I like old John. I think he's a good scout. But all I'm saying is that it's *unfortunate* that he happened to be the person Diana should have picked to turn up with on just that particular night."

"She didn't 'pick' him," Betty exclaimed exasperated. "He just happened to be there. And it was a very good thing for her that he was, because—"

"Yes—that's just what I'm saying. *Why* was he there?"

"I don't see what it's got to do with—"

"Listen," Michael said wearily. "I'm only trying to look at the thing from the angle the police are very definitely looking at it. The whole village knows John Wickham is batty about Diana. And equally they know that he hated my father's guts. Sorry to be coarse, but they do. And that being so, all I'm saying is that the whole show looks pretty bad for Diana."

Betty's colour rose.

"And the more you go on talking in that way, the worse it's going to look," she said shortly. "We don't know anything for certain yet, and I don't know why you have to assume that just because the police have been up at Oakhurst that it's a question of—that your father—"

"Why not say it openly? Go on—say it! You think he was murdered. So do I—now. I wasn't sure before—even after the way the police went on. But now I'm certain that you know something more than you're saying. That's why you're giving such a perfect imitation of the discreet little doctor's wife. Anyway, Betty, it isn't difficult to see there's something jolly queer about the whole business. One's only got to use one's head. If everything's perfectly open and above-board, what's all the mystery about? Why has Howard held up the death certificate? Why the post-mortem? Why the police? Howard isn't the sort of person to start up hares like that for fun if there's nothing behind it."

"Well, anyway," Betty said, goaded into temper. "it's nothing at all to do with me. I don't know why Howard held up the certificate and I don't know why the police have been to Oakhurst. If you're right and they're doing a routine check-up on everyone, Diana and John Wickham aren't the only people it's going to look bad for. It seems to me it's just as well for your sake that you happened to spend the evening in London and not at home."

"Oh yes," Michael agreed, readily enough. "That aspect had occurred. I see you rather fancy me in the role of suspect number one. I can't say I blame you—I expect I'll have quite a number of backers. But they won't be able to get round the fact that I wasn't anywhere near Oakhurst yesterday evening, and that I didn't get back there until after the ambulance had been and taken my father to Tunbridge Wells. And all because I happened to miss the last train home. Otherwise I suppose I'd have landed in the thick of the excitement."

Betty ignored the jibe about suspect number one and merely remarked carelessly: "Oh, I didn't realise you went to London by train—I thought you had your car yesterday afternoon."

"So I did," Michael replied rather sharply. "I left it in the station yard at Tunbridge Wells Central and hopped up to Charing Cross by train. I often do if I'm going up in the evening—it saves all that fuss about parking outside the theatre and it's much quicker in the end."

"Yes, I see. I suppose it does save time. The children were awfully disappointed you had to leave the party so early."

Michael gave her another quick sidelong glance.

"Well, the thing began at seven. I hadn't booked a seat, so I wanted to allow plenty of time. As it was, I only got there just before the curtain went up."

"What did you see?" I asked idly, not really caring in the least, but noticing that Michael was still looking at Betty in a rather belligerent way.

"A thing at the Thespian Club theatre in Charlotte Street. It was called *Emperor for Diet,* and it was pretty bad. Then, you see, what happened was that I got talking to a chap in the bar during the interval. I've no idea who he was—I'd never set eyes on him before; but he seemed a friendly sort of bloke and very interested in the theatre. And the long and short of it was that he asked me to go along after the show and have a bit of supper with him. He took me to a funny little sort of club place down some steps—I've forgotten what it was called, but it was somewhere in the depths of Soho—and then we had some food and got talking. He was an amusing chap and the next thing I realised was that it was twenty to twelve, and the last train from Charing Cross goes at eleven fifty-five. I had some difficulty in getting a taxi, and by the time I got to the station, I found I'd missed the blasted train by about three minutes. It was sickening. I asked a porter when the next one was, and he told me there was nothing until about five o'clock in the morning—and that was a ghastly sort of milk train which ambled all round the countryside and got in heaven knew when. So in the end I decided it simply wasn't good enough hanging round the station any longer, and I'd have a shot at hitch-hiking. Which I did."

"You were lucky to pick up anything at that hour of the night," Betty commented. "If I'd been you, I think I'd have stayed the night somewhere in London."

"Oh, it was quite easy. I just thumbed a lorry which happened to be going in the right direction. I wanted to get to Tunbridge Wells, you see, and the man put me down at Five Ways, which suited me all right. I walked down the hill to the station and picked up the car and drove straight back to Staple Green. Actually, it was just as well, with all the fuss that was going on, that I did get back. Diana was in a bit of a state—she came down in her dressing-gown when she heard me come in and told what had happened. I don't mind admitting I was quite shaken myself. We'd all had this ridiculous row at lunchtime as I told you, and I couldn't help feeling that it might have helped to bring on the old man's stroke. It wasn't that I was fond of him—I wasn't, even though he was my father. But one wouldn't like to feel responsible for a thing like that. Of course there was no idea then that it wasn't a perfectly ordinary stroke, although Diana kept on worrying and saying she thought there was something queer about the fact that it had happened the very night she'd been out on account of this odd telephone call. I told her not to be morbid and put the whole thing down to feminine hysterics. Then after a bit we went to bed."

I had been watching Michael's face while he talked, the mobile mouth and the way his restless hazel eyes darted about the room just lighting for a moment upon whichever of us he was addressing, but never lingering—never directly meeting Betty's eyes or mine. I was, for no rational reason, convinced that he wasn't speaking the truth. Or at any rate by no means the whole truth. He was telling the story with so much circumstantial detail—with such unnecessary frankness—that my suspicious mind instantly began to wonder what he was trying to put over on us. Should it become expedient his story could, of course, easily be checked by the police. Or, I wondered suddenly, could it? Circumstantial as it sounded at first, when one came to examine it, it was the kind of story which was going to be remarkably difficult either to prove or disprove. It was possible, but by no means certain, that he would be remembered by some of the theatre attendants. Perhaps the porter to whom he spoke at Charing Cross would be able to identify him. But supposing both these sources of confirmation failed, what then? You still couldn't say the story definitely *wasn't* true—though you might have your suspicions. The unknown chum at the theatre with whom Michael had had supper—how to discover him? And there must be literally hundreds of "funny little sort of club places" in unspecified streets in Soho. In fact, there was no London district which held more of these furtive mushroom growths.

I was aroused from these unfriendly suspicions by something Betty was saying.

"A word of advice, Michael," she said. "I hope you won't be offended if I remind you that there are a few people in the village who didn't get on well with your father, and—"

"What a masterpiece of understatement!" Michael said. "There was practically nobody who did. I know that. Why?"

"Only that I think you should warn Ann that it isn't very tactful of her in the circumstances to go round talking quite so much. She came in here this afternoon and made some rather wild remarks."

Michael's eyes narrowed.

"What did she say?" he asked.

"That several people—including Diana, John Wickham and yourself aren't going to shed many tears over this affair. I will say for her that she included herself and her father as well. But even so, you know what Ann is—she doesn't mean anything by what she says—*we* all know that, but—"

"Thanks for telling me," Michael said. There was a gleam of anger in his eyes. "I'll certainly speak to her. What *I've* been saying about Diana was—as you know—entirely confidential, and I've only said it to you because you are a friend of hers, and I'm worried about her. It's no good disguising among ourselves that my late papa wasn't exactly the most popular figure in the village—but that's quite different from having Ann rushing about making wild accusations. Silly little fool," he added violently. "Especially when everybody knows she and her father hated him almost more than anyone. Look, Betty—I don't think I'll wait for Howard now. I expect he's busy. I'll go along instead and have a word with my dear affianced and tell her to keep her pretty little trap shut."

He left the room abruptly, almost slamming the door. Betty and I continued to sit in pensive silence for some minutes after he had gone.

"Oh well," I said at last. "I think I'm going up to change. D'you know, Betty, I don't think I care awfully for that young man?"

"Oh, Michael's all right really," Betty said vaguely. "He's just a bit spoilt and selfish in his outlook. He'll stop Ann scandalmongering anyway, which is a good thing."

"It seemed to me he said even more than Ann about the 'awkwardness' of Diana's position," I remarked. "He couldn't have put his own opinion much more clearly."

"Oh, no, I'm sure you're wrong about that," Betty exclaimed. "He's really fond of Diana. That's why he's so worried about her."

"Oh," I said, getting up. "Well, you know best."

I walked slowly upstairs, brooding over other people's ideas of fondness. It didn't seem to me that leaping immediately to the worst possible conclusions about the motives and actions of your beloved step-mother—even if you then defended her integrity with your last breath—was exactly an intelligent way of expressing devotion. And whatever else Michael Metcalfe was or wasn't, I was quite sure he was in no way lacking in intelligence.

IX

SIR LAUNCELOT OF THE LODGE

As soon as dinner was over Howard departed, grumbling dismally about his lack of sleep, to the hospital at Tunbridge Wells to assist at the post mortem on Sir Henry.

Betty and I sat fidgeting in the drawing-room, she sewing a dress for Sara, and I attempting unsuccessfully to keep my mind on a very dull book about the conversion of a former Communist who had seen the light and was now wallowing in the revelation of the previous error of his ways.

"I wish," Betty remarked, reverting to the one subject in both our minds, "that Howard hadn't been so insistent on my not going up to Oakhurst today to see Diana. I can't think what harm it could have done, and it might even have cheered her up. Still, it's a bit late to go up there now. I expect she's in bed."

"Didn't you send her up a note?"

"Yes. But it's not the same thing." She snipped off a piece of cotton and put clown her sewing with a sigh. "It's no good, I can't concentrate on smocking. And then there's poor John Wickham. He's such a nice person, and he must be feeling the strain, all by himself in that gloomy little lodge. What d'you think, Lee—shall we just pop along for a few minutes to see how he is? It's only five minutes walk across the green."

"At this hour of the night?"

"It's only half-past nine. Actually, I do want to see him rather particularly to arrange about getting a turkey for Christmas. He said some time ago he'd get me one if I let him know the weight I wanted, and we measured the oven yesterday and Mrs. Padgett says—"

The naivete of this argument made me laugh out loud.

"You don't have to bother with all that elaborate process of rationalisation for my sake, honey," I said. "Which is it—sheer vulgar curiosity to hear John Wickham's story firsthand, or do you want to put in a word of good Samaritan warning about the libellous things Ann and Michael are saying about him and Diana?"

Betty looked rather hurt. "He's always been a very good friend of ours, Lee. I just thought it would be neighbourly."

"All right," I said, shutting my book with relief. "When d'you want to go? Now?"

"Perhaps I'll ring him up first," Betty said, struck by some afterthought. "I'll suggest we might come round, and then if he didn't feel he wanted to see anyone, that would give him a chance to get out of it. Wait a minute, Lee."

She disappeared into the hall and I lit a cigarette thoughtfully. I wondered if it had occurred to her—as it certainly had to me—that a surprise visit mightn't be altogether wise or tactful. It might have been distinctly embarrassing for John Wickham if we had pranced in unheralded and found him already engaged—perhaps entertaining the stricken widow from Oakhurst Place. I tried to persuade myself that the insidious propaganda put out by Ann Qualtrough was not influencing my judgment on this score, but couldn't help admitting that it probably was. And so was Michael's overdone solicitude on Diana's behalf. Heaven preserve us from our friends, I thought, who are so willing to defend our reputations from charges which might otherwise never have arisen.

Betty came back from the telephone looking relieved.

"He says he'd love to see us," she told me. "He sounded as if he meant it. So I said we'd be along in a few minutes."

I went upstairs to collect a fur coat and some snow boots. On the landing I met Nanny who raised interrogative eyebrows but said nothing. I wondered what she was making of the situation—if she knew about it. It seemed unlikely that she didn't.

As Betty and I walked up the lane the village green lay before us, shimmering with ghostly whiteness in the moonlight. Snow was falling softly. The sitting-room window of the Qualtroughs' cottage glowed amber in the darkness and inside the house somebody was playing a Scarlatti sonata on the piano.

"Who would that be?" I asked Betty. "Ann or her father?"

"Ann, I should think," Betty replied. "I don't think the old man plays the piano much these days. It's one of the things he's rather given up lately. He still listens to all the good concerts on the radio, though, and has an enormous collection of gramophone records. Mostly old Italian church music and seventeenth century stuff."

"Oh yes," I said, remembering the chest of viols.

We came to the stone pillars surmounted by shadowy eagles. Betty put her hand on the heavy latch of the iron gate.

"Remember," she hissed, "we don't know *anything*!"

I nodded. Anyway, if it came to that, just what did we know? That Howard wasn't satisfied with the diagnosis of Sir Henry's illness and that Diana Metcalfe had been interviewed by the police. John Wickham would probably know as much as that himself. I didn't feel much alarm at the prospect of being tripped up on that slender amount of information.

He came to the door of the lodge as he heard the click of the iron gate, and stood there holding it open, letting a broad shaft of yellow light shine out across the trodden snow of the drive. He was wearing a camel hair dressing-gown over grey flannel trousers and had a silk scarf twisted round his neck. His feet were encased in cosy-looking sheepskin slippers.

"Forgive the attire," he said, seeing my eyes wander idly towards the scarf. "I wasn't expecting visitors, though I'm extremely glad to see you both. Sit down, Betty. What can I get you to drink? Whisky? Mrs. Craufurd?"

"I think a small whisky would be lovely, thank you," I said. "Goodness, isn't it cold out!"

If John Wickham's silk scarf wasn't the same one Diana had been wearing over her hair that morning when she came down to see Betty at the Tithe Barn, it was its twin brother. I shook myself mentally and told myself there was no significance of any kind in that.

Betty was chattering about the snow. In a minute somebody would say that if this went on we should have a white Christmas.

The lodge was by no means beautiful, but with the aid of a blazing log fire and a couple of shelves of untidy but friendly-looking books and the deep leather armchairs, John Wickham had managed to infuse an air of comfort and snugness into the bleak little room. I caught myself glancing round for the traditional "woman's touch," but apart from one rather exotic and magnificent potted azalea which must undoubtedly have come from the Oakhurst conservatories there was nothing to suggest anything but the most monastic of bachelor apartments. John moved a handful of brightly coloured bulb catalogues off the arm of one of the chairs, and swept a sleepy and reproachful spaniel away from the middle of the rug in front of the fire.

"Pull your chairs up," he said. "Sally, lie down."

The spaniel crawled back to the rug and lay down an inch from where she had been before. John Wickham smiled and shrugged his shoulders.

"That's what I love about dogs," he said. "So obedient."

"Oh, leave poor Sally," Betty said. "We've got all the fire we can possibly want. How cosy you've made this room, John."

"Yes—well, it suits me all right," he said. His eyes strayed to a brocade cushion and a low walnut coffee table which I had not previously noticed. "Diana's been very kind in helping me to furnish it," he added. "She gave me several odd bits and pieces from Oakhurst."

Diana Metcalfe's name was a stone dropped into a pool of silence. The ripples radiated slowly outwards towards the margin of the pond.

"Have you seen her?" John Wickham went on with an obvious effort. "Since—since—"

"I saw her this morning," Betty said. "But of course that was before she'd heard the news of Sir Henry's death. Howard said she was being wonderful—very calm and controlled. But you'd expect that from Diana."

The dog Sally curled herself into a more comfortably shaped ball on the hearth rug and closed her eyes. We sat back in our chairs and sipped our whisky. I began to think that perhaps from Betty's point of view it had been a mistake to bring me on this visit. Something about the set of John Wickham's jaw as he sat staring into the fire, chewing on the stem of his pipe, suggested that he was not the sort of person likely to open up on intimate personal topics in the presence of a total stranger. However, since it was now clearly impossible for me to remove myself, I continued to sit very still and tried to look as unobtrusive and invisible as I could.

Perhaps I succeeded partially in making John forget I was there, or perhaps his need to confide in somebody who was a close friend of Diana's overcame his natural reticence. He said suddenly: "You know a Police Inspector and a sergeant have been up at Oakhurst this afternoon interviewing Diana about last night? It seems there's going to be an inquest and a lot of general unpleasantness all round."

"Yes—Howard told me."

"I didn't at all like the attitude of those policemen," John went on aggressively. "I suppose they had to ask a certain number of questions about the old man's collapse—the state he was in when we found him, and anything in the room which might have given some sort of clue about the time he was taken ill, and so on. But they could have got all that from me without bothering Diana at all. She couldn't give them any more information than I could."

"Didn't the Inspector come to see you too?" Betty asked.

"Oh yes, he was here about an hour ago. We went right through the whole set-up practically with diagrams. Even down to some ridiculous row there'd been in the morning about that blasted china slop-basin—which I'm quite glad to say we found smashed when we came in. But why rake that up? The only way the Inspector could possibly have known about the row was through Michael, and if that young man had a grain of sense he'd have kept his mouth shut. Anyone would think he *wanted* to cause even more trouble than there is already."

"He told me he brought it up because he thought the servants had heard the row going on, and would mention it to the police if he didn't."

John Wickham smiled rather sourly. "Michael hasn't so far shone as the family bright boy," he remarked obliquely. "From all I can gather from Diana, Michael's chief concern was to keep himself in the clear—says the whole thing was nothing to do with him—and never mind where that landed anybody else. A fine sort of prop *he's* been to Diana!"

"You've seen Diana since the police were up at the house?"

"No, I haven't seen her. She—she rang me up, after the Inspector had gone. She said she couldn't really grasp what they were trying to get at, because she naturally thought all they would want to know was about Sir Henry's health. Whereas what seemed to interest them much more was the story about that fake telephone call. I suppose they dragged that out of dear little Michael, too. Did she tell you about it?"

"Yes. I must admit it did sound a bit odd."

"Of course it was odd. Some damn fool trying to be funny, I suppose. It's the same sort of warped mentality which makes hooligans go through the Telephone Directory and ring up everyone with a name like Smellie and ask them what they're going to do about it."

"There must be a rather more rational motive in this case," Betty pointed out. "I mean—well, where does the joke come in? There's nothing particularly amusing about sending Diana over to Tunbridge Wells on a wild goose chase."

"There was nothing particularly amusing about the occasion when Michael and Ann Qualtrough rang up your husband last winter and said the Prendergasts' cook was having twins in the garage and would Howard come at once—and yet *they* thought it was screamingly funny."

Betty laughed. "I'd forgotten about that," she said. "Yes, Howard was rather cross. He didn't go, of course. I mean, he realised it was a hoax. But in the light of what happened I can understand that the police would have to ask questions about that call to Diana. It might—it just *might* have some kind of significance."

"Even if it had, surely the very fact that the call was made *to* Diana and not by her, lets her out completely?"

"You'd have thought so," Betty said. She moved her chair a fraction further away from the blazing fire. "Do you mean that the police think Diana *knows* who made that call?"

"I really don't know *what* they think. They completely bewildered Diana with their questions—on and on—until in the end she told me she thought they'd come to the conclusion she made the call herself. Though what would be the point of that I fail to see."

For a minute I forgot that I was supposed to be a fly on the wall and before I could stop myself I put in: "The police can trace calls. If they're as interested as all that they can find out what number rang the Parish Hall at nine o'clock—or whenever it was."

"Oh," said John slowly, looking at me for the first time. "Yes—I hadn't thought of that. So they could."

"Well, that ought to clear it up all right as far as Diana's concerned," Betty said cheerfully. "I can't imagine *why* the police think she should want to do anything so mad as to telephone to herself; but if they trace the call, she can prove that she was in the car at the time driving down from Oakhurst to the Parish Hall—because it was only about three minutes after Mrs. Prendergast had taken it that Diana arrived. And the call came from Tunbridge Wells anyway."

I relapsed into silence again, even while making the mental note that the only reason anyone had for supposing the mysterious call to have come from Tunbridge Wells was because the caller had said it did. She had also said it was Sheila Henderson speaking when it wasn't, so you couldn't place much reliance on that. The call could have come from anywhere. Even from Oakhurst Place. I reviewed this rather discomforting idea and rejected it. Diana couldn't possibly have telephoned from Oakhurst and arrived at the Parish Hall three minutes later. There wouldn't have been time. In any case, I agreed with Betty that the thing was fantastic—why *should* Diana go to such elaborate lengths to send herself off on a fool's errand the following night? It made no sense at all.

John Wickham was still complaining about the inquisition Diana had suffered that afternoon. "You've no idea how they went on, Betty. Over and over every simple little detail about what time she'd left the house—when she'd arrived in Tunbridge Wells—what Sir Henry was doing when she last saw him—what time the servants went out—oh, and of course the whisky. *How* they went on about that whisky!"

"That was the hot drink Diana made for his cold before she went out?"

"Yes. What time did she make it?—what glass was it in?—did Sir Henry drink it before she left the house?—and so on—till the poor girl didn't know if it was Christmas or Easter."

"Did he?" Betty asked. "Drink it before she left, I mean?"

"She thinks he started on it. Well, she wasn't watching him like a hawk every second of the time. Why should she? And then all the business about the radio—was it on or off when she went into the study? She told them it was off when she went out and on when she and I got back. Well, I could have told them that—and what the hell does it matter anyway?"

"I suppose they were trying to narrow down the time he was taken ill," Betty said. "That's understandable. We've got to face it, John. He was alive and well when Diana left him—and he was dying when she got back. So *something* must have happened in the meantime."

"He had a stroke," said John Wickham obstinately. "Oh, I know Howard's got some theory that there was more to it than that. Sorry, Betty, to appear to be casting aspersions on your husband's omniscience, but I'm convinced that in this case he's being a trifle imaginative."

"If he is," Betty said, "nobody will be more relieved than Howard to have his theory disproved. He doesn't *like* stirring up trouble."

"Of course I know that. I know he's only doing his duty as he sees it. But everyone's fallible. And you've obviously no idea, Betty, how these police have been letting themselves rip in chasing rainbows. Why, they practically tried to imply that there was something sinister in the fact that I happened to be walking down the road when Diana drove by on her way home from Tunbridge Wells."

"You didn't know she was going to see Sheila?"

"I—" John began and hesitated. "No, I didn't," he mumbled. I noticed a hot flush of colour creeping across his forehead. I felt suddenly sorry for him. Whatever else he might be concealing, it was painfully apparent that the rumours of his attachment to Diana Metcalfe were far from unfounded. He was quite obviously crazy about her and intensely embarrassed about it. He raised his eyes and caught me gazing at him speculatively.

"What on earth *do* these moronic police think?" he demanded angrily, to cover his momentary disadvantage. "That Diana and I were in league to do the old man in? Damn it, he was unconscious when we found him—and Howard was along ten minutes later. What do they think we did? Hit him on the head with a poker?"

At this sudden plunge into plain speaking there was a moment of rather shocked silence. Then Betty did the only possible thing, which was to laugh brightly.

"I should imagine even the police have a bit more sense than that," she said. "John, may I have one of your cigarettes? I've left mine at home."

Under cover of movement, John getting up to light Betty's cigarette and then fussing about to offer us another drink, the tension eased slightly.

"Well, anyhow," John said, settling down again and drawing fiercely at his pipe. "The blasted police can third-degree *me* as long and as often as they like. It won't do them the slightest good, but they're welcome if it amuses them. But if they go on badgering Diana again in the way they did this afternoon, I'll—I'll—" Words seemed to fail him.

Betty laid down her cigarette with deliberation and looked at his drawn face, the tense eyes and the dangerous clenching of his jaw.

"I'm going to say something impertinent, John," she said steadily. "Do you mind?"

"Go ahead," John said carelessly, but his eyes were suddenly wary.

"It's just this," Betty said. "You and I know—and Howard and Lee and *all* your friends know—that Diana has never in her whole life done anything which could even be described as indiscreet. But we live in a small village—and you know what villagers are. They talk. And if there's nothing factual for them to talk about, they'll invent something. You and Diana are a target for malicious gossip, and the more strongly you go around championing her in public, the more people will say there's something between you. So, John dear, for your own sake—and even more for Diana's—I'd suggest it would be much wiser to lay off the Galahad stuff. Especially at the inquest. D'you see what I mean?"

John Wickham bent his head. The tall grandfather clock in the corner (another contribution from Oakhurst?) ticked monotonously. Outside I could almost feel the soft stillness of the falling snow.

"What you really mean," John said without looking up, "is cut out the Launcelot stuff, isn't it?"

Betty didn't answer. A log fell suddenly from the fire basket in the grate, scattering a shower of sparks over the hearthrug. Sally uttered a yelp of indignation and lumbered over to the door with her tail between her legs. There was a strong smell of singeing, and we all began stamping busily at small smouldering patches on the rug.

By common consent nothing further was said on the subject of the Metcalfes. John recovered himself and began talking about his experiences when he was fruit farming in British Columbia. He talked well and interestingly, and it hardly seemed more than a few minutes later that Betty looked at her watch and uttered a little exclamation of surprise.

"Goodness!" she said. "I'd no idea it was so late. Howard will be back and wondering what on earth's happened to us. Good night, John—and thanks for a very pleasant evening. Come on, Lee—we must run!"

Just as we reached the front door of the Tithe Barn we met Howard coming round the side of the house from the direction of the garage. He carried a torch and was stamping the snow off his shoes.

"Hullo," he remarked. "Whatever have you two been up to? Not much night life in this part of the world—except for people like me," he added wryly.

We explained, and paused in the hall to take off our snow boots.

'Well," Howard said, "I'm glad you've been putting our young friend's mind at rest on the score that the wicked police can do nothing to him or Diana; because they're going to need all the assurances they can get. It was a very great pity that Diana gave the old man that glass of hot whisky before she left for Tunbridge Wells."

"What d'you mean?" Betty asked sharply. "What's happened now?"

"As a result of the P.M.," Howard replied gravely, "what they call in the newspaper circles 'certain organs' have been sent up to the path. lab. for a rush analysis. And I'm very much afraid we're going to have Scotland Yard on our heels any minute now."

"Oh, God," Betty whispered. "You mean, you're sure now that it wasn't a stroke?"

'Yes. I hate to say I told anyone so, because in this particular instance I would much rather have been wrong; but it's now definitely established that he didn't die naturally. It was a narcotic poison of some kind. It seems unlikely it was an accident and not very probable that it was suicide. Which leaves only murder—and that means Scotland Yard."

Betty sank down on to a small chair in the hall.

"I can't really take it in even now," she said. "What we all feared and refused to face. It's like a bad dream coming true."

Howard nodded. "And they're going all out to suspect Diana," he said. "Of course they're wrong, and she'll be all right in the end because she didn't do it. But she's in for a tough time."

"You've been talking to the Inspector?"

"To the Inspector and Colonel Wilbraham." Colonel Wilbraham was, I knew, the Chief Constable. "They're sending a bloke down from Scotland Yard tomorrow, and the inquest's fixed for Monday. And now I'm going to bed. The only ray of light I can see in the whole of this deplorable business from start to finish is that by the time it's all over I may be able to snatch a few nights' sleep because I won't have any patients left. Well, good night, girls. Darling, d'you mind seeing to the lights?"

I threw my snow-boots down the passage in the direction of the back door and walked upstairs. Betty rose automatically and switched off the light over the hall door. She bent down to pick up her bag and gloves and, as I glanced down over the bannisters from the landing, I saw her face. She was looking very much as I felt myself. We'd known all day in our hearts that this was murder and, now that our forebodings were officially confirmed, we simply couldn't believe it.

X

A VISIT TO THE BLUE BOAR

THE ATMOSPHERE WHICH HUNG OVER THE HOUSE NEXT DAY was like waiting for the result of a school examination in which you know you've failed. Betty was irritable and on edge, and Howard gruff and off-hand. I found myself starting a cold and wishing passionately that I had never set foot in Staple Green. It would have been dull in the flat in London without Bill, but at least it would have been free from the grim feeling of impending disaster which hung like a pall over the Tithe Barn.

The children had suddenly woken up to the fact that it was only ten days until Christmas, and they were demanding paste and strips of coloured paper to make chains to decorate the house. Betty produced the necessary materials and we fixed them up, sticky and contented, in the nursery. It was Nanny's afternoon out.

After tea Betty disappeared on some unspecified household errand, and I retired to my own room to consider the problem of my Christmas present list. Bill was due to join me at Staple Green on Christmas Eve; and in the meantime I was faced with the additional complication of having to look after all his Christmas shopping as well as my own. The village shop didn't offer much in the way of suggestions, and I reluctantly came to the conclusion that I should have to go up to London one day soon and put in an intensive afternoon at Harrod's or somewhere. The recurrent anxiety of Aunt Adelaide's present was always particularly difficult. She seemed to have everything an elderly widow could possibly want, but she would be bitterly hurt if neglected. It was tricky work trying to achieve a happy medium between ostentation (which might be construed as a bid on Bill's part to keep his financial expectations warm) and too modest an offering (which would look as if he simply didn't consider her worth bothering about). I sat with my pencil poised over the list frowning with concentration at the blank space opposite Aunt Adelaide's name. Cigarettes, I thought desperately? No, Aunt Adelaide had given up smoking. Bridge cards and markers? No, she had stacks of them, and, since bridge was the prevailing passion of her life she was constantly receiving fresh supplies from all her bridge-playing friends. Bath salts—talcum powder—soap? Rather mean, and in any case the glass shelf in her bathroom was smothered with such things. I had just made a tentative note: "Silk scarf?" when I was roused from my reflections by the appearance of Sara, covered with paste, who informed me that she and Robin had run out of coloured paper, and she couldn't find Mummy anywhere. Would I please get her some more from the village? *Now*—quickly, before the shop shut?

I agreed unenthusiastically to do what I could, and a few minutes later set off up the lane.

It had already begun to get dark and the moon had not yet risen. It had been snowing in a half-hearted manner all day and, though some attempt had been made to sweep the middle of the road clear, the brownish drifts lay piled up on either side under the hedges looking rather bleak and shop-soiled.

I failed to obtain paper-chain material at Mr. Perkins' general stores and had just passed the entrance to the Blue Boar on my way to the newsagent-cum-tobacconist (which, if I'd had any sense, I should have tried in the first place) when I heard my name called loudly from behind. The voice sounded oddly familiar, but for one bewildered moment I failed to place it.

I swung round on my heel and found myself face to face with our old friend from Scotland Yard, Hugh Gordon.

Hugh took the last three steps of the Blue Boar's pretentious pillared porch in one swift bound and stood beside me on the pavement. He took both my hands in his, and smiled at my surprise. I was conscious of a warm flood of relief at seeing him. "Hugh's here," I thought idiotically. "Now everything's bound to be all right. He won't let these silly local police go and arrest the wrong person, and the whole nightmare business will soon be over."

"Liane," Hugh was saying, "how lovely to see you! They told me you were here, and I was coming round this evening to see your doctor host and pay my respects."

"Are you on this case?" I asked. I knew he must be, but I wanted to be reassured on the point.

"Yes. This is a nice state of affairs you've got yourself into, I must say! Every time I let you out of my sight you go and get yourself involved in some particularly gruesome murder."

"I?" I began indignantly. *"I'm* not in the least involved. It's absolutely nothing to do with me! I only set eyes on Sir Henry Metcalfe once in my life, and then—"

"Darling Liane, how beautifully you always rise! Come into my palatial hotel and have a drink with me. You must tell me all about Bill and the Cazalets, and we'll have a lovely gossip." He was pulling me up the steps of the Blue Boar as he spoke, and all thought of Sara's paper chains went clean out of my head.

"Now where can we go?" Hugh went on, looking round a gloomy and unclean hall: "I don't think you'd care for the tap-room. It's very squalid. And the boudoir you observe through that dirty pane of frosted glass to your right has a depressing air of frowst and aspidistras which I wouldn't like to associate with our reunion. Do you think it would shock the chambermaid if I took you up to my bedroom?"

"Intensely, I should think," I said.

"Well, there's a horrible little room upstairs called 'Residents Only.' We might try that. We're quite certain not to be interrupted as there are no other residents, and in any case I can't imagine anyone choosing to sit there except in cases of the direst necessity—such as the present. Come on."

I followed Hugh up the ill-lit stairs into a hideous little room with grubby lace curtains and a depressed-looking fern in a brass pot on the table.

"What a frightful pub, Hugh. Can't you really find anywhere better than this to stay?"

"This happens unfortunately to be the only hostelry in the village. I agree it's unsavoury. I'm sure Ashley Courtenay wouldn't recommend it. But—apart from the pleasure of your company, which is none the less intense in spite of the unglamorous surroundings attendant upon it—I hope not to be here for long. The inquest has been fixed for tomorrow morning at ten o'clock, and I trust it's not going to be a very complicated affair. Spragg's here, too. Haven't you met him snooping about?"

"No." Spragg was Hugh's sergeant. I wondered what gave Hugh the idea that it wasn't going to be a very complicated affair. It seemed insolubly dark and inexplicable to me.

"Spragg often asks after you," Hugh said, ringing the bell. "He has a great admiration for your powers of deductive reasoning. You once told him that you derived inspiration from sitting in a hot bath, and ever since then Spragg's gone around looking like an advertisement for Lifebuoy soap."

A slovenly-looking youth in a baize apron appeared at the door and glared at me with deep suspicion.

"Gin or sherry, Liane?" Hugh said. "I remember your rooted aversion to beer."

"Well, it's so cold—and there's such a lot of it."

"I entirely agree—especially in this weather. Two gins, please. You like French with yours, don't you, Liane? And I'll have mine pink."

The boy shuffled off wearing the expression of one who was far less likely to bring the ordered drinks than to report to the management that there were undesirable goings-on in the Residents' Lounge.

"As I was saying," Hugh went on, leaning back in the shabby plush armchair. "I was more or less on my way round to call on your host. We've just had the result of the analysis through, and I thought he'd be interested to hear what they found."

"I'm sure he would," I said politely, and added—because I simply couldn't help it: "What did they find?"

"They found quite a lot of morphine tartrate."

"Oh," I said. There was a pause while we heard distant voices raised in altercation in the hall below. The words "gin" and "a strange young lady up there with Mr. Gordon" detached themselves.

"So he *was* murdered," I said.

"It looks like it."

The voices became more distant and eventually faded altogether. A door slammed and all was quiet.

"D'you know," Hugh remarked conversationally, "I don't believe we're ever going to get those drinks." He strode once more to the bell.

"What exactly is morphine tartrate?"

"I'm a bit vague myself. That's one of the things I was proposing to ask our friend Sandys—what it's used for therapeutically and so on. And also to discover if possible just how easy it is for a layman to get hold of a drug like that. Not at all easy, I should imagine. It's one of the things scheduled under the D.D.A., and as far as I know it isn't one of those handy little poisoning agents like arsenic and cyanide, which are also used for various commercial purposes. Nobody could obtain it on the strength of specious excuses about killing weeds or destroying wasps' nests or anything of that kind. It's a purely medical product, and the use of such a drug should narrow the field quite a lot."

I saw only too clearly that it should; but seeing it gave me no particular pleasure because the field seemed just a bit too narrow to be altogether comfortable. Where did you go to find a drug which was only used medicinally? Presumably to a chemist—or else to the house of a doctor who kept such things on the premises. I was glad Betty was not present at this conversation. She was worried enough already.

"I think you're right about our gin," I said. "And incidentally, I've just remembered what I came out for." I explained about the paper chains. "Look, Hugh, I *must* get that paper for Sara before the newsagent shuts. Why don't you come with me, and then we can go back to the Tithe Barn and have our drink there and you can talk to Howard?"

Hugh agreed that this seemed a good idea. We descended the creaking staircase again and, when we reached the hall, Hugh put his head round the corner of the tap-room door.

"You can cancel my order for those drinks," he said grandly. "I can't wait any longer."

There was a moment of stupefied silence in the tap-room, and the voices broke out again into an indignant babble as we walked down the steps into the street.

It was quite dark when we got outside. The sitting-room window of the Qualtroughs' house was brightly lit, but there was no light coming from Oakhurst Lodge. John Wickham was presumably not at home.

We got to the stationer's just in time, and I was luckily able to make a corner in the remaining stock of coloured paper. To atone for the unwarranted length of time Sara would consider I had taken over her shopping, I added an additional contribution of half a dozen silver-paper bells and some fascinating streamers, which I was sure she and Robin would enjoy throwing at each other. (Whether Nanny, clearing up the resulting debris, would be equally fascinated was another point which I didn't propose to dwell on then.)

At the door of the shop we almost bumped into a slim figure hurrying in from the darkness. Startled dark eyes looked at me for a moment without recognition from above a high fur collar which hid the rest of her face, and then their owner broke into an enchanting smile.

"Pardon, please!" Sonia Phillips said huskily. "Never in my life do I look where I am going!" She smiled again and vanished into the shop, where I heard her apologising charmingly for coming so late, but was there still left by chance one little evening paper?

Hugh's eyebrows rose and he let out the suspicion of a whistle. "Well, well!" he said. "You'll have to watch your step, Liane, to remain the belle of Staple Green if that's the sort of competition you're up against! What a perfectly lovely-looking girl. Do you know her?"

I explained, rather stiffly, the very little I knew about Sonia Phillips. I could feel Hugh's eyes on me and could have kicked myself for reacting so primly. What on earth did it matter to me if Hugh thought she was pretty? Of course she was pretty—much prettier than I was. So what?

Betty's voice from the garage at the side of the house greeted us as we walked up the drive of the Tithe Barn.

"Is that you, Lee?" she said, and without waiting for an answer went on: "Sara told me you'd gone out to get her some more paper chain stuff. How very kind of you. Howard's just come in in a great state of gloom. He's heard that the inquest's been fixed for tomorrow morning, and—"

She emerged, pulling off her fur gloves and stopped short under the porch light at the sight of Hugh.

I introduced him as we went into the hall.

"Well," Betty said, "since this awful thing *had* to happen, and I understand everybody's going to be turned inside out by Scotland Yard, I must say it's a great relief to find you're practically an old friend of the family already."

We went into the drawing-room where Betty poured out drinks and made Hugh sit in the wing chair by the fire.

Howard's voice was audible outside the door talking to Norah Wright. He sounded as if he were trying to reassure her on some point which was troubling her. I heard Norah say: "I never said it actually *mattered*. All I said was—"

Betty called out: "Howard!"

"Just a minute, darling—"

Norah was still talking. Howard's voice began to show signs of exasperation. "Anyway, Norah," he said finally, "let's not *fuss* about it. It'll probably turn up in the morning, and in any case—"

I lost interest and turned to study Hugh's profile. I'd forgotten the characteristic and slightly comic way his fair hair always stood up in a little quiff on top if he wasn't careful how he brushed it. He had on a tweed jacket and grey flannel trousers, and was wearing an old Rugbeian tie. Funny, I found myself thinking, I always thought he was at Harrow.

The door opened and Howard came into the room. When we introduced him to Hugh, and explained who and what he was, Howard looked a little taken aback.

"Oh," he said. "So you're the chap in charge? I've just had a message to say the inquest's laid on for ten o'clock tomorrow morning; but we're still waiting for the result of the analysis."

"That's one of the things I came to see you about," Hugh said. He glanced swiftly at Betty and myself. "Nobody, I know, will mention this to anyone outside before it becomes public property at the inquest, but as a matter of fact we have just received the pathologist's report. The analysis shows that Sir Henry Metcalfe died of morphine tartrate poisoning."

Betty looked merely bewildered. Howard had said he suspected a narcotic, and one poison was much the same as another to her. But I happened to be looking at Howard's face when Hugh spoke to him, and I saw a sudden involuntary frown of anxiety pass over it.

"Oh, damn," he said softly. "So it *was*—"

"Was what?" Betty asked, as he hesitated.

Howard turned abruptly to the tray on the side table and poured himself a generous whisky-and-soda before replying.

"Was what?" he echoed. "Why, murder, of course."

Although his reply sounded perfectly natural, I had somehow a definite conviction that this was not what he had originally been about to say.

"Does that, in your opinion, tie up with the symptoms?" Hugh asked.

Howard seemed to be pulling himself together. "Oh yes," he answered almost casually. "Yes, it does. The symptoms of what we at first took to be a pontine haemorrhage would apply equally well to any form of cyanotic coma. And of course opium would account for the contracted pupils and the shallow breathing. Only, of course, you understand when I first saw him there was no question of anything like that at all—no reason to suppose it wasn't a perfectly ordinary straightforward cerebral—"

"Quite," Hugh interrupted quickly.

"It did occur to me later," Howard went on more slowly. "That is, the idea of a narcotic drug occurred to me. I didn't think specifically of morphine. I'd been thinking the thing over in the ambulance on the way to the hospital and I didn't altogether like the look of it. The pulse was very slow and weak and his temperature was sub-normal. That's possible enough if it was a large haemorrhage, but in that case you'd rather expect some degree of paralysis, and as far as we could tell, there wasn't any."

"You didn't mention this to anyone at the time?"

"Well, no," Howard admitted rather sheepishly. "It seemed a bit far fetched and unlikely. It was pretty obvious he wasn't going to recover in any case—the coma was far too deep. I didn't start worrying seriously about it till the next morning. Then when Harvey told me his temperature was still sub-normal and he was in a cold sweat—well, then I did wonder a bit, and I told Harvey what I thought. The pupils were still bilaterally contracted. That worried me too. I could see that Harvey thought I was being an alarmist. It doesn't do to start hares in our profession, you know. Metcalfe was obviously sinking rapidly and there was nothing whatever we could do about it. Even when he died, we couldn't tell anything for certain without a post mortem. However, I was thoroughly uneasy about the whole business by that time, so at the risk of Harvey considering me rather an officious ass—which I'm sure he did, even though he was extremely civil—I said I'd much rather not sign the certificate. And there it was." He paused and took a gulp of whisky. "I can't say I'm surprised to hear the analysis report, but are you quite sure they specified morphine *tartrate?* I wouldn't have thought they could have been so exact as that."

"Well, that's what the report says," Hugh replied, and added with a grin: "I wouldn't have the technical vocabulary to make it up. Drugs simply aren't in my line—except good old prussic acid, arsenic and such-like. I've got it all jotted down on the back of an envelope straight from the horse's mouth when they rang up the police station from the hospital. Like to have a look?"

"No, thanks," Howard said turning away. "If they say so, it is so. These chaps don't make mistakes. He must have had a fair amount for it to be so readily identifiable, a rather unusual form of morphine to take orally, and it certainly wasn't injected."

"Is there any usual form for poisoning?" I asked bluntly.

"What I meant," Howard amended, giving me rather a dirty look, "is that it isn't a form of opium preparation that you'd expect a layman to get hold of very easily. Paregoric would be a likelier choice, I'd have thought, or one of the laudanum mixtures."

There was a long rather pregnant pause.

"I suppose," Hugh asked tentatively, "it would be impossible for you to hazard any kind of guess as to how long Sir Henry had been in this coma before you first saw him? I mean, would it be a question of hours or minutes—or can't you possibly tell?"

"Not with any degree of accuracy," Howard said. "In a witness box, I'd refuse to be tied down to any definite opinion at all. But speaking purely off the record, judging from the depth of unconsciousness and the lack of response to treatment, I'd put it at least an hour before I was called in—probably longer."

"And you got there when?"

"It must have been soon after eleven—say about ten or a quarter past. At a very rough guess I should say he must have taken his dose of morphia not later than ten o'clock."

Hugh studied his finger nails for a moment before remarking with an entirely spurious carelessness: "The symptoms would be consistent with his having taken it a good deal earlier, though? By about half-past eight, for instance?"

Howard looked at him hard before replying.

"I refuse to be quoted in any way on the subject," he reminded Hugh rather coldly. "I imagine that you are asking me whether it would have been possible for the morphine to have been in the drink Diana Metcalfe made for him before she left the house. I can't answer that either way—I just don't know."

"You can't state definitely that it *couldn't* have been?" Hugh persisted. "It would help Lady Metcalfe's position very much if you could."

Howard paused again and took another drink of whisky.

"No," he said at last. "I can't. I wish to God I could, but I can't."

He walked away to the other side of the room and began twiddling aimlessly with the knobs of the radiogram. Before any sound had come through he thought better of it and switched it off. Betty let out a tremulous little sigh and picked up her knitting.

"Well, thank you for your opinion," Hugh said. "It won't, of course, be regarded in any way as evidence, but it may be very helpful to me as a rough guide."

"Glad to have been of use," Howard said gruffly. "Well, it was very good of you to look in and tell me the result of the analysis. Will you all excuse me a minute—I've just remembered something I must see Norah about before she goes. Betty, give Gordon another drink. I won't be long."

He had made his escape before I remembered about the instructive chat Hugh had been planning to have with him on the subject of morphia in general—its uses and abuses—and most particularly the somewhat vital question of accessibility.

Hugh accepted the cocktail Betty poured for him and sat down again in the wing chair.

"By the way," he remarked soon after the door had closed behind Howard, "A chap called John Wickham called to see me at the pub this afternoon. Do I take it that he is a great friend of the Metcalfe family?"

"Well—" Betty began guardedly. "Yes—yes, he is. He lives at the Lodge at the bottom of their drive," she added helpfully.

"So I gathered. He had rather a remarkable story. He said that on Tuesday night, *after* Lady Metcalfe had left for Tunbridge Wells—he was very careful to stress that point—a mysterious motor car drove up the private road to Oakhurst Place at a quarter past nine, and returned a few minutes later. Isn't that interesting?"

"Why," Betty exclaimed in excitement, "but it's wonderful! I mean, if somebody else saw Sir Henry later on that evening after she'd gone—and he was all right then—well, it *proves* she couldn't have—that is, I mean—" she broke off in some confusion.

"It means she couldn't have doped the whisky Sir Henry drank at half-past eight," Hugh agreed. "Yes, doesn't it? Provided of course that he did drink it straight away, which would be natural, seeing that it was hot. Yes, that was the aspect Wickham was so anxious to point out to me. I just wondered—has he ever mentioned anything about this car to anybody else, do you happen to know?"

It was a pity that Betty's expression was always quite so transparent. She sat there for a moment in silence trying not to let surprise show that John Wickham had said nothing whatever about this mysterious car when we had seen him last night. Then her face cleared and she said cautiously: "Well, not to *me*, actually. But of course it's perfectly possible that he forgot about it when I saw him, and he's only just remembered about it—and realised how important it might turn out to be."

Hugh looked at her with admiration.

"You ought to be a mind-reader," he said. "That's exactly what he told me himself. He said he'd registered it subconsciously at the time—just as he'd registered Lady Metcalfe's car going down the drive about three quarters of an hour before, without really noticing it. And then this afternoon it all sort of came back to him in a flash, and he realised how significant it might be, and he felt I ought to know about it at once—before the inquest."

Somehow I didn't quite like the tone of Hugh's voice.

"Well, so it is significant," I said sharply. "I suppose you're following it up at once?"

Hugh looked at me in the way which I have always found particularly irritating, with one eyebrow slightly higher than the other and a maddening half smile on his lips.

"Of course we're following it up," he assured me smoothly. "In fact, I told Wickham that as it seemed such an important clue we'd better keep it up our sleeves for the moment and not mention it at the inquest. Because if it had been a perfectly innocent private call on Sir Henry, you'd have thought the person or persons would have come forward by now to tell us about it, wouldn't you? His death's already been announced in *The Times*."

"But," Betty gasped, "it might have been the *murderer*!"

"So it might. Well, I agree in that case you wouldn't expect him to come forward. But it seems rather a public way to commit a murder, doesn't it? To drive up openly in a car which might easily be—and in fact was—noticed by anyone in the village who happened to look out of the window. A very *careless* murderer!"

I was beginning to get a bit annoyed with Hugh.

"Well," I said. "If you'll excuse me, I think I'm going up now to have a bath."

Hugh took the hint immediately and jumped to his feet. Betty saw him to the front door, and came back looking rather ashamed of my abruptness.

"You needn't have thrown him out quite so obviously," she said reproachfully, coming back to the fireplace to warm her hands. "I thought he seemed nice. And it *is* good news that he's going to do something about tracing that car."

"Oh, don't be silly, Betty," I said impatiently. "Can't you see Hugh didn't believe a word of it?"

"You mean he thinks John made up the whole story?"

"Well, of course. Don't you?"

Betty's face clouded. "Oh dear," she said. "How terribly silly of John! And I *warned* him not to go round being so much of a Galahad."

I picked up my scattered belongings and looped the handle of my bag over one arm.

"When I find myself in a spat like Diana," I told her, "I hope you will have the kindness to allow *no* chivalrous males within twenty miles of me. The damage they do! Not," I added as I reached the door, "that there's likely to be much of a queue. I don't inspire chivalry—I'm not the type."

"Oy!" said Betty. "Come back a minute. That reminds me of something I meant to ask you. Speaking of non-chivalrous males, which day is Bill coming down?"

"He can't get away till Christmas Eve," I said. "Which means I shall have to get all his presents for him. He's got several tiresome godchildren, and I'm very much afraid that's going to involve a visit to Hamley's. I was trying to get the list sorted out this morning."

"Well, if you do have to go to London," Betty said, "would Tuesday be all right? I have to take Sara to the dentist in Tunbridge

Wells at half-past twelve, and we could drop you off at the station. There's quite a good train service from there."

"Yes, I think that would be fine," I said. "If I got a train about twelve I'd have the whole afternoon to shop."

"There's a timetable in my desk," Betty said, getting up to fetch it. She rummaged for a moment. "Yes, that would fit in all right. There's a train at twelve-four, and then you could catch the five-thirty or the six twenty-two back, and I'd come over and meet you with the car."

"Thank you," I said absently, starting for the door again. Betty's head was still bent over the timetable.

"That's a funny thing," she said slowly.

"What is?" I asked idly, my mind engaged upon the rival merits of Minibricks or Meccano for a child of nine.

"You remember Michael telling us about going up to the theatre on the evening of Robin's party—last Tuesday?"

"Yes, of course," I said, my attention switching rapidly.

"Well, he left our house at five o'clock—I remember noticing the time because I was sorry he had to go so early. And do you remember he said he went by train and got to his theatre at seven?"

"Yes."

"Well," said Betty, wrinkling her forehead in perplexity. "I don't see how he can have done. There are no trains up between the five-eight—which he couldn't possibly have caught—and the six-twenty, which doesn't get to Charing Cross till seven thirty-two."

"Oh," I said, and sat down on the arm of the sofa. "Yes, that does seem funny. Very funny indeed."

Betty returned the timetable to its pigeon-hole and shut the flap of the desk with a snap.

"Michael must have made a mistake," she said rather urgently. "He must have meant the thing started at eight o'clock, not seven."

It was apparent that having hurled this discrepancy at me and invited comment, she was now sorry she had mentioned it and didn't want to discuss it any further. I picked up my bag once more and made another determined effort bathwards. There was no doubt at all in my mind as to what Michael had said. He had said seven and I was pretty sure he had meant seven. But if Betty wished to constitute herself into a barrier of reticence between the police and the tarradiddles of the Metcalfe family, it was nothing to do with me. Nothing, that was, as long as Hugh didn't find out. He had just as much access to the railway timetable as we had, and once he had heard Michael's story, I rather fancied that young man would find himself with quite a bit of explaining to do.

I can't say the thought worried me unduly.

XI

MATERIA MEDICA

THERE WAS A GOOD DEAL OF ACRIMONIOUS DISCUSSION AS to whether Betty and I should attend the inquest next morning or not. It was being held over at Tunbridge Wells, and I had a sneaking desire to go and see what it was like. As I was a little sheepish about admitting to this unwomanly curiosity, I tried to persuade Betty that it was more or less our duty as citizens to attend, and in the end I got her quite keen on the idea. We had, however, reckoned without Howard, who immediately put his foot down and said he had never heard of such an outrageous suggestion. The chief outrage seemed to be that it would give a bad impression to the patients if it got round that Doctor's Wife had lowered herself to the level of a plain vulgar seeker after sensation; and the dignity of the practice was at stake. The same stricture applied, I gathered, in a modified way, to Doctor's Guest, so somewhat sulkily we gave way and agreed not to go.

Betty was therefore distinctly annoyed when Howard announced at breakfast that he was taking Norah Wright over to the inquest in his car, and would Betty mind pinning a notice up on the surgery door telling patients to come back in the evening instead.

"You're taking *Norah?*" Betty protested. "But whatever for? The whole thing's got absolutely nothing to do with Norah—and yet you take her, and you won't take me. I do call that mean."

I was surprised myself and rather intrigued. Once or twice during the previous evening I had caught Howard and Norah muttering together in earnest little huddles, which they had broken off quickly at my approach. Something was in the wind—something which concerned Norah—and I also had a fleeting suspicion that it was something more than mere professional propriety which had made Howard so averse to the idea of Betty and me attending the inquest.

After Howard and Norah Wright had driven off in the Daimler, Betty remembered that she had promised to take the children out to the woods beyond Horsmonden to cut some holly for decorations. Sara's school had broken up early because somebody was in quarantine for mumps and both Betty and Nanny were already finding it something of a problem to keep Sara amused. "As if the school holidays weren't long enough already," Betty sighed, "without them having to break up a week early!"

Accordingly at eleven o'clock we all packed ourselves into Betty's small Morris Minor and set off laden with secateurs, bits of string and large baskets. We had a certain amount of trouble on the return journey with Robin who became tearfully insistent about transporting practically a whole holly bush in the back seat; and in the end he travelled back wedged into a small space beside it, screaming every time we went round a corner that it was pricking him, while Sara sat precariously balanced on the back of the seat beside the driver and I held her legs.

We crawled cautiously round the bend of the Tithe Barn drive to behold Hugh Gordon's new car drawn up outside the front door. This was a long low black Lancia, incredibly sleek and shining. It was the pride and joy of Hugh's existence; and having some rough idea about the scale of salaries paid by Scotland Yard, I could only assume that the death of a rich relation or winning a football pool or something of that kind had intervened to make such opulence possible. The garage door stood wide open, and it was evident that Howard and Norah had not yet returned from the inquest.

Hugh was standing in the hall admiring Sara's paper chains, and especially the "magic lantern"—a fearsome sort of bird's nest of green and red paper which was Robin's proud contribution.

"Er—good morning," Betty said without her usual enthusiasm. "Come in. I'm afraid Howard's not back yet from Tunbridge Wells."

"That's all right," Hugh said easily. "But I'd like to wait and have a word with him, if I may. I take it you didn't go to the inquest."

"No. Howard thought it wouldn't be suitable."

"How disappointed Liane must be. Well, I didn't go either, but I was given a sort of preview of the agenda by the Coroner, and I don't think it can have been very exciting."

"You ought to have gone," I said, trying to disentangle a large branch of holly and attendant mass of trailing ivy which seemed to have fastened itself to the sleeve of my coat, "It's your job. Why didn't you?"

"I had other things to do," Hugh said evasively. He picked up a number of pieces of holly which had fallen from the bunch during my progress from the car and restored them to me.

Betty kicked off her gum boots and steered Hugh into the drawing-room. I gathered them up, and went off towards the back door to deposit the holly and remove my own boots.

I heard Howard's Daimler stop outside and voices upraised in argument. I retreated a little way down the passage.

"It's no good, Norah," Howard was saying. "They'll have to know. And if I'd been asked point blank at the inquest, I'd have told them then."

"Well, I don't see it," Norah said. "It isn't as if we knew for *certain* even now. You were the person who told me not to fuss when I first discovered about it, and—"

"Yes, but that was *before.* Now it's withholding information if we don't tell them."

"I don't agree," Norah persisted obstinately. "It's the business of the police to find things out for themselves. If you report this it will only lead to a lot of unpleasantness, and it won't do the practice any good at all."

Howard slammed the door of the Daimler and I heard their footsteps crossing the yard towards the back door.

"Don't be silly, Norah. There's nothing *negligent* about it."

"No, but you know what fools people are. They'll say you ought to have kept the beastly thing locked or something—"

I didn't particularly want to be caught eavesdropping in quite such a blatant fashion, so at this point I dropped one of my gum boots loudly on to the stone floor of the passage. There was a slight exclamation from Norah, and Howard pushed open the door.

"Hullo, Lee," he remarked conversationally. "I want to get hold of your friend Gordon. Any idea what he's likely to be doing today?"

"At this moment he's sitting in your drawing-room talking to Betty," I said. "He had the same idea about wanting to see you. Didn't you notice his car in the drive? It's fairly conspicuous."

"I saw a very gorgeous black beast—I didn't know whose it was. I hoped it was a wealthy new patient."

Norah Wright came into the passage and went towards the surgery.

"All I ask you," she said to Howard, pausing deliberately at the door, "is not to do anything *stupid.*"

Howard smiled at her and turned to me. "Norah's trying to save me from the clutches of the law," he said. "But I've made up my mind to come clean. Come on, Lee—over the top!"

I followed him through the swing doors to the hall and on into the drawing-room.

Howard greeted Hugh casually and walked over to the drink cupboard. He dispensed gin all round, and then said, looking at Betty: "I've been a bit fussed about some evidence I've been concealing. At least I think it may be evidence. Gordon will know best. But I've talked it over with Norah, and, in the light of the inquest, I thought I'd better come across with it." He took a gulp of his drink.

"Yes?" said Hugh.

"Norah and I have been checking over my drug supply," Howard went on. "And what we've discovered is that a tube containing twenty-four quarter-grain tablets of morphine tartrate is missing from my bag. Norah noticed it wasn't there last night before surgery, but I told her not to bother. I simply thought I'd mislaid it somewhere—put it in another drawer or something. Then you came in and said the analysis showed morphine tartrate in Sir Henry Metcalfe, so Norah and I began to think again. We had the most tremendous hunt right through my bag and the poison cupboard in the surgery, and I'm afraid the long and short of it is that that tube has disappeared."

There was a long silence during which I didn't dare meet Betty's eye.

"Oh," said Hugh. "I see. Well it was one of the questions I'd come to ask you, of course. Drugs like that don't grow on trees. I was going to ask you to check over your supply of morphia and make sure that there wasn't anything missing. You say you discovered the loss of this tube last night?"

"Norah Wright, my dispenser, discovered it wasn't in my bag where it's usually kept. She was checking up to see what replacements we needed. I haven't been using much morphine lately so I didn't notice it had gone."

"And you can't say at all when it disappeared?"

"I'm sorry, I can't. Except that I know it was there about a week ago. Betty, which evening was it I was called out to see Mary Webber—you know, the Prendergasts' cook?"

"Tuesday," Betty replied promptly. "Not last Tuesday—the one before. I remember because it was the day we had those people in for drinks, and I'd hoped you'd get back early to help me cope."

"This woman had scalded herself," Howard explained to Hugh. "She was in considerable pain, and I decided to give her a shot of morphia before I dressed it. I remember taking out an unopened tube of morph. tart. and then noticing that the one next to it, which was morph. sulph., had been half used already, so I thought I'd use that instead. There's very little difference, except that morph. tart. is more readily soluble for a hypodermic and I generally prefer it for that reason. But as the other was open it saved bother to go on with the same tube. So that's how I know it was there then."

"Had you any other tubes of morphine tartrate in your bag?"

"No. That was the only one. And Norah's checked over the surgery supply, and that's all accounted for."

"Mmm," said Hugh thoughtfully.

I was a bit thoughtful myself. Tuesday, I reflected. That was the very evening when Sir Henry Metcalfe himself and his wife and son, not to mention several of his less loving neighbours, were all milling round the house, in and out of the surgery where Howard's bag was sitting on the table—probably unlocked. As far as I could see, any single one of these people might have helped themselves to a nice lethal dose.

"Of course it mightn't have been taken that particular day," Howard pointed out. "That's just the last time I know for certain it was there. It could have disappeared any time *since* then. And I'm afraid that unless I'd suddenly wanted to use the stuff, I wouldn't have noticed it was missing at all. That is, until Norah did one of her routine checks."

There was another rather uncomfortable silence. I think it was in all our minds that Tuesday was much the likeliest day for the morphia to have disappeared.

Hugh voiced what was probably the same idea a few minutes later when he said: "Allowing that it could have vanished any time since last Tuesday week, it might still be a good idea to check over the people who happened to be in this house that night. All those with access to the surgery, that is. Mrs. Sandys, can you remember exactly whom you invited that evening?"

"Yes, of course," Betty said. "There was Sir Henry and Lady Metcalfe, and his son Michael. Then there was Mr. Qualtrough and Ann, his daughter—oh, and a Mrs. Phillips, who's a newcomer to the place and lives in a cottage about two miles outside the village. I think that was all. Besides ourselves, of course."

"John Wickham looked in, too," Howard reminded her.

"Oh yes, so he did. But, Mr. Gordon, these people are all *friends* of ours—we've known them for years. Except, of course, Mrs. Phillips—but she's a stranger and probably wouldn't even have known there *was* such a thing as morphine tartrate—certainly not that Howard kept some in his bag. Besides, what motive could a girl like that possibly have? She didn't even know Sir Henry—she'd never set eyes on him before that evening."

"Mrs. Phillips," Hugh murmured, turning to me. "Wasn't that the name of the glamour-girl we met coming out of the newspaper shop last night?"

I nodded.

"You're sure she didn't know Sir Henry?"

"Oh no," Betty put in quickly. "I'm sure she didn't. She's only been in the place a few weeks. It was to introduce her to a few people that I asked her in."

I wouldn't have been nearly so sure myself, if Hugh'd asked me the same question. But then Betty hadn't caught the fleeting expression of alarm in Sonia Phillips' dark tip-tilted eyes at the moment when she noticed Sir Henry being steered across the room to be introduced to her. She had recovered herself very quickly—almost instantaneously—but the impression remained. If she didn't know Sir Henry personally, his name rang a bell with her in some way. And Sir Henry himself—he had behaved rather oddly too. I remembered the look on his face as he had stood hesitating by the fireplace and the deceptive softness of his voice as he said: "I beg your pardon, but I don't think I quite caught your name, Mrs.—er—?"

"About Howard's bag," I said slowly, "Mrs. Phillips could have seen that, you know, Betty. Don't you remember she told us she'd lost the way round to the front door and she'd come in through the surgery? Well, if the bag was on the table—"

"Well, even so," Betty said. "It seems rather far-fetched. If it comes to that, *anyone* could have got into the surgery. It's empty after Norah goes home, and everybody in the village knows our habits."

"They'd have to get past Mrs. Padgett," Howard said. "She's bound to see anyone who comes in through the surgery door."

"Yes. You're right. I'd forgotten Mrs. Padgett."

"By the way," Hugh said, fishing out the little black notebook I used to know so well. "I'm shockingly ignorant about drugs, I'm afraid. You say this stuff was in quarter-grain tablets. The analyst seemed to think he'd had about four grains. That would leave a further two grains—say eight tablets—unaccounted for?"

"Just about," Howard said. "You can't be accurate about post mortem figures. You can only judge it on the amount recovered from the body and then calculate from that what sort of dose he probably had."

"Four grains would be a pretty stiff lethal dose?"

"I should say it would polish off most people. There again it's difficult to lay down any hard and fast rules. The usual therapeutic dose is anything from an eighth to a third, but it's a tolerance forming drug; and it would take far more to bump off a hardened addict—or even somebody who'd been having regular morphine injections from a doctor—than it would to kill a person who was unused to it. I've never prescribed opium in any form for Sir Henry, so unless he had a private supply of his own—which you'll agree is unlikely, and one would have noticed the symptoms before—I should have thought two grains of morphine, or at any rate three, would have been enough to settle his hash."

I shuddered slightly. Somebody either hadn't known very much about the properties of morphia—or else they'd wanted to make very sure that Sir Henry would never wake up again.

"Would the morphine have been readily soluble in say—whisky-and-soda?" Hugh asked. "There was a tray beside him with a glass and various indications that he'd been drinking something—but of course the frustrating thing from our point of view is that everything was tidied away and washed up long before we ever got to the scene at all."

Howard looked a little guilty about this. He turned away to light a cigarette and remarked: "It wouldn't have been soluble in alcohol anyway, and I don't know how you'd introduce about sixteen tablets into a siphon. It sounds a bit clumsy to me."

"It's *infuriating,*" Hugh said, "about the glass he was drinking from. We've rescued the decanter from the dining-room, but if as you say the stuff isn't soluble in alcohol we shan't get anything from that. Do you remember if there *was* a siphon on the table beside him?"

Howard shook his head. "Now you mention it," he said, "I'm pretty sure there wasn't."

"Was there *anything* besides the decanter and the glass?" Hugh persisted. "Of course Lady Metcalfe and Wickham have both been asked the same question, but they say they were too upset over Sir Henry's condition to remember anything about the state of the room at all."

"Well, I was fairly taken up with the patient myself," Howard said. "I can't say I noticed anything particular about the room."

"Do you remember what Diana said about the radio being on—and something about a book on lilies which he wouldn't have been reading, because he was busy examining his china bowl, the one they found broken beside his chair?" I asked Betty. "I suppose they told you about that, Hugh?"

"The Inspector did mention it," Hugh replied. "It *may* have some significance, I suppose, but I confess I can't for the moment see it. You aren't suggesting the morphine was in the china bowl, are you?"

"Well, I hadn't thought of that," I said tartly. "Anyway, it was broken, so you can't even analyse the pieces. I was thinking more about the radio being on. If Sir Henry was well enough to turn it on at nine o'clock for the news, it seems unlikely that the morphine what-have-you was in the whisky Diana gave him before she went out at half-past eight."

Hugh made no reply to this and I felt more snubbed than ever. If I had known him less well I might have taken comfort from the thought that my logic had bereft him of speech. As it was I gathered he considered such a theory simply too silly to waste time discussing. I sat seething with impotent indignation.

"About that table," Howard said suddenly. "There *was* something else on it besides the glass and the decanter. It comes back to me that Wickham moved the tray for me to put my bag down—and there was something else. Now, what on earth could it have been?"

"Oh darling," Betty exclaimed. "Do try to think—it may be a very important clue."

Howard shut his eyes in an agony of concentration and we all sat round hardly daring to breathe lest we should disturb his thought processes.

"Yes," said Howard, emerging at last from his trance. "I've remembered. There was a silver hot water jug. One of those things with a lid like a coffee-pot. I can see it quite clearly. It was on the tray Wickham moved for me to park my bag."

"Whatever would Sir Henry want that for?" Betty asked in surprise. "I can't see him sitting there drinking hot water."

"D'you think Diana brought his hot drink in it?" I asked.

"She might have done, I suppose," Betty agreed doubtfully. "But it seems much more likely she'd make it in the pantry or somewhere and bring it along in the glass, I mean, you don't generally put whisky in a jug, do you?"

"It'll be quite simple to ask her, any way," Hugh said. "Thanks very much for remembering that, Sandys, it may be useful."

"The morphine would be more soluble in hot water, of course," Howard remarked. "Perhaps he had another drink later on—made it himself, I mean. I wish we'd thought of the poison idea at the time, and then we could have saved the evidence from being all cleared away. But at that stage it had simply never entered my head."

"Don't worry," Hugh said. "It's annoying, of course, because we need every scrap of evidence we can get, but I daresay it wouldn't have helped much in any case. Even if we'd found traces of morphine in the jug or the glass or both we should still be a long way from knowing who put it there. I don't somehow fancy that the character who went to so much trouble to arrange this business would have been naif enough to have left any finger prints. The knobs of the radio have been tested, of course, and the door handle. In fact they've gone over the whole place pretty carefully; but speaking for myself I don't expect any results at all from that. It's just one of those routine affairs, which has to be done."

There was an apologetic scuffle outside the door and Mrs. Padgett's head appeared round the corner. She coughed nervously and mumbled something about lunch being ready. Her diffidence conveyed that it had been ready for a long time, only she hadn't liked to intrude before.

"I'm so sorry—" Hugh began, rising to his feet. "I'd no idea—"

"Please stay and have something to eat," Betty said quickly. "It's only rabbit pie, but there's plenty of it. The children have theirs upstairs, and Norah isn't staying today, so it will just be ourselves."

During lunch Howard and Hugh talked fishing, and Betty and I consumed rabbit pie in silence with our thoughts miles away.

We had just left the dining-room and were returning to the drawing-room for coffee when the telephone in the hall rang. We left Howard to answer it and went on and sat down by the fire.

"It's for you, Gordon," Howard said, coming in from the hall. "Colonel Wilbraham."

The Chief Constable, I reflected, must have put in some quite creditable detective work on his own account to have tracked Hugh down to the Tithe Barn. Or had Hugh intended all along to come and scrounge some lunch off Betty? Remembering the

Blue Boar I felt I could hardly blame him if he had. He went out to the telephone, leaving the door slightly ajar, and I am ashamed to admit that we all three continued to sit in complete silence with our ears flapping. Howard picked up the current number of the *B.M.J.* and pretended to be reading an article on blood groups, but Betty and I just sat.

Hugh's end of the conversation was clearly audible from the drawing-room and we could even hear a few faint and distant cackles from Colonel Wilbraham.

"Yes, sir—I did," Hugh was saying cheerfully. "Spragg took a man up to search the house during the inquest. It seemed a good opportunity. No, I haven't had his report yet."

Betty made wild signs at me across the hearthrug which I took to mean what house—had I known about this—and if so, why hadn't I told her? I shook my head in bewilderment.

The cackles went on for some time.

"Oh," said Hugh. It was impossible to gather anything from his tone which was just a shade too carefully level and matter-of-fact. "Well, that's very interesting—and as it happens it ties up with something else, which has just come in."

Betty's eyebrows waggled madly. I shook my head again. None of it made the remotest glimmer of sense to me.

Colonel Wilbraham seemed to be talking at some length.

"I see," said Hugh, speaking in the same carefully flat voice. "Yes. Well, in view of Spragg's report, I agree that it seems the only thing to do. In fact we haven't any alternative. Yes—yes—yes. I shall be ringing the Yard at six o'clock and I'll have a word with the A.C. Yes. Right you are, sir. Sorry, I didn't catch what you said? All right, sir—I'll come straight over now."

There was a ping as the receiver went back, and Betty and I jumped guiltily and tried to look as if we hadn't been eavesdropping at all. Actually, knowing Hugh, I was perfectly certain that he realised how avidly we had been hanging on every word he spoke, and had regulated and censored his conversation accordingly.

He walked back into the drawing-room with a slightly puzzled expression on his face. I deduced that something had happened for which he had not been altogether prepared, and that he was trying to fit it into the pattern of events as he now saw them.

Betty handed Hugh a cup of coffee. He accepted it and drank it standing up by the fireplace. To Betty's remarks he gave polite and pre-occupied replies. It was quite obvious that we were going to get nothing out of him in the way of low-down on his conversation with the Chief Constable. The look on his face rather precluded any fond hopes I might have cherished about doing better later on, if I managed to catch him in a, more mellow mood at the Blue Boar. Whatever this particular thing was, he wasn't going to let me in on it; and as I knew from bitter experience, nobody could be quite so much of a clam as Hugh when he had made up his mind that he wasn't going to divulge something.

He finished his coffee and put down the cup.

"Thank you very much for a delicious lunch," he said formally to Betty. "Will you forgive me if I dash off now? I have an appointment to see Colonel Wilbraham."

Howard went out with him to his car, and a few seconds later I heard the supercharged roar of the Lancia engine receding down the lane.

"Something's happened," Betty observed unnecessarily to me. "You'll have to put your best Delilah foot forward, Lee. *Whose* house was searched during the inquest? It can't have been ours, can it? We were all out, but surely Nanny or Mrs. Padgett—"

"They'd have to have a search warrant," I reminded her. "And of course Nanny would have told you if they'd been here."

"More likely it was Oakhurst," Howard said coming back into the room and reaching for the *B.M.J.* "Fingerprints on the study carpet or something. Diana says there hasn't been a minute's peace since Wednesday, what with photographers and half the Metropolitan police force creeping round on all fours looking for clues."

"What I want to know," Betty said, "is what tied up with something which had just 'come in.' Was that something we said?"

"Or what Hugh and Colonel Wilbraham haven't any alternative about," I put in.

Howard rustled the pages of the *B.M.J.*

"You don't suppose," Betty said slowly, "that it's your morphia they've found? Could *that* be what ties up?"

"That," said Howard bitterly, "seems the one thing they couldn't possibly find. According to the analyst they've already found it—inside Sir Henry."

"Not all of it," I said. "They could have found the tube and any tablets there might be left over."

Howard regarded me sourly and heaved himself out of the armchair.

"I leave you two dear little things to a happy afternoon of speculation," he said acidly. "Personally I've got to work. And by the way, Betty, when Norah comes in, you might ask her to leave the surgery keys somewhere where I can find them. I foresee the most rigid security precautions being taken from now on—everything will be kept locked day and night—my bag will never be out of somebody's sight—and Norah will end up by making me sleep with it chained to the bottom of my bed. D'you know, the ridiculous girl first of all didn't want me to mention the morphine was missing at all—and then just before lunch, she said she thought is was pretty damn careless of me to have left it in the surgery that night anyway. There's no logic in women. Well, so long, ghouls. See you later."

"That's all very fine," Betty said, when the door had closed behind Howard. "But there *are* people who might think Howard had been careless with that bag. Norah's perfectly right to think of the effect it would have. Lee, who *could* have taken that beastly morphine?"

I shrugged my shoulders helplessly. I would have given a good deal to know the answer to that myself.

XII

TRYING IT OUT ON THE DOG

THE LOCAL NEWSPAPER NEXT MORNING DID FULL HONOUR to the inquest and there was even a photograph of Howard, with Norah Wright beside him, leaving the court. This amused Betty and me and annoyed Howard very much indeed. There was also a blurred and unrecognisable picture of Diana Metcalfe under the heading: "Widow of Deceased Judge." There was luckily no portrait of: "Boy-friend of Widow of Deceased Judge," though obviously John Wickham would also have had to attend the inquest. On the whole the report was disappointingly unsensational. The paper was not able openly to announce the thing as murder, because the inquest had been adjourned *sine die* with an open verdict; but the local reporter had done his best to cram as much heavy innuendo between the lines as he possibly could without actually laying the proprietors open to a charge of libel.

I half expected Hugh to drop in during the course of the morning for a matey chat on the progress of the case, and when he did I was determined to demand an explanation of his cryptic conversation with the Chief Constable. But I had no opportunity to pump him on that point or any other, because he never appeared.

The only person who did appear—somewhat unexpectedly—was Mr. Qualtrough. He roamed into the house at about half-past eleven while Betty was upstairs and I was in the hall struggling to arrange some outsize branches of holly in an earthenware pot much too small to hold them. At the sound of footsteps I looked quickly round towards the door, and the whole vase overbalanced heavily on to the floor, as I had always knew it eventually would.

"Allow me," said Mr. Qualtrough gallantly, scooping among the débris.

The ostensible purpose of Mr. Qualtrough's visit, it turned out, was to present Betty with a small bunch of Christmas roses from his garden; but actually I am quite sure that he was simply brimful of curiosity about the Metcalfe case, and had come along to what he supposed might be regarded as a clearing house for current gossip to see what crumbs of news he could collect.

"Quite a little commotion, is it not," he observed, his beady eyes falling on a copy of the local paper which was draped conspicuously over the hall table. "How our late lamented neighbour would have deplored such vulgar publicity! And I understand, Mrs, Craufurd, that you yourself are practically in the thick of the investigation?"

Somewhat startled, I asked him just what could have given him such an idea.

"My daughter tells me," he said gently, "that the young man from Scotland Yard, who is staying at the Blue Boar—such a very unattractive inn, is it not?—is an old friend of yours."

For the hundredth time I wondered exactly how the grapevine of village intelligence functions. Nobody could possibly have seen me with Hugh—the only time I had ever emerged with him from the precincts of the Blue Boar, it had been pitch dark and the only person we had encountered was Sonia Phillips. It seemed unlikely that she would have relayed this piece of information to Ann Qualtrough—or anybody else. (When I put the point later to Betty she accepted it without any surprise at all. "Oh," she said, "that's nothing. I expect Mr. Willis told her. He notices everything that goes on. You don't seem to have grasped, Lee, that strangers like you and Hugh Gordon are practically celebrities. You can't expect to get away with any clandestine little appointments in a village like this—so don't you think it. It isn't surprising, poor dears, when you realise that other people's goings on are all they have to interest them from one year's end to the next. Why, I wouldn't mind betting that my Mrs. Padgett knows exactly what the Prendergasts had for dinner last night, and how much Diana paid for her last new hat.")

Sara and Robin hurled themselves down the stairs, followed by Betty, which relieved me from the necessity of replying to Mr. Qualtrough's rather awkward leading question.

"It really seems quite providential in the unhappy circumstances," Mr. Qualtrough pursued, when the children had gone off into the garden on their tricycles, and Betty had disappeared in the direction of the kitchen to rustle up some mid-morning coffee, "that I am able to produce what I believe is known in detective fiction as an unimpeachable alibi." He smiled, pleased with the phrase. "Otherwise, I might find myself in a somewhat equivocal position." He peered earnestly at me and added in a hoarse whisper: "My relations with my late neighbour are known to have been a little strained."

"I hardly think anyone—" I began uncomfortably.

"Oh no, you can't say that," Mr. Qualtrough reproved me, holding up his finger and wagging it at me in an admonishing manner. "I am—I quite agree—an Unlikely Person. Therefore I am all the more worthy of your attention as a potential suspect."

Oh well, I thought. Since he was determined that I wanted to play Sherlock Holmes with him, I might as well string him along and get all I could out of the old thing. It wasn't at all likely to be of the smallest interest or importance, but it might just possibly help Hugh a bit in clearing the ground. After all, I remembered, this comic old character was definitely one of the people who was wandering about the house on the night that Howard's morphine tartrate probably disappeared, and—on his own admission—he certainly disliked Sir Henry Metcalfe very much indeed.

"Yes, I think on the whole it is fortunate," Mr. Qualtrough said precisely. He placed the tips of his fingers together and regarded me owlishly from over the top of his spectacles. "It is definitely fortunate that I spent the entire evening of my unhappy neighbour's seizure at home with my daughter, and that neither of us stirred from the house." He shot me a childish look of triumph. "I have never been interrogated by an officer from Scotland Yard," he went on, almost wistfully. "And true though my statement is, I feel they would hardly be disposed to accept it on the strength of my bare word alone, without investigation, would they?"

"Well," I said, a little uneasily, "I suppose they'd have to try and verify it a bit. You know, with exact times, and so on."

"I think—yes, I am sure—that I can remember most of the relevant hours," Mr. Qualtrough said. "Dear me, this is rather an amusing game, isn't it? Let me see. Ann was out in the afternoon—yes, of course, there was a children's party here. She told me about it afterwards. There was some anxiety, was there not, as to the gastronomic capacity of the son of the house? I trust that he, in modern parlance, 'made the grade?' Yes. Ann came back and prepared the supper. We dined, I remember, at eight o'clock. We have no servants, and my daughter looks after me when she is at home. When she is away, I 'fend for myself,' as the expression has it. As I was saying, we dined. We ate haddock, I recollect, which I must confess is not one of my favourite dishes, followed I seem to remember by cheese and biscuits. Frugal you may consider, but I assure you entirely adequate. The nutritive value of casein—"

I began to glance furtively towards the door. *Why,* I asked myself, was this extraordinary little man telling me all this? Was it really a mild form of parlour game? Or had it some deeper significance—did he intend that I should be the messenger who would pass it on to Hugh Gordon? Or what?

"After dinner," Mr. Qualtrough continued, shutting his eyes and tilting his grey imperial straight up towards the ceiling, "we partook of coffee in the room Ann calls my study. It is, in fact, our only sitting-room. I drank my coffee and then—then, what did I do?" He opened his eyes suddenly and fixed me with a penetrating glare. "Ah, yes. I think that was the moment when I indulged in a short nap."

I began to take a bit more interest in the story. This might, I considered, be informative after all; because what, in fact, Mr, Qualtrough was giving me as well as his own activities—or lack of them—was an account of Ann's movements too. And Ann Qualtrough was definitely not a young woman to be lost sight of.

"A nap?" I repeated tentatively. Anything might have taken place during Mr. Qualtrough's nap. Ann, armed with morphine tartrate stolen from Howard's surgery, could have crept up the drive to Oakhurst Place—it wasn't more than five minutes walk from door to door—and done all sorts of nefarious things. "I suppose you wouldn't know what time you—er—dropped off? That," I added hastily, to reassure him that I was playing the game properly according to the rules, "is the sort of question the police would be *bound* to ask you."

"Oh, it was a very short nap," Mr. Qualtrough replied disappointingly. "Not more than a quarter of an hour—twenty minutes at the outside. I should say it was about five minutes to nine when Ann brought in the coffee. Then she retired to the kitchen to wash up. I have frequently noticed that a woman will take at least twice as long as a man in the same circumstances over a simple task like washing up. The trouble is that women have no method.

Now when I wash up—" He caught my eye and remembered that he was making a statement. "Yes, that is what Ann was doing. I heard the familiar clatter of earthenware. Then I dozed off. I woke up when Ann came back to fetch the coffee tray. She asked me, I remember, if I would like another cup of coffee and I declined. That would have been about a quarter past nine. Yes, that is exactly what it was, because I had just resumed my book when Ann called out from the kitchen to remind me about a concert of chamber music I wished to listen to on the wireless."

This was the kind of statement Hugh would like. Nice definite times, confirmed by the B.B.C. No vague "I suppose it must have been soon after nine by my watch, which is usually unreliable." Nine-fifteen by Big Ben was nine-fifteen, and no getting away from it.

"Ann came in and turned on the wireless," Mr. Qualtrough went on. "And it was exceedingly vexing, because the concert had just started. They were playing the A major violin concerto of Mozart—Köchel 219, if I remember rightly—an exquisite work if one ignores the unfortunate interpolation of a Turkish march in the third movement—what can have been the point of that, I wonder? It is totally irrelevant to the theme. Can it have been inserted with a desire to flatter Salzburg, do you suppose? Or did the composer imagine that the minuet as it stood lacked eloquence?"

I shook my head rather blankly. Mozart hadn't confided his intentions to me.

Mr. Qualtrough hummed a few bars of the offending tune.

"Not that we got as far as that," he said regretfully. "The battery failed about half-way through the first movement. *Most* annoying." He clicked his tongue at the memory.

"Battery?" I said.

"Oh yes, we have practically nothing in the way of modern conveniences at Little Hodges," Mr. Qualtrough informed me. "Our landlord did not see his way to installing electricity when the main cable was brought to the village from Brenchley. Consequently we illuminate the house with oil lamps—which I admit I personally much prefer to the harsh glare of electricity—and we run our wireless off a battery, which I take to be charged at intervals at Power's Garage. It is a small inconvenience which does not incommode me unduly, but my daughter does not share my archaic tastes."

"And what happened after the battery failed?" I asked with interest. There was still plenty of time left during the rest of the evening for Ann to slip up to Oakhurst Place. I had reluctantly abandoned the theory that she could have accomplished this while the old man was asleep—twenty minutes was really running it a bit too close—and the risk that Mr. Qualtrough might have woken up at any moment and discovered her absence was altogether too hazardous.

"Oh, after that I played a short game of chess with Ann. I went to bed earlier than my normal hour because I was still feeling distinctly sleepy owing, I think, to the fact that the atmosphere was heavy with snow. It is strange how it affects some people in that way. I remember once—"

I led him gently, but deliberately, back to the subject of his bedtime. Unless the game of chess had been very short indeed, there simply couldn't have been time for Ann to have got up to Oakhurst Place and back before the return of Diana and John Wickham.

"I suppose you wouldn't remember the time you went to bed?" I asked, just like a real police interrogator.

"Indeed I would," Mr. Qualtrough said triumphantly. "Because I wound the clock in the study before I went upstairs. It was exactly half-past ten."

"Oh," I said, shattered. This was no good at all. Howard had put Sir Henry's dose of morphine as ten o'clock at the latest, and

Ann would have had to allow a few minutes for her parent to settle down before she would have dared to risk going out into the night and being missed by him in case he called her for anything. Of course, it was possible that Howard was wrong—he had said himself it was only a rough guess and he refused to swear to any definite opinion. I added as a hopeful afterthought: "I suppose your clocks are right?"

"Certainly," said Mr. Qualtrough with dignity. "I set them myself by the wireless signal every week, and they keep remarkably good time. The study clock said half-past ten, and this was confirmed by the clock in my bedroom. I do not rely on a wristwatch as I consider them on the whole untrustworthy timepieces. The carriage clock in the study, on the other hand—"

But I had lost interest in the carriage clock in the study. I didn't want to hear anything about its date or its inside or its history. The carriage clock had let me down and had proved conclusively that—unless they were in the plot together—neither Ann nor her father could possibly have been out of the house for more than a very few minutes between the operative hours of eight o'clock and half-past ten.

I was savouring the dead sea fruit of my failure to unearth some juicy clue from under the very noses of Hugh Gordon and Sergeant Spragg when Betty returned carrying a coffee tray, full of apologies at having kept us waiting so long.

"We ran out of coffee," she explained. "I had to send Sara up to the shop. I hope my guest has been entertaining you nicely, Mr. Qualtrough."

"Excellently, excellently," said the little man smiling. "Or rather, as it is I who have been doing most of the talking, I trust that I have been entertaining her. Now, Mrs. Craufurd, here is the prisoner at the bar. How say you—is he guilty or not guilty?"

Betty looked up startled, with the coffee pot in her hand.

"Guilty of what?" she exclaimed. "Whatever are you two talking about?"

"Murder," said Mr. Qualtrough with a grim little chuckle of amusement. "I have been arraigned and subjected to a gruelling cross examination as to my every movement on the night of the illness of our departed neighbour. Mrs. Craufurd is about to pronounce judgment. Pray silence in the court."

"It was just a game," I explained sheepishly. "Mr. Qualtrough has been telling me about his alibi. It was his idea," I added hastily, seeing the outraged expression on Betty's face.

"I have been rehearsing," Mr. Qualtrough said. "I have, as Ann would put it, been going over my lines. I trust they were convincing?"

"Very convincing," I mumbled. "Of course you must remember I'm only an amateur at this game, Mr. Qualtrough. I don't know how many other searching questions a real police interrogator would have thought up to ask you. But as far as this humble member of the jury is concerned, you leave the court without a stain on your character."

"I am greatly relieved to hear it," Mr. Qualtrough responded gravely. "Really, I was beginning to get quite nervous. Thank you, Betty my dear, this delicious beverage will revive me after my ordeal in the witness box."

Betty was still looking rather disapproving as she handed me the sugar basin, and when Mr. Qualtrough was looking the other way she tapped her forehead significantly and raised her eyebrows. I could see her point. Mr. Qualtrough was an exceedingly eccentric old party.

Betty and I both tried in various devious ways to change the subject, but Mr. Qualtrough refused to be diverted from his little game.

"Now that I have received my acquittal at the hands of the learned judge," he remarked, "I feel that I may speak more freely. And I don't mind confessing among friends that I, for one, am immensely gratified that the late Sir Henry Metcalfe is no longer with us."

He grinned impishly at Betty and took a sip of coffee.

"Of course I know he wasn't always a very considerate landlord," Betty began doubtfully, "but—"

"My dear lady, I do assure you that there is nothing personal in my gratification," Mr. Qualtrough interrupted severely. "Do not imagine that I am so petty-minded as to be swayed only by such fiddling considerations as my own domestic comfort. Indeed no. My aversion to Sir Henry is founded on very much wider ground. The man was a charlatan—a public menace—a disgrace to the name of English gentleman."

"I know he wasn't popular," Betty agreed soothingly. She glanced reproachfully at me, and I could see her dying to ask what on earth I had been saying to the little man to start all this.

"He was a fraudulent nincompoop," Mr. Qualtrough said with great energy, obviously enjoying himself. "He talked of art. Bah! What does a man like that know of the Muses? He pretended to be enthusiastic over an indifferent collection of largely spurious specimens of oriental porcelain. But what does a man like that appreciate of design or colour? Nothing! I tell you he was a Philistine—a pedantic popinjay—a—a—"

Just as I thought Mr. Qualtrough was going to blow up, there was the sound of the front door being flung open and footsteps in the hall.

"Hullo, Dad," cried Ann Qualtrough, running in with her arms full of parcels. "I thought I'd find you here. Morning, Betty—how d'you do, Mrs. Craufurd! Now," she said accusingly, turning back to her father, "what were you getting so steamed up about when I came in?"

"Nothing," said Mr. Qualtrough, pouting up his face like a sulky baby. "I was expressing my opinion of a man I disliked."

"I could hear your voice right down the lane," Ann said. "I said to myself: 'There's the aged parent at it again.' Look, you've got to come home. Harper wants to see you."

Harper, I afterwards discovered, was the manager of Lewis Qualtrough's shop in Tunbridge Wells.

"He can wait until I've finished my coffee," Mr. Qualtrough said crossly. "What are all those parcels?"

"Oh, food and things," Ann said vaguely. "Forgive my barging in like this, Betty, but Mr. Perkins said he'd seen Dad walking along in this direction and I had to find him. It's about that Toby jug," she added to her father.

"My Ralph Wood Toby jug?"

"The one in the window that you won't put a price on."

"It's not for sale."

"Well, I told Harper that; but he's got somebody who wants to buy it, only the customer says it isn't a genuine Ralph Wood and as far as I can gather Harper agrees with him. Anyway—"

"The day that Harper's judgment on a piece of china is taken in preference to mine is the day I retire," Mr. Qualtrough snapped. "Why can't the man stick to furniture—he knows little enough about that, but at least he can tell the difference between Sheraton and a late Victorian wash-stand. Not a genuine Ralph Wood indeed! There's only one man in the county who knows less than Harper about china. And he isn't in the county any longer," he added with satisfaction.

"Who—? *Oh*!" Ann said, enlightened. "Is *that* who you were talking about when I came in? That accounts for it!"

Mr. Qualtrough continued to stick out his lower lip like a spoilt child. "I shall say what I like about Sir Henry Metcalfe," he said defiantly. "I repeat—and I shall continue to affirm—that the man was a charlatan. Do you know, Mrs. Craufurd, that he actually had the impertinence to invite me—*me,* an authority—up to his unspeakable abode only last week in order to show me a small china slop-basin purporting to be an authentic specimen of Imperial *famille rose* ware, which he had picked up from some second-rate dealer in the Ladbroke Grove area. I ask you! Of course I told him at once that the thing was a Samson copy—it even had the 'S' mark on the bottom—but he remained unconvinced. Quite apart from the unlikeliness of such an object being for sale in an establishment of that kind, I pointed out—"

"Oh, Dad," Ann protested, "how beastly of you to prick his little bubble like that! He was so proud of his slop-basin. Everyone in the village was invited up to see it—even Mrs. Prendergast, who doesn't know *famille rose* from the Swiss Family Robinson. And actually, you know, it wasn't *nearly* one of his worst floaters. The 'S' was very inconspicuous—I hardly recognised it myself—and anyone but an expert would have missed it. The reason he didn't see it was because he didn't want to. But don't you remember the time he bought the famous blue-and-white Ming dish and had a large dinner party in honour of it, and you took a fiendish delight in telling him in front of everybody that it was a nineteenth century Japanese reproduction made at Mikawachi?"

They both laughed heartily at the recollection of Sir Henry Metcalfe's discomfiture.

"One may laugh," Mr. Qualtrough observed sententiously, wiping his eyes with a large spotted silk bandanna. "But the world of ceramic art is a better and a healthier place without the patronage of such ignorant, opinionated, bigoted and bombastic fools as the late Sir Henry Metcalfe."

"Well, of course it is, darling, everyone knows that," Ann said soothingly. "But *I* was advised not very long ago to keep quiet and not say rude things about the dear dead departed. It might," she mimicked mischievously rolling her eyes at Betty, "it *might* be misconstrued!"

Betty laughed.

"You're a hopeless pair," she said. "And it's just as well the police can't hear you. Luckily they can't go round arresting everybody who didn't like Sir Henry—there wouldn't be enough handcuffs in Kent—but all the same, I really did mean what I said to you the other day, Ann. Remember?"

Ann nodded brightly till her fair hair came tumbling into her eyes.

"I am a model of discretion now," she said. "It's a pity I can't control the aged parent a bit better. He'll land us both in Maidstone Gaol. D'you know, Dad, I'm beginning to see what you came down here for. Did he bring you any flowers?" she asked Betty suspiciously.

"Over there on the desk," Betty said. "In the small white vase. Lovely Christmas roses."

"I knew it!" Ann said. "It was bribery and corruption. He thought he'd be able to get all the latest low-down out of you because Mrs. Craufurd's got inside information. By the way, is there anything new? Michael said the inquest was very dull. I wanted to go but Dad said it was unmaidenly, didn't you, you wicked old man? He really meant if I went he was afraid he might have to cook his own lunch. The only thing that interested *me* about the inquest was that Mrs. Phillips was there."

"Mrs. Phillips?" Betty repeated in surprise. "Why ever would she be there?"

"I can't imagine, darling," Ann said. "That's what makes it so intriguing. What is even more curious is that Michael, who could have hardly failed to spot her, never mentioned it at all. It was Norah Wright who told me."

"How funny," Betty said. "As a matter of fact Howard didn't mention it either."

Ann shot her a swift sideways glance.

"There seems to be a sort of conspiracy of gallantry, doesn't there?" she suggested drily. "Protecting Mrs. Phillips' fragile reputation from the charge of vulgar curiosity."

"There seems no such sense of filial piety on your part," Mr. Qualtrough complained, "to protect *my* reputation in the same way."

"*You*!" Ann said. "You're revelling in every minute of this case—you know you are! The only thing you're afraid of is that they might catch the murderer and hang him, whereas in your opinion he ought to be knighted for his service to the nation."

Mr. Qualtrough forebore to reply to this accusation, but there was a gleam in his eye which did much to testify to its truth.

"Come on," Ann went on briskly. "You've finished your coffee now, and you can't keep poor Harper waiting for ever."

She picked up her various parcels and hustled her protesting parent to the door. We went into the hall to see them off, and long after they had turned the corner of the drive and been lost to sight as they walked back up the lane to the village, Mr. Qualtrough's high-pitched querulous voice floated clearly back on the cold winter air.

"I am not interested in *what* Harper thinks. The man's a booby. And in any case I have no intention of selling that Toby jug to *anyone*."

XIII

NOT AT HOME

AT LUNCHTIME BETTY REMARKED THAT SHE FELT SHE'D neglected Diana Metcalfe for long enough, and she was going up to Oakhurst Place that afternoon to see her.

"Yes, I should think that would be quite a good idea," Howard said. "She's feeling a bit low. Take Lee with you—you might be able to cheer her up a bit. And while you're, at it, Norah's made up some dope for her—some mild sleeping powders which I think she needs—so I'd be very grateful if you'd take them along with you. It would save me a journey."

As we made our way up the snowy drive towards Oakhurst, Betty demanded: "What *was* all that nonsense you and Mr. Qualtrough were talking this morning? You weren't really cross-examining him, were you?"

"No, of course not. It was a sort of game he insisted on playing. Apparently Ann had told him that I knew Hugh—so all I can suppose is that he was sort of trying it out on the dog before he had his proper interview with the police. He went into every second of their evening with the most meticulous details. Is he usually so punctilious about looking at clocks and noticing the exact moment he does everything?"

Betty scuffled a clod of snow off the heel of her gum-boot. "I've never known really *what* to make of Mr. Qualtrough," she said frankly. "He's a funny old thing. Actually, I'm awfully fond of him, but he's got a terrific strain of small boy in him—rather wicked small boy. You know—he likes teasing the grown-ups and getting them all worked up. And all the time it's he who's laughing at them. People who've known him a long time say that most of his eccentricity is put on, and that it dates from the time his wife died. He was comparatively normal before that. I don't know. I think he must always have been a bit naughty about pulling people's legs. It isn't a habit one develops overnight. He was probably having some kind of obscure little joke with you, Lee, over his alibi."

"You mean he was playing up to baby?"

"Well, not exactly—because *he's* the baby. But maybe he was teasing you just a little over what he imagines to be the methods of Scotland Yard. All the same, I think you'll find, if his story was bristling with exact times, that they *are* exact—and accurate. The game wouldn't be any fun if it could be disproved. He's probably deriving a lot of simple pleasure from the idea of you relating his story to Hugh Gordon, and then all the machinery of Scotland Yard being put on to check every precise little detail of his evening—which after all only boils down to a very ordinary evening in the home, which simply couldn't matter less, and has absolutely nothing to do with the murder."

"That seems to me," I said crossly, "a very great waste of everyone's time."

"Yes, but that's just the point. I told you he was like a wicked small boy. Oh look, Lee—there's a hawthorn covered with mistletoe! I must ask Diana if we can cut a bunch to put in the hall."

The park was looking very lovely in the snow. The avenue up to the house was bordered with magnificent elms, and away down to the left I caught a glimpse of a small lake with an island in the middle. To the right of the drive orchards had been planted, and beyond the bare fruit trees I could see the roofs of several rows of greenhouses. These I took to be part of the nursery gardens tended by Diana and John Wickham.

Oakhurst Place, when we came to it, was quite an impressive job in the Palladian Georgian manner. It didn't quite live up to the style promised by the eagles on the entrance gates, which I imagine dated back to something earlier than the present house. But the wide stone facade with its Corinthian pillars and flight of steps up to the front door was easy on the eye, and accorded well with the formal lawn in front and the cluster of dark cedars which rose behind the stable-wing, complete with Wren-shaped clock-tower and air of spacious leisure and the days gone by.

The heavy oak front door was closed but not locked. Betty gave it a gentle push, and we walked into the hall. There didn't seem to be anyone about.

Betty called: "Diana!" but there was no reply.

"We'll just have a look in the drawing-room," Betty said.

The drawing-room was a long, light, beautifully proportioned room, papered cheerfully with yellow and white stripes. Flowers, presumably from the greenhouses, were everywhere. It had a polished parquet floor and some lovely Persian rugs which struck envy into my heart. Along one wall was a glass-fronted Chippendale china cabinet, and I wandered across to admire some charming Dresden shepherdesses and a number of attractive old china snuff-boxes which were displayed on the shelves.

"Is this part of Sir Henry's famous collection?" I asked.

"Oh, no," Betty said, over her shoulder. "I think most of that lot belongs to Diana. Sir Henry's stuff was all oriental—you know, dragons and ginger jars and things. He kept it in the study and refused to let the maids touch it for dusting or anything. I wonder where Diana can be. It looks as if she must be out."

"Perhaps she's upstairs lying down or something," I suggested.

Betty crossed to the fireplace and rang the bell.

I wandered round the room examining the pictures, which were mostly Victorian water-colours in gilt frames—not in the least valuable or important works of art, but pretty and pleasant to have around.

After a few minutes a parlourmaid appeared at the door. She looked unaccountably nervous and seemed to be registering relief at the sight of Betty and myself.

"Oh, madam," she said to Betty, "I'm so glad it's you. I didn't know who it could be ringing from the drawing-room, and I said to Mrs. Harding, 'I'll have to go,' I said, 'though who it could possibly be there after all the business we've been through, what with the police all over the place and everything'—"

"It's all right, Alice," Betty said, smiling reassuringly. "We let ourselves in at the front door. Did you think we were burglars? I hoped to find Lady Metcalfe in here. Is she at home, d'you know?"

"Well, madam, she isn't. Her ladyship's been called away."

"Called away?" Betty echoed in surprise. "Oh. Have you any idea when she'll be back?"

"No, madam," the girl said, twisting her apron strings and looking embarrassed. She hesitated for a moment and then went on with a rush: "There's been ever such a lot of funny things going on here, madam, ever since the master died. First we had those police all over the house, taking photos and I don't what else. Then we had the gentlemen from Scotland Yard asking all sorts of questions, and poking round the master's study and all. And then today, madam, just after I'd taken in her ladyship's coffee after lunch two other gentlemen called—I think one of them was some sort of Inspector, and the other was Colonel Wilbraham—I recognised him from having been here to dinner when the master was alive—and I showed them in here to her ladyship. And they'd been here only a few minutes, madam, when her ladyship rang the bell and said to me, 'Alice,' she said, 'tell Mrs. Harding that I have to go away for a few days,' she said, 'and ask Gladys to pack me a small suitcase,' she said, 'with just the things I need for the night, and a change of underclothes.' So I did what she told me, and Mrs. Harding and the other girls were all very surprised, madam, but we thought it must be something to do with the arrangements for Sir Henry's funeral. So Gladys packed the case like she was told, and brought it down here to her ladyship, and then they all went off together in the Colonel's car. That would be about an hour ago, madam. And Mr. Michael wasn't at home either, so I'm sure I don't know if he could tell you where her ladyship's gone, because we don't know, madam, and that's a fact."

Alice paused and continued to gaze at Betty with wide enquiring eyes. Betty shot me a worried glance and turned back to the maid.

"Thank you very much, Alice," she said. "I see. Well, if Lady Metcalfe does come back today, perhaps you would tell her I called to see her, and ask her to ring me up."

"I will, madam, thank you," the girl said. She continued to hover anxiously by the door.

"It's a terrible thing about the master, isn't it, madam?" she ventured. "Such a thing to go and happen in the house—and then an inquest and all. Mrs. Harding says—"

"Yes, it's very terrible," Betty interrupted repressively. "If I were you, I'd try not to think about it too much. By the way, when Mr. Michael comes in you might ask him—"

As she spoke there were footsteps in the hall and the door of the drawing-room burst open. Michael Metcalfe, his face the colour of putty, almost fell into the room. He took no notice of Alice, standing goggle-eyed just inside the door, but went straight over to Betty and grabbed her in a distraught way by the arm.

"Thank God you're here," he said. "I've just been round to the Tithe Barn trying to find you. I was down at the Qualtroughs about an hour ago when Diana rang up and told me. She said to let you and Howard know at once."

"Know what?" Betty demanded tensely.

"But don't you *know*?" Michael said. "Isn't that why you're here? Don't you know that Diana was arrested at two o'clock this afternoon and they've taken her off to Maidstone Prison?"

To say that Betty and I stood there stunned with surprise is an understatement. We literally gaped.

"Oh, but they *can't* do that," Betty exclaimed weakly. "There must be some mistake!"

"I don't know about whether they *can*," Michael said grimly. "All I know is that they *have.* I've spent hours on the telephone to the family solicitors in London, and they're just as staggered about the whole thing as we are. And just about as useless, too," he added bitterly. "We'll have to find a new lawyer for her—that firm's hopeless. I might get hold of Dick Henderson, I think. At least he'd take some personal interest in the thing. Just after Diana rang up, while I was on the phone to London, Ann saw John Wickham crossing the green, so of course she immediately rushed out to tell him what had happened, and now he's gone roaring over in the bus to Tunbridge Wells to dig out Colonel Wilbraham and find out what the hell it's all about."

Betty and I exchanged agonised glances. It seemed to us that of all the unfortunate things John Wickham could have done, from everybody's point of view, this was quite the worst.

"But you've got to have *evidence*," Betty protested, harping back to the subject of Diana. "You can't just go round arresting people without any evidence."

"They were up here again yesterday morning," Michael said. "They turned up with a search warrant while Diana and I were over at the inquest. Maybe they found something then."

"But what *could* they find? You can't find evidence to incriminate somebody who never did anything wrong in her whole life."

"Well, I'm sure I don't know," Michael said unhappily. "And I'm damned if I can see what to do about it."

"I know what *I'm* going to do about it," I said, making up my mind. "I'm going straight down to the Blue Boar to find Hugh Gordon and ask him what the devil he thinks he's doing."

I was furious with Hugh. First, I admit, for holding out on me in this unfriendly way; and secondly for the sheer stupidity of imagining that a woman like Diana Metcalfe could ever have done such a thing in such a manner. You only had to *look* at her to realise she wasn't a murderess. Surely, I thought irritably, if I could see this, then Hugh, with his much greater experience of criminal types, might have had the sense to see it too. I recollected bitterly how pleased I'd been to recognise him that evening outside the Blue Boar, and the snug feeling I'd had that everything would be all right now. I'd relied on him to manage the case properly—and this was what he had done!

"I suppose there's nothing I can do?" Betty asked Michael in a doubtful way.

"Well, I don't quite see what," Michael admitted helplessly. "The first thing of course is to get her out on bail or something. Look, I'll run you both back to the village in my car—it's outside—and then I'll go over to Tunbridge Wells and have a word with Dick."

I should have thought Michael's legal background would have made him aware of the fact that people being held on a murder charge are never granted bail, but Dick Henderson would be able to point that out to him. Betty and I got into the M.G. and went skidding rapidly down the snow-covered drive.

I asked Michael to drop me on the green, while he drove Betty on to the Tithe Barn.

The more I thought about Hugh's duplicity and obtuseness, the crosser I felt. I stumped up the steps of the Blue Boar; kicking lumps of snow right and left from my boots as I went. I began rehearsing what I should say to Hugh when I saw him.

The landlord, seedy and smelling of stale gin, told me with a leer that "my gentleman friend from Scotland Yard" was out. He added that he had gone off in his car directly after breakfast and had not returned for his lunch.

I stumped down the steps again, feeling that it was just as well for "my gentleman friend" that he wasn't in. Perhaps by the time I ran him to earth my indignation would have cooled off a little. Half-way across the green it occurred to me that it was perhaps not altogether my business to be attempting to control the workings of Scotland Yard and that Hugh might not entirely welcome my outspoken criticism of the way he was running his case. By the time I got to the top of the Sandys' lane I was remembering that Hugh—no matter how incomprehensible his behaviour now seemed—was as a rule nobody's fool. I was still very cross with him indeed; but perhaps it would be only fair to hear his side of the affair before condemning him out of hand.

It was, therefore, with rather mixed feelings that I panted round the end of the Tithe Barn drive and beheld the shining black Lancia standing parked on the gravel outside the front door.

Hugh was in the drawing-room sitting comfortably in front of the fire with Howard and Betty, having, as far as I could make out, an entirely amicable discussion as to whether he should or should not come to dinner that evening.

"I can't continue to batten on your rations at the rate of two meals a day," Hugh protested half-heartedly, turning to Betty with the deprecating smile which in weaker moments during the past I had once mistaken for charm. "And the standard of my hostelry is such that I hesitate to return your hospitality by inviting you to—"

"What is all this about your having arrested Diana Metcalfe?" I demanded abruptly. "I do think you might have warned us. And, I must say, Betty, that seeing she is supposed to be one of your greatest friends, you seem to be taking the whole thing remarkably calmly."

Betty had the grace to blush slightly. So I should hope, I thought, sitting there practically feeding the hand that bites you.

"Lee, of course it's awful about Diana," she said swiftly, "but Mr. Gordon has just been explaining the position to us, and he says it's for Diana's own protection—"

"Her *protection?*" I said scornfully. "Protection from what?"

"Sit down, my dear crusader, and listen to me," Hugh said, pulling me across to the sofa and giving me a little push, which I resented very much. "Lady Metcalfe hasn't been arrested at all. She's simply been taken over to Maidstone for questioning. It may be more convenient to keep her in custody for a day or two until—"

"Well, anyhow," I interrupted, "Michael thinks she's been arrested, and so does John Wickham. They're in an awful stew. And just what is the difference between arrest and what you call protective custody? You're simply quibbling to keep me quiet."

"There's a very great difference," Hugh said. "In one case the prisoner is charged with some specific crime, while in the other—"

Betty interrupted him eagerly: "Lee, Mr. Gordon's been telling us some things we didn't know. He says there's been fresh evidence—"

"What evidence?" I said.

"Liane," Hugh said. "I hate to be so crude as to remind you that I am supposed to be in charge of this case, and that, in spite of what you obviously think, I haven't entirely taken leave of my senses. Hasn't it ever occurred to you that most circumstantial evidence is open to at least two interpretations? Suppose, for example, I find one day that my gold cigarette case is missing. And suppose it is subsequently discovered by Spragg or somebody, hidden at the back of a drawer in your bedroom, what would most people assume from that?"

"If it was Spragg, he'd probably be silly enough to think I'd pinched it," I said shortly. "And I don't see what—"

"Just a minute. Another explanation might be that you hadn't pinched it at all, but that somebody else—disliking you—had pinched it and planted it in your drawer to incriminate you. Yes?"

"I suppose so," I said grudgingly. "But I can't see what all this has got to do with your arresting Diana. Do you mean somebody's planted something on her?"

"It could be," Hugh said, suddenly serious. "Anyway, we have now reached the very definite conclusion that either—(a) Lady Metcalfe murdered her husband, which I'll allow sounds unlikely on the face of it, or (b) that she didn't do it herself, but she knows who did and is trying to shield that person, or (c) that somebody is deliberately trying to frame her by planting incriminating evidence against her. If any of these alternatives is true—and one of them must be—don't you agree that she's considerably safer in custody at Maidstone than wandering about loose and unprotected in Staple Green? In the first two cases she would be a menace to others, and in the last alternative somebody else is a menace to her."

"I could see that," I admitted unwillingly, "*if* you had any evidence. Planted or otherwise. But you haven't. All you've got is just a lot of vague nonsense about a telephone call, and the fact that she—"

Hugh turned to Howard.

"What I came here to ask you, before all this started," he said, rudely interrupting my sentence, "is a very simple question. Would you be able to identify for certain your own missing tube of morphine tartrate tablets if you saw it?"

"Well—" Howard began doubtfully. "They're all turned out exactly alike, you know. I mean, provided it was the same make and the label wasn't too new—because I'd had mine in stock for some time—I don't think I could possibly say for certain."

There was a little disappointed pause.

"Oh dear," Hugh said sadly. "What a pity."

"Wait a minute!" Howard exclaimed suddenly. "I believe I could. Hold on a second."

He went into the hall and returned carrying his black medical bag. He unlocked the top of it and carefully lowered the flap. He pulled out one of the little drawers at the top and held up a small metal container. Betty and I got up from our chairs and came over to look. Hugh's head was bent over the row of tiny phials inside the metal box. One of the tubes was missing. On the labels of all the others a faint yellow stain was visible.

"You see what I mean?" Howard said, "One day I spilt some picrid acid in the surgery while this case was open. Some of it went over those labels. I can't say for certain about the morph, tart.—that's the one that's missing—but as the acid went over all the other tubes, I should think that one probably got stained too. If you ever find the tube, I daresay—"

Hugh put his hand in his pocket and drew out a small phial wrapped in tissue paper, an exact replica of the ones in Howard's bag. It was labelled "Morphine Tartrate grains ¼" and was empty. Across the bottom of the label ran a distinct yellow smudge.

Howard stretched out his hand.

"You can examine it," Hugh said, handing it over. "It's been tested for fingerprints—and I may as well tell you there weren't any at all. Not even yours, you'll be surprised to hear. Which is in itself suggestive."

"Yes," Howard said positively. "That's it. Look, you can see where the pattern of the stain fits, in between these two tubes. Are we allowed to ask *where* you found this?"

"Of course," Hugh said. He wrapped the little tube carefully back in its tissue paper and restored it to his pocket. "It is my sole justification in the eyes of Liane for my deplorable action in the matter of detaining Lady Metcalfe. I ordered a search of Oakhurst Place to be carried out yesterday morning during the inquest. That tube was discovered by one of Spragg's boys hidden in Lady Metcalfe's bathroom, about half-way down a jar of bath salts. Now, Liane, do you see my point?"

XIV

TANGLED WEB

THE NEXT DAY WAS SUNDAY. AT ABOUT HALF-PAST TEN HUGH appeared with the Lancia and said that he was going out to call on Mrs. Phillips. He wondered if I would like to go with him. From this invitation I assumed that Sergeant Spragg was otherwise employed, and the idea of taking me instead was intended as an olive branch to soothe my wounded feelings. I was still smarting slightly from our argument the day before; because, right as Hugh undoubtedly was, I dislike being made to look an incompetent ass in front of my friends. An interfering and officious ass at that.

Betty came down the stairs and said she was taking Sara to church. Robin, with Nanny's assistance, was busy on his Christmas cards and Howard had gone out on some visits. I decided I might as well go with Hugh, although I took great care not to sound too keen.

Hugh, presumably still with some dim desire to make amends, astonished me by suggesting in an off-hand manner that I might like to drive the Lancia. I am quite sure he was confident that I would refuse, and tried not to show his alarm when I accepted the offer with alacrity. I stepped into the driving-seat, very much on my dignity, and switched on the engine. Almost before Hugh had the passenger-side door properly shut we were off like a rocket. We whizzed down the lane making a noise like twenty dirt-track riders and very nearly came to grief in a large snowdrift piled up under the hedge at the first turning we came to. I was shaken to the core, but Hugh merely turned a shade paler, gritted his teeth and said nothing. I admired his self-restraint. We adjusted ourselves and took the next hill at sixty. It was the first time I had ever driven a car in which the lightest pressure on the accelerator sent you practically flying into the next county, and it was great fun.

About a mile beyond the village we came to a sign post which said: "Lower Bunnet 1 mile" and I remembered that Howard had told me that Sonia Phillips' cottage was at the cross-roads of the hamlet. We turned down a steep narrow lane with high banked hedges which almost grazed the wheels of the car on both sides. I prayed that we should not meet anything coming in the opposite direction. I wasn't too sure where the reverse gear was, and I certainly wasn't going to demean myself by asking Hugh.

"By the way," Hugh said, speaking with a forced air of calmness which I know he was far from feeling. "You may be interested to hear that Spragg has been over the post office records of every call that went through the Staple Green exchange last Monday night, and has managed to trace the mysterious telephone call to Lady Metcalfe."

"Oh?" I said, swerving sharply to avoid a large dog which suddenly bounded out from the hedge into the middle of the lane from literally nowhere. "Well, I should imagine that must have put in a nasty spoke in your theory that Diana made the call herself. I worked it out that if she'd telephoned before she left Oakhurst she would have had to travel two miles in something under three minutes, including crossing the village. I don't see her doing that—even in a car like this. And as there was nowhere else for her to make the call, that seems to let her out. Now you tell me what Spragg so cleverly discovered."

"I agree with your deductions that the call didn't come from Oakhurst," Hugh said, clinging tightly to the door handle as we swept past a couple of pedestrians huddled nervously in the recess of a gateway into a field. "But you're wrong in saying there wasn't any other place Lady Metcalfe could have telephoned from. In fact, the call came from the only spot on her route where she could possibly have made it herself to correspond with the time factor."

"And where was that?"

"The public telephone box outside Mr. Perkins' shop on the village green. Just exactly where, according to her own story, she would have been at the moment when the call was made. About a three minute drive from the Parish Hall."

"Oh," I said again. There didn't seem to be anything else to say. I managed to add: "So what do you assume from that?" in a defiant tone.

"I assume either that Lady Metcalfe did, in fact, make that call herself—which makes things look pretty black for her. Or that we are up against a very clever murderer, who thinks of everything."

"But that's absurd—" I began and stopped. It seemed equally impossible either way. I resolutely refused to accept Hugh's first alternative; which left only the theory that somewhere in Staple Green lurked a malevolent person who hated Diana Metcalfe so much that he was prepared to frame her on the charge of a murder she hadn't committed. Who could possibly want to damage her like that? From what I had seen of her it was obvious that she was a sweet person and popular in the village. Everybody liked her and she had never done an ounce of harm to anyone in her life. It sounded absolutely crazy to me, and I said so.

"Well, then, what other suggestions have you to offer?" Hugh asked politely. "Can you produce any other likely candidate to put in her place?"

"Well," I said doubtfully, "I don't know about a likely candidate, but there was Mr. Qualtrough. He came round yesterday determined to fill me up with a very copper-bottomed alibi for himself and Ann, which I suppose he wanted me to pass on to you. That in itself's always a bit suspicious, isn't it? The only trouble was that I couldn't see any flaws in it at all. You may be able—Oh, Hugh, wait a minute! I think this must be the place. Howard said it was by a pond. Remind me to tell you later about the Qualtroughs."

The lane had widened out into a miniature green with a small semi-frozen duck pond in the middle, and a farmhouse with its outbuildings on the right. A few disconsolate ducks who were straggling about in the road fled at our approach, quacking noisily. On the left of the road stood a low whitewashed house which had evidently at one time been two very small cottages later knocked into one. It wasn't very big even now. I slowed down and tried to read the name on the gate.

"Holly Tree Cottage," Hugh said. "That's it."

Somewhat to my surprise the Lancia stopped quite meekly at the spot I had selected for parking, and we got out. From the corner of my eye I could see Hugh's anxious glance wandering rapidly over the wings of the car in search of probable scratches on the paint, but he made no comment.

We walked up the path of Holly Tree Cottage and rang the bell. The door was at once opened by Sonia Phillips herself. She was wearing a flowered cretonne overall, and was obviously surprised to see us, but the effect was by no means that of a harassed housewife taken on the hop in the middle of her morning chores. Her exquisite complexion was flawless, her dark hair coiled smoothly on her neck, and her hands could have been photographed there and then in glorious technicolour for a strip advertisement on

"How to Keep Soignée While Washing-Up." I must confess that, having been previously disposed to like Mrs. Phillips, I found this immaculate perfection at eleven o'clock on a Sunday morning a little hard to forgive.

If Sonia Phillips felt that there was anything unusual in the fact that Hugh Gordon should have been accompanied on an official visit by Mrs. Sandys' house guest, she did not show it.

The front door opened into a small dark passage, and without flurry she led us through into a tiny sitting-room which held nothing but the barest minimum of furniture and yet managed to convey an impression of great charm and taste. There was a rosewood cottage piano in the corner, a narrow upright writing desk, a couple of rather shabby wing chairs covered in faded rose brocade, a few small tables and some white-painted bookshelves, and that was all. It was in a way rather an impersonal room, because like its owner it gave nothing about itself away. It held no past and no future. It was friendly and pleasant and a little aloof.

In the brick fireplace a log fire had been laid but not yet lit. Mrs. Phillips bent down and applied a match to the paper. It began to burn competently. Then she carried the music stool from the piano over to the middle of the room, and sat on it, her bands folded in her lap, regarding Hugh calmly with clear dark eyes. She was a very still person. She seemed enveloped in quietness, and I never once saw her fidget or assume an ungainly position.

Even Hugh, going with less confidence than usual into his routine patter about being sorry to disturb her on a Sunday morning, but there were one or two small points in connection with the death of the late Sir Henry Metcalfe, etc., etc., on which he hoped she might perhaps be able to shed some light, seemed to sense the atmosphere of impermeability. His usual method of shock tactics wasn't going to prove of the slightest avail here.

While he was talking, I glanced round the room again. The white bookshelves held a number of books on the ballet, some modern poetry, several volumes of French plays, a beautifully bound copy of the *Religio Medici* and one or two books on gardening. There were no novels and no biographies. It struck me as being the most completely escapist collection of literature I had ever seen. My eyes wandered to the piano on which a decorative arrangement of catkin branches and stripped holly berries in a painted jug made a gay patch of colour against the white wall. There were one or two photographs scattered about the room, one of which I recognised with some surprise as a well-known ballerina. Apart from this, there was nothing even remotely personal, and certainly nothing which gave the slightest indication as to her past life or interests; and of the late Mr. Phillips there simply wasn't a clue.

Hugh reached the end of his preamble, cleared his throat hopefully and waited.

Mrs. Phillips said: "Of course I will tell you anything I can, but I am afraid it will not be a great deal. What is it, in particular, that you wish to ask me?"

"I understand," Hugh said carefully, "that you met Sir Henry Metcalfe for the first time about a week ago at the house of Dr. and Mrs. Sandys. You had never seen him before?"

The faintest shadow of expression passed fleetingly over Mrs. Phillips' clear brow. If I hadn't been watching her like a hawk, I should never have noticed any change in her face at all, and even as it was it was gone almost before it came.

She replied steadily: "No, I had never seen him before."

"But you had met Lady Metcalfe, hadn't you?"

"I had not met her to speak to—no. I had seen her in the village, and I knew who she was. But I had not before spoken to either of them."

"And when was the next time that you saw Sir Henry?"

Her big eyes widened in surprise.

"I did not see him again," she said positively. "Never. The next thing I hear, a week later, is that he has been taken ill and is at the hospital. Then I hear that he is dead. It is true that the police are interested in the manner of Sir Henry's death?"

"Certainly it's true," Hugh said evenly. "But I understand that you were present at the inquest, so surely you heard the medical evidence that was given?"

Mrs. Phillips' calm gaze did not waver. She said quietly: "I heard the evidence, yes. There was talk of poison. But they did not say how Sir Henry came by the poison. It might have been an accident."

I remembered that Howard had told us that the inquest had been adjourned *sine die* with an open verdict, but all the same I felt Mrs. Phillips was slightly overdoing the naivete. Nobody could have attended that inquest and still express surprise that the police should be interested.

"I merely ask myself," said Mrs. Phillips demurely, "how such a terrible thing should have occurred."

"The police are asking themselves the same question," Hugh replied. "We hoped perhaps you might be able to help us."

"I?" Sonia Phillips repeated in astonishment. "But how should I be able to help the police?"

'I think you might be able to," Hugh said slowly, watching her. "Mrs. Phillips, please don't think I'm being impertinent, but I am interested to know why you should have bothered to attend the inquest on this man—a man whom you had only met once before in your life. Do you mind telling me that?"

Mrs. Phillips stretched out her hand for a cigarette. She picked up a spill from the little table by the fire and bent down to light it.

She returned to the music stool and sat down quietly holding the cigarette in her fingers.

"Of course I do not mind telling you," she said smiling. "I confess that I am—how do you say it?—intrigued. I am curious. Here is this harmless old man who dies so suddenly. I have met him—and I have met his wife and son. I am interested, and I wonder for them why this strange thing should have happened. I am also interested in your English law. I have never before seen an inquest. I am curious to know how they conduct such things in England. So that is why I went. Your host and his secretary," she added, turning to me, "they were also interested, were they not?"

"Y—yes," I said. "But of course Howard was needed for the medical evidence." I couldn't think up any reasonable explanation for Norah, so I left it at that.

Hugh said thoughtfully: "You described Sir Henry Metcalfe as a harmless old man. Was that really your opinion of him?"

At this, her head went back a fraction, but she answered in the same level tone: "I did not know Sir Henry. Why should I have any other opinion of him?"

"No reason, I suppose," Hugh said. "But it seemed an odd choice of adjective. Most people disliked him rather actively, I gather. You know Michael Metcalfe quite well, don't you?"

She didn't like that one either, and this time there was a distinct moment of hesitation before she replied: "I have met him two or three times. He seems a nice boy, but weak."

"Did he ever speak to you about his relationship with his father?"

"I do not understand you," Mrs. Phillips said coldly.

"It is a matter of fairly common knowledge that Michael Metcalfe and Sir Henry did not get on well together. I merely wondered if he had ever mentioned any disagreement to you?"

Sonia Phillips raised her chin and looked Hugh coolly in the eyes. "I am not English," she reminded him, "so you must forgive me if I do not always conform to your English customs. In my country young men of good family do not discuss the private affairs of the home with strangers."

If Hugh had felt as rebuffed at this point as I did, the interview would have ended there and then. However, he merely bowed faintly, as one who concedes a point, and went on unruffled: "Very well. Now, I should be grateful if, for the sake of my routine check-up, you would kindly describe to me as fully as you can remember exactly what you were doing last Tuesday evening from, say, eight o'clock onwards."

"That is the evening on which Sir Henry was taken ill?"

"It is," Hugh said shortly.

Mrs. Phillips pleated a fold of her cretonne overall between long, beautifully manicured fingers.

"I am not sure that you have any right to ask me such a question," she remarked finally.

"Oh, I've no right at all," Hugh replied cheerfully. "This isn't a formal interrogation. If you have any objection to making an informal statement, you are, of course, perfectly at liberty to refuse. Only in that case, I should have no alternative but to subpoena you as a material witness and to ask you the same question through the medium of prosecuting council, when I think the learned Judge would be empowered to insist on a reply. The jury would then be free to put whatever interpretation they liked on your previous refusal to answer a simple question."

Mrs. Phillips suddenly laughed. She said: "In the crime books about America, I have read that the police lock people into cells and shine bright torches on them and hit them over the head with little rubber coshes when they will not answer questions. It has always seemed to me a very barbaric procedure."

"If such a thing were true, it certainly would be," Hugh agreed stiffly. "You will forgive me if I fail to see the point of your analogy."

The smile on her face deepened. "It is just that here you do not seem to need the little rubber coshes," she said. "You use the threat of the law instead."

A slight hardening round the corners of Hugh's mouth was the only outward sign that his patience was wearing thin. He said nothing.

Mrs. Phillips continued to sit very still. One of the holly berries dropped off the branch on the piano and fell with a small plop on to the floor.

"Of course I will tell you," she said gaily. "I have no reason to refuse—I just wondered what you would say if I did. I am so interested in the working of the English law. On that Tuesday evening I was here—alone by myself from about six o'clock, when I came in from a little walk, until the time I went to bed. I think that would have been about eleven o'lock. So you see I cannot help you."

"You have no maid living in the house with you?"

"No, Mr. Gordon. I have a woman from the village who comes for two hours in the mornings three times a week. The rest of the time I am by myself."

Hugh said tentatively: "That must be rather lonely for you."

She regarded him with a quizzical expression in her dark eyes. "Loneliness is no hardship to me," she said quietly. "I have plenty of things to occupy me. I like to be alone. That is why I came to this house."

"Oh yes," Hugh said. "That reminds me. I understand you have decided to give up the lease of this charming cottage and move elsewhere?"

For the first time Sonia Phillips was really taken aback.

"I cannot imagine who can have told you that," she said frigidly. "It is not true."

"Doesn't it just show how house-agents get things muddled?" Hugh said. "It happens that a friend of mine was wanting a house in this part of the world, and I looked in on the agents in Tunbridge Wells yesterday, and they told me this cottage was on the market."

Something Howard had said came back to me.

"Yes," I said uncertainly, "I remember about a week ago Howard said—"

Sonia Phillips' face cleared.

"But, of course," she said, "I remember now. One day I did say to Dr. Sandys that I thought I would go away. It was the English weather—so cold and depressing. I have not been well since I came here. I thought the climate was not suiting me. I may even have mentioned it to the house-agents. But then the sun shone again, and I changed my mind. This is a nice little house, do you not think so?"

We agreed that we did think so. I avoided Hugh's eye. He would, of course, give me credit for seeing through the mythical friend who had suddenly developed an urge to live in Lower Bunnet—but what in heaven's name could have put him on to the house-agent? Howard had mentioned Mrs. Phillips' impending departure long before Hugh arrived on the scene—and I had never given it a thought since. Could Hugh have been doing a good deal more extensive beavering into Mrs. Phillips' plans than he had divulged to me? Looking at his smooth impassive face, I knew he could. But what far-fetched hunch could possibly have led him to assume that she was likely to be wanting to leave the district? I became suddenly convinced that he was holding out on me again, and was accordingly chagrined.

Hugh was saying: "There's just one more point, Mrs. Phillips. You have kindly told me where you were on Tuesday evening last.

Can you possibly cast your mind back a bit further and tell me also about Monday? That is, the evening before?"

Sonia Phillips' delicate eyebrows rose.

"*Monday* evening?" she asked in a puzzled voice. "What can you wish to know of Monday? I think—yes, surely that was the day I went to London. I took a train in the morning—you understand, I do not like driving my little car in the crowded streets. So I left her at Tunbridge Wells station, and came back to her in the evening."

"What time did you get back?"

"I do not know why you ask me all these questions. On the Monday there is nothing. I suppose I returned at about half-past nine. There was a train from Charing Cross—"

"Oh, well, that makes it perfectly easy," Hugh said reassuringly. "It's simply a formality, you see—but the station people will probably remember about the car, and we can check up from them."

"Check up?" Mrs. Phillips repeated. Her level gaze went past me and was directed towards the bare tops of the elm trees on the other side of the lane. "No," she said, after a slight pause. "I am wrong. It was Saturday that I went to London. How stupid of me."

Again I managed with a super-human effort not to look at Hugh.

"Then what happened on Monday?" he prompted.

"On Monday—I really cannot remember. I expect I was here. Perhaps I went out to post a letter—a little walk down the lane—I do not know. Is it important that you should know where I was on the day before Sir Henry Metcalfe took his poison?"

"I'm not saying it has anything to do with Sir Henry," said Hugh mendaciously. "But I am anxious to trace a telephone call which was made on Monday evening at about eight o'clock from the call-box at Staple Green. I suppose you didn't go as far as that to post your letter?"

"No," said Sonia Phillips definitely. "There is a little box in the wall, here by the farmhouse. That is where I posted my letter."

"I see," Hugh said. "By the way, do you know anyone called Mrs. Henderson?"

She threw her cigarette into the fireplace and missed it. She walked over to pick it up and returned to the music stool.

"I am sorry," she apologised, "what was that you said?"

Hugh repeated his question. He added: "She is a daughter of Sir Henry Metcalfe, who is married and lives in Tunbridge Wells."

Mrs. Phillips shook her head regretfully.

"No," she said. "I have told you, I do not know the Metcalfe family—only casually. I did not even know that he had a married daughter."

I said tentatively: "Michael never mentioned her to you?"

The telephone bell rang.

Sonia Phillips glanced quickly at Hugh. Her hunted gaze went on to me. The telephone bell continued to ring. She walked across the room and picked up the receiver, standing with her back towards us.

"Yes?" she said. "Oh, but—"

I suppose we should have burst into animated conversation about the weather or something. We should have helped her out of an obviously awkward spot. But we didn't. We sat glued to our chairs listening avidly to every word she spoke.

"I am busy now," she said as coolly as she could. "No—I do not think it would be a good thing if you came over now. I am engaged. Yes—yes—yes. *Bien compris?*"

There was a short pause while the telephone quacked.

"Yes," said Mrs. Phillips. *"A bientot."*

She replaced the receiver with deliberation and picked up another cigarette as she passed the table.

"I am afraid," she remarked pleasantly, "that I am expecting a visitor soon. Is there anything else you wish me to tell you?"

"Not at present, thank you," said Hugh, accepting this extremely plain hint and rising to his feet. "I don't think there's anything else for the moment. You have been most helpful, Mrs. Phillips."

I gathered up my belongings, wondering whether the irony of this simple remark had escaped her, and concluding that it certainly hadn't.

Hugh and I beat a hasty retreat into the hall. Mrs. Phillips accompanied us as far as the door and waved to us as we departed, a charming figure in her gaily-patterned overall, standing gracefully on the threshold, one hand resting on the old iron latch.

"Enigmatic type," Hugh remarked as we reached the road. "How much would you be inclined to believe of what she says?"

"Practically nothing," I replied. "But she's got charm all right. Did *you* believe her?"

"Frankly," Hugh admitted, "I didn't. But then I'm in a stronger position than you are, Liane, inasmuch as I have definite proof that she was lying in her teeth throughout our entire interview."

I looked at him suspiciously.

"You *were* holding out on me," I said. "I knew it."

"Liane—darling—you must forgive me. I had to. You've got such a terribly expressive face, and it was important to me to know the impression Mrs. Phillips' story made on you before I showed you something."

"What do you mean?" I demanded unmollified.

Hugh glanced back at the cottage. We were hidden from view by the thick yew hedge. He delved into his pocket and produced a rather crumpled piece of paper.

"Spragg's search up at Oakhurst was productive from several aspects," he said. "As well as the morphine tablets in Lady Metcalfe's bath-salts, he and his merry men also found this—in a pigeon-hole in Sir Henry's desk in the study."

I snatched the piece of paper out of his hand. It was a sheet of Sonia Phillips' writing paper and was dated Monday, December 12th. The day before Sir Henry received his cup of cold poison.

"Dear Sir Henry," I read. "I shall be grateful if I may see you on a personal matter which is urgent and important to me. It will not take many minutes of your time. I understand that you will be alone in your house tomorrow evening. May I please come to see you at half-past nine? I ask you to be so kind as to destroy this letter."

It was signed: "Sonia Phillips," and there was, a P.S.: "Unless I hear from you to the contrary I will come."

XV

THE VICAR'S LADY

I WALKED ACROSS TO THE LANCIA IN SILENCE AND GOT INTO the left-hand seat.

"You can drive," I said to Hugh, who was standing hesitantly waiting to see what I was proposing to do about it. "Why didn't you show me that letter before?"

Hugh let in the clutch with something more nearly approximating a jerk than anything I had ever seen him do to the engine of a car. "I've told you," he said. "Because your face would have given the whole show away."

"I'm surprised," I said nastily, "that you waste your time in the police force. You ought to be a professional poker-player. I must say I'll be sorry for your wife—if you ever have one. The poor girl will never know if she's coming or going. Do I gather that the case is now over, bar the shouting, and that Sonia Phillips did it all the time? Because if so, why have you arrested Diana Metcalfe?"

"The case is a very long way from being over I'm afraid," Hugh said, avoiding a stray duck by inches. "I want a lot more proof on a number of things. That letter of Mrs. Phillips' isn't nearly so conclusive as you appear to assume. The only thing it actually proves is that there was some sort of connection between her and Sir Henry Metcalfe. And we had already suspected that. There's absolutely no evidence to show that she ever kept that appointment."

"But you didn't even ask her about it!"

"No. I didn't want to put her even more on her guard than she was anyway. But I can assure you that Spragg and I have not been entirely idle, and—"

"I can't understand you," I said. "There you go arresting Diana Metcalfe on the strength of a miserable little bit of circumstantial evidence, which you admit yourself was probably planted on her, and yet you get something as concrete and damning as that letter—making an appointment for the very evening that Sir Henry was alone and was given a lethal dose of morphia by somebody who went to see him—and you do absolutely nothing about it."

"You misjudge me, you know. Actually, I'm doing quite a lot about it. But I'm not going to be precipitated into messing up the whole case. I want to find out a great deal more about Mrs. Phillips before I confront her with that letter. If I showed it to her now, she'd simply invent some story which we should be in no position to disprove—and then where should we be? Do be sensible, Liane, and stop letting your partisan spirit about Diana Metcalfe swamp your judgment. I explained to you that we haven't arrested her—she's not been charged with any crime. But she's got considerably more sense than you have, because she knows quite well that for the moment she's much better off where she is. At least she's safe."

I was by no means convinced, but instinct warned me that if I went on arguing much longer Hugh would start regretting that he had ever shown me the letter at all, and certainly wouldn't let me in on the next bit of evidence which came along, no matter what it was.

"Well," I couldn't refrain from saying, "you may be right. But at least that letter indicated that she knew Sir Henry was going to be alone in the house that evening. And how could Mrs. Phillips have known that—*unless* she was the person who made the telephone call to get Diana out of the way and leave the coast clear?"

"I understand," Hugh said, "that in a village nobody has any private life at all. The grapevine works overtime. I don't think it follows that she couldn't have known about the Metcalfes' plans unless she made that call herself. However, that's just one of the many things we've still got to investigate. Her past life, too. Did you get the impression that she might have been on the stage at one time?"

"Yes," I said. "At a guess I should say she was a ballet dancer. There's something about the way she walks. And didn't you notice those photographs she had in her sitting-room?"

"Yes, actually I did. I should think you're probably right. But I've got to find somebody who knows something about her past history, and—"

I explained about the remark Sara had made to me the evening the Metcalfes came in for drinks.

"Howard didn't say anything about her being a patient," I added, "until Betty asked him point blank where he'd been one afternoon. It seemed a bit odd that he never mentioned her before the party."

"Well, I don't know," Hugh said doubtfully. "Professional etiquette and all that, you know. Still, I'll ask him about it. And in any case, Liane, don't worry that we're going to lose sight of a promising suspect, because we aren't. There's a hell of a lot we've still got to clear up—"

"The *car*!" I exclaimed sharply. "It might have been hers."

"What car?"

"Oh, Hugh, don't be obtuse! The car John Wickham saw going up the Oakhurst drive that night. Mrs. Phillips has got a little Ford, and—"

"You don't really believe in that car, Liane, do you?"

I felt myself turning rather pink.

"Well," I said, getting huffy again, "I should at least have made some effort to see if it existed. Have you done *anything* about trying to check the car at all?"

"Spragg is still working on it. It was a dark, cold night and there were very few pedestrians about in the village. Nobody we've found so far remembers seeing it, but—"

"What about the wheel-marks?"

"My dear sweet child, it was *snowing*! And by the time we were called in on the case it was Thursday and it had snowed a whole lot more. So, dear Liane, there were no wheel marks—and I should like to have seen Spragg's face if I'd suggested he should start digging up the drive to—"

"All right," I said, "you needn't go on."

It seemed pretty obvious that the car was a dead end. I stared out of the window across the bleak acres of hop-gardens and decided regretfully that I would never make much of an amateur detective.

"I resent being accused of inactivity," Hugh was saying. "I assure you that I am leaving no stone unexplored or avenue unturned in the sacred interests of my calling. *Fiat justitia ruat coelum,* I don't know what I'd do, Liane, if *you* ever became a serious suspect. Resign, I suppose. However, we are still mercifully on the same side of the fence, even though you consider I'm not doing my job properly. And now, what was all that you were beginning to tell me, just as we arrived at Holly Tree Cottage, about Mr. Qualtrough and his alibi?"

In the excitement over Sonia Phillips' letter I had more or less forgotten about the Qualtroughs. As briefly as I could I explained to Hugh about the ridiculous game Mr. Qualtrough and I had played, and his peculiar insistence on impressing me with the exact times of every one of his entirely innocuous movements.

"Rather as much as to say," I added, "'Make what you can of that!'"

Hugh didn't make a lot of it. He simply said: "I don't think there's anything very remarkable in that. These precise elderly characters *are* apt to be pernickety about details, and you say he's an accurate, scholarly sort of old bird. Did you gather why he was so anxious to try his story out on you, rather than on Betty or Howard or any other of his friends?"

"Well, he did let it out that Ann had told him I knew you."

"You mean he thought he could rely pretty confidently on anything he said to you being passed on to me?"

I wasn't flattered at this role of District Messenger Girl.

"Yes, if you like to look at it like that," I admitted a trifle sulkily. "But I shouldn't get too worked up about it, because Betty says that's just the sort of childish amusement which would appeal to him—to send you and Spragg off on some tremendous wild-goose chase, wasting endless time checking up a completely true and harmless story, which will get you nowhere."

"We'll have to do that in any case," Hugh sighed. "Though I daresay Betty's right. You'd be surprised at the amount of trouble caused by the law-abiding. The zealous citizen is almost more of a nuisance to the police than the downright malefactor. He resents having his word taken for anything, and unless you rush about checking and double-checking everything he tells you, he thinks he isn't getting his money's worth as a tax-payer."

"Well, anyhow," I said placatingly, because there seemed no point in our both getting peevish on the same morning, "if Mr. Qualtrough's story is true—and I really don't see why he should have made it up—it does give you quite a number of definite times to work on."

"Only as far as the Qualtroughs are concerned," Hugh grumbled. "I agree that if they're covered until ten-thirty, they're in the clear. Howard Sandys wouldn't commit himself officially to any time, as you know, but he thought Sir Henry must have had that dose of morphia by ten o'clock at the latest; and I'm prepared to accept that as a basis to work on. It's a bit disappointing because I've seen the Qualtroughs' cottage with all those suggestive french windows leading out of the back, and it looks an absolutely ideal set-up for the left hand not to know what the right hand's doing. Only unfortunately, in this case, both hands seem to have been tied."

"You don't think," I suggested tentatively, "it would have been possible for Ann to nip out earlier—while Mr. Qualtrough was asleep? It wouldn't have taken long to get up to Oakhurst, it's only just across the green—"

"And what would have happened if Mr. Qualtrough had woken up from his little snooze and called out to her—or gone into the kitchen to see what she was up to?"

"Yes," I had to agree. "I'd thought of that. It would have been a terrific risk. And the same snag applies to Mr. Qualtrough having sneaked out while Ann was washing-up. She might have come into the study for something and missed him."

We came to the turning which led up to Staple Green. There was a patch of blue sky behind the oast-house on the horizon, though the dark skeletons of the elm trees still looked cold and forbidding.

"Suppose," I suggested brilliantly, "they were in it together?"

Hugh shook his head. "I daresay it's technically possible," he admitted rather grudgingly, "but I don't somehow see this thing as a syndicate effort. Nor do I fancy the combination of Mr. Qualtrough and Ann as a murder-team. From all I've heard he is inclined to be cautious and pedantic—she is the direct opposite, and she treats him as a cross between an amiable lunatic and a small child. I don't think they'd be able to get together very harmoniously on their *modus operandi* and they'd certainly come unstuck in their interrogations afterwards. But I promise you I'll bear it in mind when I go and see them."

I hadn't much faith in the theory myself—it was just a random idea. I was still convinced that the only really sinister proposition we had come across yet was Sonia Phillips, especially in view of the note to Sir Henry. Whatever Hugh might say about its not being conclusive, it was remarkably suggestive, and I didn't want this promising clue to share the same fate of oblivion as John Wickham's motor car.

"You are going to follow up Sonia's letter, aren't you?" I said, as we turned into the Tithe Barn drive. Glancing up, I could see Robin leaning perilously over the sill of the nursery window, waving. He was fascinated by Hugh's Lancia.

"Eventually, of course," Hugh said with a slightly exasperated can't-you-stop-nagging expression on his face. "But for the moment I want to keep it up my sleeve—and I'd rather you didn't mention it, either, Liane—not even to Betty or Howard."

"O.K.," I said offended. "Wild horses will not drag it from my lips."

Hugh dropped me at the front door and drove off rapidly towards the village. I watched him as far as the lane, and then wandered into the house. Betty and Sara had not yet returned from church, but as I came in I noticed that Howard's car was back in the garage.

I found him upstairs with Robin, who began calling out eagerly that he wanted to show me his Christmas cards. He had been chalking busily all the morning, and there were plentiful signs of his activity all over the floor, the table and Robin himself.

"I like this one," I said, picking up a spirited impression in the Picasso school which represented an immense brown robin with a flaming scarlet shirt-front sitting on what I took to be a haystack.

"Oh," exclaimed Robin in acute embarrassment. "I didn't mean you to see that one. That one was for *you*. Will you forget you've seen it? Promise?"

I promised to forget about the robin, and was then shown the Christmas-pudding card which had been designed for Sara; the black cat for Mrs. Padgett—"because of Sooty"—(Sooty was the kitchen cat); and a remarkably faithful reproduction of one of the council houses on the Brenchley Road for Howard. The *pièce de resistance* was a militant-looking angel, bearing a sprig of holly. This was for Betty.

"I think they're lovely," I told him, "and very appropriate."

"Very what?"

"Very suitable. Pudding for Sara, and a house for Daddy and Mrs. Padgett's Sooty. And I'm sure Mummy will love her angel."

"The angel was what Nanny made me draw," Robin admitted. "I was going to do Mummy an engine."

"Why an engine?"

"Because—because—well, sort of to *remind* her." Robin grew very pink. He began to gabble: "She-said-if-I-was-good-boy-and—and—well, Dickie Henderson's got an engine and he's only *four*—and so I thought perhaps—but Nanny said an angel would be nicer—and she didn't think Mummy *would* forget about the engine. Auntie Lee, you don't think she'll forget, do you?"

Howard put his head in at the nursery door.

"Come down and have a glass of sherry," he said to me. "And tell me the latest developments. That's some car your boy-friend's got. Don't tell me that he bought *that* out of his salary!"

"I've no idea what he bought it out of," I said rather stiffly. "And he is *not* my boy-friend."

In the drawing-room Howard poured out some sherry and began searching for the current copy of *The Radio Times*.

"It is quite remarkable," he said, "the way one can never find *anything* in this house. All last week I was looking for this damn thing, and now that it's out of date, here it is sitting on Betty's desk. And now the new one's disappeared!"

I picked up the old copy and turned idly to the programmes for the previous Tuesday. Yes, there was Mr. Qualtrough's chamber concert on the Third, followed by a reading from *The Revenger's Tragedy*. On the Home Service there was the news as usual at nine o'clock, then a variety programme, and the evening finished with "Excerpts from the Operas" played by the Studio Orchestra. The B.B.C. seemed to be about the only wholly reliable witness we had so far.

Suddenly Howard, who was standing by the window with a glass of sherry in his hand, exclaimed: "Oh, my God, look what's coming!"

I went over to the window and looked out. I saw Betty walking up the drive with Sara and a wispy little woman of middle age, wearing a musquash coat and a most unfortunate hat trimmed with purple velvet pansies.

"Who's that?" I asked.

"Mrs. Prendergast, the Vicar's wife. I *hope* I'm wrong, but it looks hideously as though Betty is bringing her back to lunch."

"What about the Vicar? She can't leave him to eat his Sunday joint in solitary state."

"You can't bank on that," Howard said sadly. "I bet you anything you like the Vicar's been called off to minister to some outlying member of his flock, and Betty's fatal sense of hospitality has triumphed again. Look, Lee—you hold the fort in here, like a good girl. I've remembered something I've simply *got* to see to in the study."

Pausing only to refill his glass of sherry from the decanter on the table, Howard bolted from the room.

It transpired that his diagnosis was correct. The Vicar had been called out, and Mrs. Prendergast was staying to lunch. She was a nervous, twittery little person with a habit of embarking on long, complicated anecdotes of which she lost the thread half way through and never by any chance arrived at the denouement. She spoke in a series of breathless little gasps, and every second word she uttered was in italics.

Lunch passed off uneventfully with local gossip about the Women's Institute and the Wolf Cub Concert, which was to be held shortly in the Parish Hall in aid of funds for something which I never quite grasped. Sara and Robin, who lunched downstairs on Sundays, were on their best behaviour, and no reference was made to the Metcalfe affair.

Afterwards, however, when Sara and Robin had gone upstairs for their rest and Howard, with some muttered excuse, had escaped to his study to read the Sunday papers, and Betty and I were left sipping our coffee in the drawing-room alone with our guest, Mrs. Prendergast let out a deep sigh.

"Poor Diana!" exclaimed Mrs. Prendergast. "Poor, *poor* Diana!"

Betty and I exchanged glances.

"Unthinkable!" said Mrs. Prendergast. "The very *idea*—!"

There was a short pause while we all meditated on the unthinkable.

"Of course one didn't like to say anything about it in front of the dear *children*," our visitor continued. "Such *impressionable* little minds! There is, alas, plenty of time for them to learn about the *darker* side of life later on when they grow up. But it is a *tragedy* for the village, don't you agree, dear? I suppose the police must have some *grounds* for taking such a *decisive* step?"

At this point she swung round to gaze avidly at me, her nose literally quivering. I wondered just how many other people in the village were to be told that I was a friend of the Man From Scotland Yard—and to regard me, accordingly, as a mine of inside information. Little did they realise what a barren seam they were attempting to work.

"I'm afraid I don't really know anything about what the police think," I said regretfully. "Unfortunately they don't go round confiding in lay people much, you know."

"One of them actually came to see *me*," Mrs. Prendergast said with pride. "A man called Sergeant Spragg—such an *odd* name. I wonder what part of the country he comes from? There were some people in the village in Dorset, where my husband had a living before we came here, called Spragg. Farmers, they were. Possibly they may have been in some way *related?*"

"You should have asked him," Betty told her, to save me.

"Oh, my dear, I was *much* too nervous to ask him anything! It was *he* who was doing all the questioning. It was about that *extraordinary* telephone call from poor Sheila Henderson, which I now understand to have been a *hoax* and *not* from Sheila at all. I explained to Sergeant Spragg that we haven't been in Staple Green very *long*—it is just three years next Whitsun that my husband became the incumbent—and, of course, Sheila Metcalfe had married and gone to live over in Tunbridge Wells some *years* before we came to the village. Well, I've *met* her, of course, with Diana up at Oakhurst once or twice, though *not* latterly. I think the last time I saw her must have been at the Conservative Fête at Brenchley last summer—or was it the Flower Show at Cranbrook? Well, anyway, I *told* the Sergeant that I had never known Sheila *well*, and that I could *not* guarantee to recognise her voice for certain—let alone swearing in a witness-box that the woman who spoke to me on the telephone that evening *was* Sheila Henderson. But then, as I explained to him, *at the time* I had no reason to doubt it. She *said* it was Sheila Henderson, and I never *thought* of questioning it. I mean, I didn't say: 'Are you *sure?*' because that would have sounded so peculiar—almost *rude*—and, of course, I *was* sure in my own mind! And it was not more than *three* minutes later that dear Diana came in, and *naturally* I gave her the message at once. Diana asked particularly whether Sheila had wanted her to ring back to *confirm* the arrangement about her going over to Tunbridge Wells the following evening, but I simply repeated what Sheila had said—that her own telephone was out of order and she was speaking from the house of a *friend*. There was never the *slightest* reason for *anyone* to imagine that the call was other than genuine. And then, when *all this happened*—!"

"I suppose you could at least be certain that the person who rang up was a woman?" Betty asked casually. "I mean, it couldn't have been a man disguising his voice to make it sound like a woman?"

"Well, I don't *think* so, dear," said Mrs. Prendergast helplessly. "I must confess that at the *time* I was convinced it was a woman—well, she'd *said* she was Sheila Henderson, so I'd just assumed she *was*!"

"I wouldn't worry about it too much if I were you," Betty said. "I expect the police will be able to find out all about it. And in any case, it may have had nothing to do with—with this other business at all. Let me give you another cup of coffee."

"Thank you very much, dear. *Well,* as I said to Arnold only this morning at breakfast, it may not be a very *Christian* sentiment, but it is a *distinct relief* that if this very terrible thing had to happen to *somebody* in the parish, it should have been Sir Henry Metcalfe who was taken, rather than a man who would have been more universally *mourned.*"

Betty's mouth twitched slightly as she poured out the coffee.

"And did the Vicar agree with you?" she asked wickedly.

"He hardly went so far as to *agree,* dear, but I think he saw my point. The workings of Providence are often so *very* obscure, are they not? One scarcely likes to suggest looking on the *bright* side of anything so—so distressing as *sudden death,* but I couldn't help thinking that there must be a great many people who are probably—er—*better off* without poor Sir Henry Metcalfe. Oh," she exclaimed hastily as I looked up and caught Betty's eye, "I didn't mean *financially* better off! Indeed, *indeed* I meant nothing of that kind! I just meant that Sir Henry has not always shown himself as *sympathetic* as he might be in his dealings with the people around him. Take his disagreement with Michael, for example. I *quite* agree that the stage is not a profession I myself would have *chosen* for my son, but Michael was so *very* enthusiastic. I understand he showed *distinct* promise—and after all, some of the very *best* families now permit their children to take up theatrical careers. Look at Mr. Churchill's daughter—and—and a dear friend of mine was *at school* with Lilian Braithwaite! I mean, it isn't at all the *same* nowadays. But there was Sir Henry *insisting* on Michael giving up the whole idea and studying law instead. I always thought it was very *hard* on the boy. And *now,* you see, he will be free to choose for himself, and he will be able to marry that nice child Ann Qualtrough without *any opposition.* I think Ann is going to be a *very* clever little actress! Don't you remember, dear, those charades she and Michael got up last winter in aid of the Organ Fund? A little *daring* in parts, perhaps, for a village audience—but nowadays people are so much more *broadminded* than they were when I was a girl. There *are* people, I know, who disapprove very much of men dressing up as women—though I have *never* heard of anyone taking exception to *Charley's Aunt!*—but there was nothing *offensive* in what Michael and Ann did. And the song Michael sang dressed up as one of those old Piccadilly flower-sellers was really *most* amusing!"

Mrs. Prendergast's eye fell suddenly on the clock.

"Good gracious!" she exclaimed. "Can that *really* be the time? I must *run,* or I shall be late for my Sunday School class! It has been so delightful, Betty dear—and I have so *much* enjoyed meeting Mrs. Craufurd. You must both come round to the Vicarage for tea one day soon. *Goodbye,* dear—no, *don't* bother to see me out—*so* delightful—*goodbye*!"

XVI

STALEMATE

I DIDN'T SEE HUGH AGAIN UNTIL LATE ON MONDAY AFTERNOON. Sir Henry Metcalfe's funeral was due to take place in Tunbridge Wells in the morning. Howard refused flatly to attend, on the grounds that he was far too busy and had mislaid his top hat. Betty, having a dim feeling that she ought perhaps to go for Diana's sake, was fairly easily persuaded to compromise with a large wreath instead.

"Diana won't be there anyhow," Howard pointed out, "and it would only embarrass Michael to have the whole village rolling up in squads. He knows nobody loved his late Papa, and the only reason for anyone from here to go would be plain vulgar curiosity. Anyway, he's got Dick and Sheila Henderson to support him, and I know they're anxious to keep the whole thing as quiet as possible. They haven't announced the funeral in the papers."

About half-way through the morning Ann Qualtrough wandered in. She was wearing her blue slacks and the familiar duffle coat and her fair hair stood wildly on end.

"*Whew!*" she exclaimed, flinging herself down on the sofa in an exaggerated attitude of exhaustion. "You've no idea what's been happening to us! *Straight* from the inquisition, darling! I'd always thought that young man from Scotland Yard looked rather a poppet, and I was all set to enchant him in my simple girlish way—but, d'you know, Betty, it didn't work out a bit like that? He's much harder-boiled than he looks. *How* he put us through it! The elderly parent and I have been on the mat since half-past ten—and for sheer jitter, give me an audition any day!"

"I don't see what you had to be in a jitter about," Betty said. "Would you like some coffee to restore you?"

"Darling, I'd adore some if it isn't a bore. Well, of course it was a very good thing that our strength was as the strength of ten, because our hearts were pure—but even so, that man had us both tied up in knots, contradicting ourselves all over the place; and in the end the aged parent got so confused about whether he'd had his little nap before or *after* he'd drunk his coffee—as if it mattered!—that he practically gave way and confessed to the murder from sheer nervous exhaustion."

"He told me," I remarked, "that he had his coffee first and then dozed off. He seemed to remember it all very clearly indeed."

"Yes, darling, but you weren't Torquemada in person! You know, if I really *had* done something nefarious, like murdering Sir Henry instead of merely wanting to, I should simply hate to have that Gordon after me. It's the quiet unobtrusive way he goes about it. You can never tell from his face *what* he's thinking, or whether he's believing a single word you say. I just sat there, looking like Bergner in the second act of 'Escape Me Never,' gazing at him with huge trustful eyes—but I don't think he was in the least melted. After all, how can you *prove* that you were in the kitchen drearily washing-up—and not dashing off to Oakhurst to inject old Sir Henry with morphia-whatever-it-was? He kept looking dirtily at the french windows and I could see him picturing us creeping out into the snow—it was snowing that night, wasn't it?—muffled in cloaks like the Phantom of the Opera going about our fell purposes. I don't know which of us he suspected more—Dad or me. And then, just when I was wondering what we'd look like with the handcuffs on, and whether I'd be allowed to take the script of 'Behold, The Moon' along with me so that I could mug up my lines behind the cruel prison bars, he suddenly smiled charmingly and thanked us both for being so helpful—and that was that! *Whew!*"

After Ann had gone, I walked up the village with Robin to buy some stamps. It had turned into rather a lovely day, with a pale wintry sun shining from the colourless sky on to the half-melted snow and gleaming distantly between the black branches of the bare trees. It was still cold and I think probably freezing a little. Robin had his tricycle with him and was anxious to show me how fast he could ride it. By the time we had done a wide detour of the village, and come back by another road which joined the Tithe Barn lane at the far end, it was half-past twelve.

Betty greeted me abstractedly and sent Robin upstairs to wash his hands before nursery lunch.

"For heaven's sake, come and have a gin," she said. "I feel I can do with it."

"Why?" I asked. "You look a bit harassed. What's been happening?"

Betty poured out some gin-and-French and sat down with a sigh.

"Really, you know, Lee," she said, "there's simply no end to this wretched business. It seems to crop up all day long. While you've been out, I've been having the most tremendous session with John Wickham. He's absolutely beside himself with anxiety about Diana—and now he's taking some idiotic line that it's all *his* fault."

"How could it possibly be his fault?"

"Oh, he thinks he's compromised her in the eyes of the village, or some such nonsense. Of course he's madly in love with her—he came clean at last, and admitted it. But there's nothing new in that.

And he also admitted he loathed Sir Henry—which, again, we all knew. But now he seems afraid that his feeling for Diana will go against her with the police, and that they will think she did this in order to get rid of the old man and be free to marry him."

"Well, you've already tried to point that aspect out to him once," I said. "I was there."

"Yes, I know. But it only just seems to have sunk in. Of course he still maintains that Diana doesn't know anything about the fact that he's so crazily in love with her. He says he's never said a word to her. But he doesn't expect the police or anybody else to believe that."

"Do you?" I asked sceptically.

"D'you know—with John—I really think I do. I wouldn't if it had been anybody else. And besides, I know Diana pretty well. She must have gathered of course, that he's very fond of her. But I think if she'd ever realised how completely besotted he is, she'd have done something about it. She'd have made him go away, or something."

"She might possibly reciprocate."

"If she did, she'd never admit it," Betty said positively. "Not even to herself. Well, anyhow, poor old John went on and on about what a chump he'd been to hang around waiting for her to come that night. He knew perfectly well she was going over to see Sheila, and he spent the whole evening pottering about like a lost dog waiting for her to come back. He walked down the road towards Brenchley, hoping to meet her. And then when she asked him in for a drink he *knew* it would be a silly thing to do because it would annoy Sir Henry and make him more waspish than ever with Diana; but he suddenly sort of made up his mind, and he thought: 'Well, hell—it's got to come some time!' So he stormed into the study, firmly determined to tell Sir Henry once and for all exactly what he thought of him. He planned out what he was going to say—something like: 'Sir, you are a cad, and I have come to inform you that I love your wife,' and so forth."

"Does Diana realise all this?"

"Good heavens, no! Well, you see, it never came off. All that happened was that they arrived at Oakhurst—they walked into the study—and there was the old man unconscious in the chair. John was knocked sideways with surprise. He almost felt that it was an act of Providence or something."

I leaned back and gazed out of the window, and wondered how much of this story I ought to pass on to Hugh. Or how much of it he had already grasped for himself. Probably all of it, in which case there was no need for me to say anything at all.

"Has John Wickham got the shadow of an alibi for the way he spent the evening?" I asked.

"No, I don't think so. He says he was pottering about in the Lodge mending a bookcase and doing various odd jobs. But he can't prove it. And about ten o'clock he set off walking. He didn't know what time Diana would be coming back, but he guessed the road she'd have to take. That all ties up, because she met him plodding along at the bottom of the hill, just this side of Brenchley—and Brenchley's about four miles from here."

"Diana's story," I said carefully, "was that she'd *overtaken* him on the road—that is, that he was going the same way that she was."

Betty laughed. "Oh dear, Lee, you're being much too clever—it must be the association with Hugh Gordon! Don't you see that as soon as John recognised the lights of her car coming, he turned round and *pretended* to be walking back the same way. Because he didn't want Diana to realise he'd gone out on purpose to meet her. He wanted it to look like a *casual* encounter!"

"Oh, for heaven's sake!" I said impatiently. "Why do people in love have to be so idiotic? I rather agree with Hugh when he once said if you found somebody behaving in a thoroughly furtive, illogical and suspicious manner half the time it wasn't a sign of guilt at all—it was just that the poor ass was in love!"

"Well, as long as Hugh Gordon understands that," Betty said, "there's a bit more hope for John. I've known John ever since he came here, so naturally I—"

"By the way," I interrupted, remembering something. "What about the mysterious car which drove up at quarter past nine? Did John Wickham admit that he'd invented that too?"

"No, oddly enough, he didn't. He stuck grimly to the car, and said he hoped Hugh Gordon was investigating it."

"He isn't," I replied shortly. "He thinks it's all moonshine. And anyway—" I stopped suddenly, remembering how I had tried to persuade Hugh that this might have been Sonia Phillips' car. But surely he or Spragg would have had the sense to ask her neighbours—the people in the farmhouse opposite—if they had noticed her taking out the Ford that night? He *couldn't* have overlooked anything quite so elementary.

Betty remarked, changing the subject: "I've got to take Sara and Robin over to a children's party at Goudhurst this afternoon. Are you sure you don't mind being left? I didn't think you'd want to come with us. It will be pretty deadly."

I assured her that I didn't in the least mind being left. In fact, I thought it was rather a good idea. It would give me a chance to get my muddled thoughts into some kind of order.

However, by the time I settled down to a solitary tea in the drawing-room at about half-past four, I hadn't made any progress at all. I kept wondering rather irritably what Hugh was up to, and what fresh bits of evidence he was unearthing to keep from me.

He had an annoying way of presenting me with some totally inexplicable clue—or, even more infuriating, something like the letter from Sonia Phillips which looked so conclusive and subsequently turned out to be nothing of the kind—and then going drifting off to investigate it at his leisure with the assistance of Spragg and his minions, while he left me to chew on the meagre fact and to work it out like Mycroft Holmes on the strength of pure logic. It simply wasn't a fair distribution of mental effort.

Hugh turned up just as I had finished my tea. He looked tired and downcast, which immediately made me feel maternal and forgiving. I hurried off to fetch him a fresh pot of tea and hastened to ply him with scones and home-made jam.

He said rather bleakly: "I've been to see the widow."

"Oh dear," I said sympathetically. "Poor Diana! Did you confront her with the evidence?"

"Yes. She nearly fainted clean away when I told her where the tube of morphia had been found. She couldn't offer any explanation at all. Not that I really imagined she would be able to. Either she put it there herself—or she didn't. In neither case would she be likely to produce an explanation. I also asked her about the hot-water jug."

"And what," I asked with interest, "did she say about that?"

"She said she was positive she'd never taken in any hot-water jug. She said it lived in the pantry. She'd made Sir Henry a hot whisky-lemon-and-water before she went out, and she could only assume that he must have gone out to the kitchen and made himself another hot drink later on."

"Or that somebody else went out to the kitchen and made it for him," I suggested.

"Exactly. It was perfectly possible either way. So I didn't press that point. After that she opened up quite a bit."

"Yes?" I said.

Hugh helped himself to another scone and applied a generous quantity of raspberry jam.

"She's a very nice woman," he remarked at a tangent.

I refrained from comment.

"She admitted that Sir Henry was a difficult character—which, of course, was only too obvious. She said he was terribly harsh with the children and she'd had a lot of trouble with him on that account. She stalled a bit about John Wickham, and then finally admitted that he and her husband didn't get on. She agreed that Sir Henry had had rows with the Qualtroughs and had talked of evicting the old man from Little Hodges. But when I tried to pin her down to any definite suspicion that one of those people might have poisoned her husband and tried to fix the blame on her, she wasn't having any. She resolutely refused to believe that any of them *could* have wanted to frame her. She kept saying pathetically: 'But they were my friends—they liked me—they'd never do a thing like that.'"

"I feel sure she's right," I said.

"Well, *somebody* did," Hugh retorted. He took a final gulp of tea and pushed away his cup. "Then I went on to the subject of Sonia Phillips. I asked her if she'd had the impression at the Sandys' party that Mrs. Phillips had ever met her husband before. She said she had—so much so that she'd mentioned it to him on the way home. He replied that he'd never set eyes on anyone called Sonia Phillips in the whole of his life, and couldn't imagine why she should think he had."

"Well, we know *that* wasn't true," I said.

"We know there was some connection—no more than that. I asked her again about the Qualtroughs and she said she liked the old man and was quite sure he would never go to the lengths of murdering anyone. She added that she'd known Ann since she was a small child, and while she wasn't altogether satisfied she was the right wife for Michael, she couldn't see her murdering anyone either. Altogether a thoroughly useless, negative and frustrating afternoon."

"And how long does Diana stay in Maidstone?" I asked.

"She hasn't got to stay there a minute longer than she wants to. I understand that Michael is in conference with the son-in-law, what's-his-name Henderson in Tunbridge Wells, to draw up a writ for *habeas corpus* and get her out straight away. She laughed when I told her that, and said Michael was wasting his time. I refrained from embarrassing her by relating the efforts of her amateur Don Quixote who had been inventing mythical motor-cars on her behalf, because it was well meant on his part—if over-zealous—and it would have worried her. She's very fond of John Wickham."

"How I shall laugh," I said, "when that motor-car is tracked down and found to be the pivot of the whole mystery."

"I shan't grudge you your girlish mirth. Do you think it would be possible to squeeze out another cup of that delicious Orange Pekoe?"

I put some more logs on the fire and regarded Hugh's averted profile. He seemed to have brushed his hair better than usual, or at least done something to it. The tuft on top was much less conspicuously untidy.

"So what," I asked him at last, "do you conclude from all that?"

"Very little," he admitted. "I've had Spragg's reports on the servants, and there's absolutely nothing to be got from them. They came in about twenty-past eleven—saw the lights on in the study, and assumed Sir Henry was still up, but nobody went to see. They had a cup of cocoa in the kitchen, after which they all pushed off to bed. They didn't know until the following morning that there was anything wrong at all."

"What about the washing-up?"

"They did that in the usual way next morning. Nobody told them not to touch anything in the study, so they just went ahead and cleared things up. It wasn't until Diana's maid took up her breakfast tray in the morning that they even discovered Sir Henry had been taken ill. They mentioned that they'd found 'one of the master's bits of china' broken on the floor in the study, and asked what they should do about the bits. Diana told them to throw them away."

The front door bell rang suddenly.

I waited for a moment, as usually whoever it was walked into the hall and yelled for Betty, but when nothing happened I concluded it must be a patient and I'd better go.

It wasn't a patient. It was Sergeant Spragg, very apologetic about disturbing me and interrupting Hugh over his tea. He explained that he had recognised Hugh's car outside, and as a report had just come in from London which he understood Mr. Gordon wanted without delay, he had taken the liberty of bringing it along in person.

"Come in, come in," I said with alacrity, realising that this was a bit of jam for me. Hugh couldn't very well disappear abruptly into the night, replete as he was with Betty's scones, without looking extremely rude. And if the report was all that urgent, the chances were that he would open it on the spot and I would be in a very favourable position to receive the low-down on its contents.

I urged a rather reluctant Sergeant Spragg into an armchair by the fire and pressed a piece of cake upon him. He was at first inclined to refuse, arguing that it would "spoil his tea," and it wasn't until I glanced at the clock and noticed it was past six that I realised what he meant.

The report turned out to be the official check-up on Michael Metcalfe's movements in London on the Tuesday night.

Hugh read it through slowly, turned it over, and read it again. Then he raised his eyes and looked quizzically at me.

"Three guesses," he said maddeningly.

"Nobody remembers Michael at the theatre; nobody can find the 'funny little club' in Soho; nobody can identify the unknown chum who was so interested in the stage," I said glibly. "There wasn't any milk train—or if there was, Michael didn't ask about it. Personally, I don't believe Michael ever went to London at all that night."

"I wonder what makes you so sure?" Hugh asked. "As a matter of fact, the milk train's the one thing you're wrong on. There *was* a milk train. But he probably knew that anyway."

I explained about Betty's discovery with the timetable.

"You might have told me," Hugh said reproachfully. "Not that it makes any difference. No chum—no night-club—no porter. Yes, I'm inclined to agree, no London. I wonder where he was. *Lord,* what a bore these people are, who won't tell you the truth! *Was* he murdering his Papa, or wasn't he? When I first saw him I didn't think he'd got the guts to murder a wood-louse, but now I'm not so sure. What do you think, Spragg?"

"I think, sir, that there's more in that young man than meets the eye."

"D'you know, Spragg, I believe you're right. So perish all first judgments! Liane, what's your opinion?"

I could feel Sergeant Spragg's fishy eye fixed rather disapprovingly on a spot on the wall somewhere about a foot above my head. He said nothing.

"I really haven't the least idea," I said. "I knew Michael hadn't gone to London because, even apart from the fact that there was no train he could have gone on, he also said he'd been fiddling round at Charing Cross missing the last train, etc., at five minutes to twelve, and then he'd decided to hitchhike back—he'd thumbed a lorry to Five Ways—walked down to the station to pick up his car, driven all the way back to Oakhurst and arrived at half-past one. Well, he couldn't have done it. Not unless the lorry was jet-propelled."

Sergeant Spragg let out his breath with a slow hiss. His gaze shifted to my face. He almost beamed. I felt a wave of pure thankfulness that I hadn't let down the class.

Unorthodox as it might be for Scotland Yard to be sharing its innermost secrets with the boss's lady friends, at least the woman wasn't a complete and utter fool.

"That was a very nice piece of cake, ma'am," Sergeant Spragg said. "I enjoyed it."

"I'm so glad," I said hysterically. "Have another piece?"

"Well," said Spragg magnificently, sealing our bond for ever, "I don't mind if I do."

Hugh glanced impatiently at his watch. He said "I wonder if I'd catch young Master Michael if I went up to Oakhurst now."

"There's just one other thing, sir," Sergeant Spragg said. There was a barely perceptible pause while he weighed up how much, in the present cordiality of our *entente,* it was permissible to say before me. "It was about the—er—the local side of the enquiry. About the other party, sir—the lady."

For a moment Hugh looked blank.

"Oh yes," he said. "That's all right, Spragg. Mrs. Craufurd came along with me when I first went to see her. I take it you're referring to Mrs. Phillips?"

"Well, yes, sir. I went to the Food Office, like you said, and they had her change of address registered there all right. It was a block of flats in Kensington she lived at before, sir, and I telephoned the Yard to put Hawkes on to it that end. But it seems it all fizzles out there, sir. They remembered her all right at the flats—said she'd been there about a year. A very quiet lady, they said she was, didn't go out much and never entertained. Kept herself to herself, like. It didn't seem she had many friends, and none of the people at the flats knows anything about her or where she came from. Hawkes took it up with all the leading theatrical agencies too, sir, like you suggested, but none of them had any record of anyone of that name. Of course they're going on with that line still, sir, only it would probably be easier for them if they had a photo they could work on."

"Yes, of course," Hugh agreed. "The most likely thing is that's she changed her name. She's properly registered here, you say, with a ration book and everything?"

"Oh yes, sir. It's only in London we can't seem to trace any back record."

"Try the *London Gazette* or whatever it is," Hugh said. "There must be some record of people who change their names by deed poll. I'll get you a photograph for the theatrical agencies and then Hawkes can have another shot at them."

"Did you ask Howard about her?" I asked.

"Yes, I spoke to him—but, as I thought, there wasn't much there. He said she is a patient, and she's suffering from some kind of injury to the spine—an accident, he gathered, though he didn't know quite what, which happened about three years ago. He got the impression that she'd been a dancer and had had to give it up on account of this accident. Apparently she has a good deal of pain from this back of hers, and he's been giving her morphia injections."

I sat up abruptly and opened my mouth to speak.

"No," Hugh said before I could get a word out, "I'm afraid that line's no good. Sandys has been giving her injections of morphine sulphate; but he's never let her have any tablets to administer to herself, and he has never at any time given her morphine tartrate."

"Oh," I said, deflated.

Sergeant Spragg rose ponderously to his feet. I accompanied him to the door and returned to find Hugh staring broodily into the fire.

"Everything seems to fall through as soon as one gets down to it," I said thoughtfully. "I suppose Howard didn't say anything about her personal background?"

"That was all I could get out of him. He doesn't know anything about her private life—her husband, or anything of that kind. In fact, he was extremely disinclined to talk about her at all, and the amount I got was like squeezing blood out of a stone."

"Perhaps he's fallen for her, too, in a mild way," I suggested. "Ann Qualtrough wasn't so far wrong when she said Sonia Phillips was a bit of a man-trap."

Hugh ignored this remark. I picked up the tea plates and stacked them on to the trolley and made for the door. I declined Hugh's abstracted offer of assistance and wheeled the trolley out into the kitchen. When I came back he was still sitting exactly where I had left him, gazing unseeingly at the same smouldering log.

"By the way," I said, "Betty told me to ask you, if you came along, to stay for dinner. Howard's been given a brace of pheasants by a grateful patient."

"That's very kind of her," Hugh said absently, his thoughts obviously still miles away.

In the drive outside the door of a car slammed and there were footsteps from the direction of the garage. I gathered that Betty and the children had returned from their party.

"Look, Liane," Hugh said suddenly. "I don't think I am going up to Oakhurst now. I'm going back to the pub to have another word with Spragg. Will you tell Betty that I'll be delighted to accept her invitation and I'll be back in about an hour?"

"I think this is Betty coming in now. But what about Michael? Aren't you going to—"

"I've decided to pay another call on Mrs. Phillips after dinner. Would you like to come?"

"Yes," I said. "Of course I would. But I thought you said Michael—"

"I've got an idea," Hugh said, "that maybe Mrs. Phillips might be able to shed some light on Michael, too."

XVII

SERENADE FOR SONIA

HUGH AND I SET OFF IN THE LANCIA TO CALL ON SONIA Phillips at about half-past nine. As we parked the car beside the duck-pond and walked across the road to the gate of Holly Tree Cottage, I distinctly heard the sound of voices coming from the sitting-room window. I hesitated and turned to speak to Hugh, and as I did so, noticed the dark shape of a small car standing under the yew hedge a few yards from the gate.

"She's got somebody there," I said. "Do you think—"

"Certainly she has," Hugh agreed. "I rather thought she might have."

Undeterred he walked briskly up the path and rang the bell. I trailed along behind him, feeling for some obscure reason a little uncomfortable. Detectives, I supposed, had to develop a pachydermatous approach to their problems. Otherwise sensibility would be continually preventing them from thrusting themselves into the houses of suspects who were obviously unwilling to receive them, and they would never be able to extract any information at all. It occurred to me that for a living I would rather be selling vacuum cleaners any day.

Sonia Phillips opened the door. She was wearing a long dark-red housecoat which exactly matched her lips and fingernails. The rest of her was etched in black and white. Her face, tense in the shadow, looked very pale and her eyes were wide with surprise. She gave a swift hesitant glance at the closed door leading from the passage behind her, and remained standing in the doorway.

"I am sorry," she said firmly to Hugh, her foreign accent more pronounced than usual, "but I am at present engaged. Perhaps tomorrow morning—?"

"It was really Mr. Metcalfe I wanted to see," Hugh explained politely. "I understood I might find him here?"

Mrs. Phillips was silent for a moment; her dark slanting eyes seemed to be summing him up.

"Very well," she said at last. "Will you come inside please?"

We followed her into the sitting-room. Michael Metcalfe, sitting in one of the pair of shabby wing chairs drawn up to the fire, turned a startled face towards us. He stood up quickly, and a slow red flush began to spread over his forehead. He was an extremely embarrassed young man.

"I must apologise for intruding like this," Hugh said easily. "But I thought you might be here, and I particularly wanted to catch you this evening if possible. There were one or two little things I wanted to ask you. I brought Mrs. Craufurd along to infuse a spirit of informality. This isn't really an official visit."

Sonia Phillips had drawn up the piano stool, and now brought in a big cushion which she placed on the floor by the fire.

Michael Metcalfe continued to stand leaning against the chimney piece scowling.

"I must say, I don't see quite what—" he began rather shrilly, and was interrupted by Sonia, who put her hand on his arm and shrugged her shoulders in a tiny gesture of helplessness.

"We shall do no good, Michael," she said, "by refusing to answer Mr. Gordon's questions. He has taught me that once. And as I have just been telling you, I think we have both been quite foolish enough already."

"I suppose," Michael growled, "it's about the story I told you about my going up to London the night my father was taken ill?"

"That, among other things," Hugh said. "You never went near London, did you?"

Before Michael could reply, Sonia Phillips said calmly: "Michael did not go to London, but neither did he poison his father, Sir Henry, with morphia. He could not have done so, because you see he was here with me all that evening—here, in this room."

"I—I—" began Michael, and broke off, stammering. He ran his fingers through his dark curly hair and the red flush deepened.

"It would have saved us a lot of trouble if you'd said so before," Hugh pointed out mildly. "Don't you think so?"

I thought of the indefatigable Hawkes and his assistants ploughing their way through the cosmopolitan jungle of the smaller Soho restaurants, interviewing theatre commissionaires, interviewing porters, running to and fro far into the night, and considered that Hugh was being very forebearing indeed with this tiresome young man.

Michael was still silent. He seemed to be looking to Sonia for guidance, but she was standing gazing pensively into the fire, with a withdrawn expression on her face.

"All right," he admitted finally. "Yes—it would. I'm sorry. You see, I—I made up that story about going to London before any of this happened. I mean, about my father. So I had to stick to it." He hesitated again. Nobody made any move to help him out, so he swallowed nervously and continued: "It was because of Ann. I—she—I mean, I couldn't tell her I was coming here that night. She—she wouldn't have understood."

"I think," Sonia Phillips put in gently, "I think you mean she *would* have understood."

There was a rather awkward pause.

"Oh, hell," Michael said suddenly, flopping down into one of the chairs and searching his pocket for cigarettes. "Look, Gordon, you must see how frightfully awkward it was. I—I'm supposed to be engaged to Ann. And—well!" He threw up his hands in an eloquent gesture. "After I met Sonia it just wasn't any good any more. I knew it was hopeless. I fought against it—Sonia, I *did!* You *know* I did. I didn't want to hurt Ann's feelings—but I felt I must see Sonia. I *had* to talk to her—and it was so difficult. You've no idea, Gordon, how impossible it is in a small village like Staple Green even to *speak* to anyone without the whole place buzzing! Ann wanted me to take her over to the cinema in Tunbridge Wells that night—she'd asked me about a week before, just after that night we went to the Sandys' for drinks and I'd half said I would. So to get out of it, I invented this story about going to London so that I didn't have to explain to her where I really was going. And even then it was difficult, because I was afraid Ann would want to come to London, too, but luckily she didn't go on about that. She just dropped it, but I think she was a bit hurt. Anyway, there it was. And once I'd given out to everybody at Betty's kids' party that I was going up to town, I couldn't go back on it. I just had to go on pretending I'd been there. I realised afterwards I'd made a floater about the trains—the one I was thinking of was a train I'd once been up on which gets to Charing Cross about half-past six, and then I discovered afterwards that it only runs on Saturdays. It was too much to hope *that* wouldn't be spotted by the police, so then I didn't quite know what to do. I told Sonia, and she advised me to come and tell you. I—I didn't want to do that, because—well, because I felt such a fool."

"I see," Hugh said gravely. He sat down primly on the music-stool. Mrs. Phillips was sitting on the cushion on the floor, her back propped against one of the oak beams running up from the fireplace, and I had sunk into the other armchair.

"You realise, don't you," he said to Michael, "that by concealing this story until now you have put Mrs. Phillips into a very awkward position?"

Sonia Phillips' hand tightened for a moment on the edge of the cushion.

Michael said: "But why—how?"

Hugh put his hand into his pocket and brought out a small crumpled piece of paper. Without a word he handed it to Sonia, and watched her unfold it. She drew in her breath in a long gasp of horror and looked at Hugh with, enormous frightened eyes.

"I thought he would have destroyed it," was all she said.

Michael grabbed the piece of paper out of her hand.

"What is all this?" he exclaimed in a high-pitched voice. "Oh my God, Sonia—you never told me—"

"No," she agreed sadly. "I didn't tell anyone. I was going up to see Sir Henry that night because I heard Lady Metcalfe in the village say she would be out that evening, and that you were going to London. I didn't know then that you had made it up—that you were really coming to see *me*. Then, when you came, I could not go to Oakhurst to see Sir Henry, because you were here. I was a little worried afterwards about that letter, but as I heard nothing from the police about it, I thought he must have burned it as I asked him to."

"But *why—?*" Michael demanded urgently. Oblivious of the presence of Hugh and myself he seized her hands and flung himself down on the floor beside her. "Sonia, *why* were you going to see my father?"

"I—I wanted to ask him a favour," she said.

"But you didn't *know* my father!" Michael protested. "You'd only met him that once at the Sandys' house. *What* are you talking about?"

Instead of replying directly, Sonia Phillips rose to her feet and crossed the room to the little writing-desk in the corner. She took a small bunch of keys out of the pocket of her housecoat and unlocked one of the drawers. She picked up a bulky envelope and came back to her seat by the fire. She held out the packet to Hugh.

"That will explain everything," she said simply. "I didn't want anyone to know—ever. But I see now it is no good."

She folded her hands in her lap, and Michael swung round to see what is was that Hugh was examining. Hugh opened the envelope and drew out a thick wad of press cuttings. One of them fluttered to the floor at my feet, and I picked it up curiously.

It was an account, dated just over two years before, of the trial for murder of a young Italian named Giovanni Felipo and his Russian-born wife, Sonia. It had been a particularly brutal murder. An old lady living near Bournemouth had been attacked and robbed one night in her home. She had died in hospital a few hours later from multiple injuries, and had never recovered consciousness. The case for the prosecution was that the Russian woman, who had been acting as companion to the old lady, had plotted with her Italian husband to leave one of the downstairs windows unbolted on the night in question, and had been throughout an accessory before, during and after the murder. The summing-up of Mr. Justice Metcalfe had been strongly against both the prisoners, but in the end the jury had found a verdict of guilty for the man and not guilty for the woman.

"I did not have anything to do with it," Sonia said in a low voice. "But I could see that the judge did not believe me. I had left Giovanni some months before. I was dancing then in the Russian ballet company, and one evening he came home very drunk and he hit me and I fell. I hurt my back, and I could not go on dancing. When I came out of the hospital, I ran away. I took a job as companion with the old lady through an advertisement I saw one day in the paper. I told her the truth, and she was kind—oh, so kind! I do not know how Giovanni found me. But he did find me. He started coming to the house. At first he tried to make me go back to him and I refused. I did not know that he was planning to steal the old lady's jewels. She had been kind to me, and I—I do not steal. So I never thought. Then Giovanni came one night when I was shutting up the windows and I let him into the kitchen. It was foolish of me, perhaps, but I did not know what he had come for. He locked me into the pantry and went upstairs. I could not get out and I heard—I heard the most *terrible* sounds from above!" She covered her face with her hands, and after a moment went on, her voice hardly more than a whisper: "Giovanni came back. He let me out of the pantry, and I saw that there was blood on his hands. He said that if the old lady died and the police caught him, they would hang me also, because he would tell them that I had helped him to steal the jewels. He said our only chance was to run away quickly. I didn't know what to do. I was frightened, and I knew that if I refused he would kill me also. He was so strong. And then when we were both still there, standing in the kitchen, the police came. Somebody had heard the old lady's cries and had sent for them. Giovanni tried to run, but they caught him and took him away. They took me away also. I tried to tell them that it was not my fault, but they didn't believe me. Giovanni was my husband. And at the trial, the judge still did not believe me. I do not know now why they didn't hang me with Giovanni. I thought I was going to be hanged."

A long shiver passed over her, and she buried her face in her hands. In a flash, Michael was beside her, his arms round her heaving shoulders.

"I believe you," he said steadily. "I believe you, and I'm going to marry you and take you away and look after you all your life."

I glanced across the fireplace to Hugh. His face was completely impassive. Then he stretched out his hand, picked up Sonia Phillips' note to Sir Henry Metcalfe and dropped it into the fire. The flames licked eagerly at it, and in a moment it was gone.

Some minutes later, Sonia raised a not unattractively tear-stained face. I observed with envy that she was one of those lucky women who could even cry gracefully.

"That was why I wanted to see Sir Henry," she said to Hugh. "I wanted to beg him not to tell the people here who I was. I knew he had recognised me that night. When I first came to this village and heard the name Metcalfe, I did not think of that judge, I had forgotten his name—but never his face. Never that cruel, cold, hard face which did not believe a word I said."

She shuddered again, and Michael's protective arm went round her.

"It was *you* I was afraid he would tell," she said to Michael, smiling suddenly in a way that obviously turned his bones to water. "I didn't want you to know about me. But now I am so very, very glad that you do know—and that it does not make any difference."

"I don't think he would have told anyone," Hugh said. "You've got to give the old devil his due—I beg your pardon, Metcalfe. But when his wife asked him later if he'd met you anywhere before, he told her he had never heard the name Sonia Phillips in his life. And he didn't add that he *had* heard of Sonia Felipo. He may have been a harsh judge, Mrs. Phillips, but he did adhere to the ethics of his profession. You needn't have worried."

Michael Metcalfe continued to sit on the floor holding Sonia's hand and gazing idiotically into space. I began to feel distinctly superfluous.

Hugh cleared his throat and looked at his watch.

Sonia Phillips rose swiftly, dabbing at her eyes with a small white handkerchief.

"I am sorry," she said, "to be so stupid as to cry when I am so happy. I also have been as bad as Michael in giving you trouble, Mr. Gordon. We should have told you these things before. May I make you a cup of tea before you go?"

"Yes," I put in rapidly, before Hugh could refuse. "I think that would be lovely. Let me come and help you."

Out in the tiny kitchen Sonia smoothed her hair and put some powder on her nose. The extraordinary thing was that she didn't really need it. I thought ruefully of the spectacle I myself should have presented if I had just been through a similar orgy of emotion, and imagination boggled.

Sonia put on the kettle, and then poured some milk into a saucepan and put it on the gas ring.

"Your Dr. Sandys," she said, "advised it. He said I should take a cup every night when I go to bed. I do not much like milk, but Dr. Sandys has been so kind—I must do as he says."

We returned to the sitting-room with the tea-tray and Sonia's milk. Michael, who was looking like somebody who has just been informed by a *Daily Express* reporter that he had won the Irish Sweep, immediately became almost embarrassingly uxorious. He insisted that Sonia was looking tired—as indeed she was, poor girl, and no wonder—and that she should go to bed as soon as she had drunk her milk.

"D'you mind hanging on just for a moment?" Michael said to Hugh, as Sonia left the room. "There's something I must ask you before you go."

He hurried off to say goodnight to his betrothed, and we were left sitting by the fire. Personally I was feeling pretty exhausted myself, with strain and various other vicarious emotions.

"I suppose," I remarked rather acidly to Hugh, "that with your marvellous insight, you had already foreseen all this!"

"Hardly all," he said. "I expected we'd find young Michael Metcalfe here—and I rather fancied that Mrs. Phillips might prove to be the explanation of that mythical journey to London. But I certainly didn't foresee *this.*" He jerked his thumb in the direction of the scattered press cuttings.

"And you believe her story?"

"Well, as a matter of fact, I do. I remember hearing about the case at the time, of course, though it was nothing to do with me—I mean, I wasn't on it, and I never saw any of the people concerned. But enough came out afterwards about that young blackguard Giovanni Felipo to have warranted hanging him a dozen times over. I should think he must have given any woman he married utter hell."

"I wonder," I said irrelevantly, "how many of that jury were men."

Hugh looked at me with some approaching genuine anger in his expression.

"Liane, that really is one of the most shocking remarks I've ever heard you make! The verdict was right—and it was in accordance with the weight of the evidence. There was a lot of criticism of Metcalfe's summing-up, I remember, and, if the verdict had gone against that girl, there would have been very good grounds for an appeal. You don't mean to say *you* don't believe she was innocent?"

I threw my cigarette into the fire and laughed at him.

"Of course I believe she was innocent," I said. "Only having a face like that must help. Do you think she'll marry Michael?"

"I should say it looks extremely probable at the moment," Hugh returned drily. "She's really much more suitable for him than Ann Qualtrough. It's the difference between quick-silver and a mountain lake. Michael's inclined to be a bit jumpy himself, and he needs a woman with calm. Sonia Phillips has more than calm—she's got a sort of esoteric stillness which would hold a man like Michael till the end of the world."

I picked up the tea-pot, observed with chagrin that it was empty, put it down again and remarked lightly: "I believe you're half in love with her yourself."

"I said she could hold a man like Michael," Hugh reminded me quietly. "And shall we not re-open the unprofitable subject of who I am or am not in love with? You may remember that the summer before last—"

Michael Metcalfe came into the room radiating that God was in His heaven and all was right with the world. His eyes were shining and there was a faint smudge of lipstick below his left ear.

"Gosh!" he said, like a small boy, "isn't she marvellous? She's going to be awfully good for me, too, because she says she thinks I ought to go on with this law business my father was so keen about—but somehow, coming from *her,* it makes the whole dreary business seem quite different and not really dreary at all. She's so intelligent about things—she understands everything in such an amazing way! Somehow reading for the bar, if I had her there to talk to and discuss things with, seems quite an exciting sort of prospect. We could go away somewhere first, you see. I think she ought to go away—at any rate until her back's strong again. I thought we might go to Spain—she's never been to Spain. And then when we come back—"

"What about your stage career?" I suggested. "Don't you want to go on with that?"

Michael shrugged his shoulders. "I don't know," he said simply. "I seem to have gone off the idea of the stage a bit lately. I'm not really an actor, you know, and I don't think I would ever make the grade. I was awfully keen on the idea once, but somehow—well, at best I'd only be a poor player who struts and frets his hour upon the stage and all that. Oh!" He broke off suddenly and a sort of shudder went over him. He glanced quickly over his shoulder, and then seemed to pull himself together and laughed nervously. "Sorry," he said. "Habit. Ann always used to fly off the handle if anyone quoted *Macbeth*—she said it was unlucky."

I made no reply. The mention of Ann Qualtrough's name had put a feeling of constraint on Soma's little sitting-room.

"Ann—" Michael began uneasily. "That was what I wanted to ask you, Gordon. You—you won't say anything to Ann about all this, will you? I shall have to tell her myself, of course, eventually, but somehow—"

"I won't say anything about it to Ann," Hugh promised. "But if I were you, I'd go and have a talk with your step-mother. I think you'd find her sympathetic."

Michael's face clouded for a moment.

"Yes," he agreed sombrely. "I must go and see Diana. I've been pretty selfish, really—I haven't been over to Maidstone to see her at all. I've been so—so taken up. Have you *got* to keep Diana in that place, Gordon? Dick Henderson's getting out a *habeas corpus* writ or something, I believe, but naturally one doesn't want to go on with that if it can be avoided. Because you can't still seriously think that she had anything to do with all this?"

"You go over and see her," Hugh advised. "I'm as keen as you are to get Lady Metcalfe released, but until this case is cleared up she's better off where she is."

"But will it ever *be* cleared up?" Michael asked hopelessly. "I mean, *who*—"

"Listen," Hugh said slowly. "I've got an idea, and I want your co-operation. You asked me just now not to mention to Ann that you were here with Mrs. Phillips that night you told her you were going to London. Now, how many other people knew you were going to London?"

"Why, practically the whole village I should think," Michael said. "I broadcast it pretty widely. Nobody knows I *didn't* go—nobody, that is, except Sonia and you."

"I want you to stick to your London story," Hugh said. He rose from the piano stool and went and stood by the fire. He looked very serious. "I shall ask Mrs. Phillips to say—as she did originally—that she was here by herself that! evening. Do you understand? I don't want *anyone* to know that you and Mrs. Phillips are in a position to give each other an alibi for that night."

Michael nodded.

"O.K.," he said. "But what about Ann? I mean—well, I do feel such a frightful cad about Ann. But it's no good going on with something when you know it's all wrong. And I knew our engagement was wrong the first minute I ever set eyes on Sonia. All the same, I've got to tell Ann some time. I only didn't want her to get it from you first."

"Yes, I see what you mean. But just for the moment, I'd rather you didn't even tell Ann. You know how these things get around, and it's just possible she might let something drop—"

"I know," Michael said. "You don't have to tell me. Ann is awfully indiscreet sometimes. What about Diana? Can I tell her?"

Hugh seemed to be considering for a moment.

"Well," he said, "I don't think that could do much harm. Lady Metcalfe isn't in a position to pass anything on—even by accident. And she isn't seeing any visitors—"

"Yes, she is," Michael interrupted. "John Wickham went over to see her on Saturday. I met him on the way to the bus."

"Have you seen him since?"

"No."

"I think you'll find," Hugh said gently, "that poor Wickham had his journey in vain. Lady Metcalfe hasn't seen anybody at all since she went to Maidstone, with the exception of Spragg and myself. If you want to go and see her, I'll give you a note to the prison authorities. But you won't get in without."

"Oh," Michael said. "I see. Well, thanks." He wandered over towards the door and paused with his hand on the latch.

"Have you got some idea about all this, Gordon?" he asked. "It—it sounds as if you have."

Hugh stooped to pick up his overcoat and handed me my fur gloves. We all went into the hall together. At the front door Hugh stopped.

"I've got several ideas," he said evasively. "I think the case will be over very soon. I think I know who poisoned your father, Metcalfe, and why. But so far I have absolutely not one iota of proof. Goodnight."

He walked off rapidly down the path. I trotted behind, and my last glimpse of Michael was an incredulous pair of hazel eyes staring after us as he stood in the lighted doorway watching Hugh's retreating back.

XVIII

CHRISTMAS SHOPPING

OF COURSE I BADGERED HUGH ALL THE WAY HOME TO explain just what he had meant by telling Michael that the case would be over very soon, and that he knew who'd done it and why. But you might as well have tried to open a Whitstable native with an invisible hairpin.

"Think!" was all he would say. "Use the intelligence God gave you! There's only one person who *could* have done this thing, and if you can't work it out for yourself you're not the girl Spragg takes you for. Now, you won't go and mention any of this business about Michael and Sonia Phillips to Betty and Howard, will you?"

"Oh, all right," I said crossly as I got out of the car. "But just what *am* I to say, because Betty's sure to ask? She knows where we went. That Sonia Phillips confessed all—or what?"

"You can tell her," Hugh said seriously, "that we had a pleasant cup of tea with a very charming woman. Now go inside quickly. I know you look sheer heaven standing there like that with the moonlight shining on your hair, but you'll catch your death of cold—and I shall have to spend the rest of my life nursing nothing but a beautiful memory. I'd much rather have you around to torment with my conundrums, so hurry up and get inside the house. Goodnight."

He drove off in a roar of acceleration and I walked slowly up to the front door.

I lay awake half the night brooding over one thing and another, and was consequently feeling both tired and irritable the next morning when I went down to breakfast. Betty reminded me that I had said I wanted to go to London that day, and told me that she and Sara would be ready to start for the dentist at half-past eleven. They would drop me off at the station at Tunbridge Wells.

In my present exhausted condition, the very thought of the London Christmas shopping crowds appalled me. I said rather feebly that I had thought it over and decided I could probably manage to get everything I wanted in Tunbridge Wells.

"Oh good," Betty said. "Then we can attack it together. I've got a lot of presents to get, too, and really the Tunbridge Wells shops aren't at all bad—and much less crowded than London. I thought we'd have lunch over there, and make a day of it."

We deposited Sara at her dentist at half-past twelve and made for the shops. Betty consulted her list and found she had to go to several shops in the High Street, so we drove down to the bottom and parked the car opposite the Pantiles and walked back. We called in at a bookshop to pick up some books which Betty had ordered for Howard, and paused at the window of the next shop to look at some toys. The window was gaily decorated with tinsel and holly and we were fascinated by a family of brightly coloured clockwork beetles, scarlet, green and yellow with black spots on their wings, which we thought seemed suitable for Robin's stocking.

"His proper present is a set of trains," Betty said. "That's coming from London, and Sara's having a bicycle. But it's the stockings which are the hardest things to think of. I think I'll get him one of the red ones, Lee. He's got a green frog already. Are you going to come in with me, or go on and see if you can find the sort of socks you want for Bill? There's a shop just across the road where

I got some very nice ones for Howard, and I'll come over and meet you there."

I got the socks and was staring in at the window of a gramophone shop when Betty joined me again.

"Oh, that reminds me," she said. "I promised Sara I'd see if they had any of the 'Alice in Wonderland' records."

I followed her into the shop, and wandered round examining lists in the vague hope that there might be something suitable for Aunt Adelaide, who, I remembered, had a gramophone and a taste for what Bill and I privately considered the most frightful Victorian ballads. I had just rejected the idea on the grounds of packing difficulties, when one of the salesmen came up to speak to Betty.

"Excuse me, madam," he said, "but you are Mrs. Sandys from Staple Green, aren't you? I wonder if you would be so kind as to tell Miss Qualtrough that the records she ordered last week have come in, and we will send them along just as soon as we have a van going in that direction."

"I'll take them for her, if you like," Betty said. "I've got my car. Do you want me to pay for them, or has she got an account?"

"That's extremely kind of you, madam. It will be on account. Mr. Qualtrough buys a number of records from us—a very musical gentleman, Mr. Qualtrough, as I expect you know, madam. We always do our best to oblige Mr. Qualtrough, though there is not much general demand for the type of record he fancies. A little too high-brow for some people's tastes!" He tittered deprecatingly, and I could well imagine that there wouldn't be exactly a universal rush among the local inhabitants to buy up chests of viols or records of early Italian harpsichord sonatas.

Betty took the parcel and we left the shop rather hurriedly, because we had just realised that Sara would be finished with the dentist and was probably champing impatiently for her lunch.

As we drove up the hill to the dentist, Betty gave a little exclamation and said: "That's another thing I meant to do! Isn't it awful how the time flies? Lee, I really think I *must* call in and have a word with poor Sheila Henderson. She must be so worried about Diana. You needn't bother, of course, but I think I'd better just run in for a minute after lunch."

"I'd rather like to meet her," I said. "That is, if I wouldn't be in the way."

"No, of course not—she'd like it. We can park Sara in the hotel after lunch—she loves going there, because they've got a tank of fishes in the hall and Sara watches them for hours. We needn't stay more than five minutes with Sheila."

We collected Sara and drove back to the hotel, where we disposed of an extremely expensive and uninspired meal which Sara adored because it wasn't at home. She insisted on a second helping of chocolate blanc-mange which, as Betty pointed out, she would have refused to touch if it had been provided in the nursery. Afterwards Betty told her that we were going to see Mrs. Henderson, and would come back later to pick her up.

"Goody," Sara said pleasedly. "Can I go and watch the fish?"

We left her with her nose glued to the heated tank and drove up the Frant Road. The Hendersons lived in a modest little house with a small garden, in a turning about half-way up on the left.

Sheila Henderson was a fragile feminine edition of her brother Michael. She had the same restless hazel eyes and curly brown hair. She would have been a pretty girl if it hadn't been for the permanent pucker of worry on her wide forehead, caused presumably by the difficulties of trying to cope with a house, two children and a husband on a definitely very restricted income. We listened to a long tale of woe about the rapidity with which Dickie grew out of his shoes and the gross favouritism displayed by the butcher in the matter of offal.

"Yes, of course it's all pretty awful about father," she said in reply to Betty's tactfully framed condolences. "But quite frankly Dick and Michael and I are all much fonder of Diana than we ever were of him. He's never done a thing for any of us, and the children hardly knew him by sight. D'you know, on Dickie's last birthday he never even sent him a card? Diana was marvellous—she gave him a lovely wooden horse on wheels and ten shillings for his Savings Account and a new pair of gum boots. I don't khow where I'd have been without Diana. They don't *really* think she had anything to do with it, do they? I mean, she *couldn't* have done! She arrived over here at about nine o'clock and she stayed till half-past ten. Michael told me they were keeping her at Maidstone for her own protection or something, but it all sounds quite insane to me."

"Well, I suppose the point is that whoever *did* do it seems to be trying to put the blame on Diana," Betty said. "Look at that peculiar telephone call. I agree it sounds insane either way. But you see, there's still just the possibility that Sir Henry had that dose of morphia much earlier—even before Diana went out. I don't mean, of course, that she—"

Sheila Henderson ran a distracted hand through her thick mop of hair.

"If only there was some way of tying down the time," she said. "Yes, I do see that. It's only the people like us who really *know* Diana who realise how impossible and absurd the whole idea is."

There was a rattle at the front door and the sound of letters falling on to the mat.

"Well, let's hope it gets cleared up soon," Sheila said gloomily "People keep writing me letters of condolence—I bet that was another batch arriving just now. As you know, none of the spicy details got into the London papers, and all most people have seen is a discreet little obituary notice in *The Times*, which gives no indication of what really happened; and then they write saying how much I must miss poor papa until it nearly makes me sick. If only they knew!"

She went into the hall and came back with a bunch of letters in her hand which she tossed distastefully on to the table.

"Go ahead and read them," Betty said. "We mustn't stay any longer anyway—we've left Sara watching the goldfish in the King's Arms, and we must get back and rescue her. Besides, I've still got a mass of shopping to do."

A yell from upstairs indicated the presence of Dick Henderson junior who had recognised Betty's voice and wished to be visited.

"Well, he's supposed to be having his rest," Sheila said doubtfully. "I won't come up, if you don't mind, because he always plays me up if I go in when he's resting. He may behave better with you."

"Is the baby up there too?"

"Yes—you will be careful not to wake him, won't you, Betty? Perhaps it would be a good thing if you popped in for a moment to see Dickie—it will stop him calling out."

"I'll only go in for a second. Lee, you must just come up and take a look at the baby. He's a honey."

We went upstairs and had a few words with Master Henderson and peered at the sleeping infant in the cot. He looked much like any other baby to me, but Betty found him entrancing. I had literally to drag her away.

When we came down, Sheila Henderson was standing in the middle of the sitting-room with an open letter in her hand.

"Betty," she exclaimed in a voice shaking with excitement, "*Betty*—come and listen to this! It's a letter from Blanche Fitzroy—you know, the girl I went to Switzerland with the winter before

I was married—she's seen about father's death in the paper—but *Betty!* She says she *saw* father the very night it happened!"

"*Saw* him?" Betty echoed sharply. "But where? When?"

"Well, listen! She says they've been away—only just seen the news—very distressed—yes, here it is! 'Jack and I were driving through Staple Green about a quarter-past nine on Tuesday night and we thought we'd drop in for a few minutes to see Lady Metcalfe and ask about you. Your father came to the door and he said everybody else was out. He asked us to come in, but as we were in a bit of a hurry we refused. It's awful to think that it must have been so soon after we saw him that he was taken ill, because we read in the paper that he had died the very next day. Was it a heart-attack or something? Poor you, what a terrible shock it must have been for you and Lady Metcalfe—'" Her voice trailed away.

"Quarter-past nine!" Betty repeated wonderingly. "Why, that means—"

"It means that it lets Diana out altogether!" Sheila gasped. "Because at a quarter-past nine she was *here*—here in this room! And if he was all right then the stuff *can't* have been in the whisky Diana left for him. That was hot and he drank it straight away. She saw him start on it. Oh, Betty, we must let the police know at *once*!"

"We certainly must," Betty agreed. "Do you think it would be possible to get hold of Hugh Gordon, Lee—now, on the telephone?"

"We can try," I said, and went out into the hall to ring up the Blue Boar. I hung on for several minutes in a frenzy of excitement listening to the bell ringing the other end, but eventually the grating voice of the unpleasant Mr. Willis informed me that Hugh was out, and he had no idea when he would be back.

"Damn," Sheila said. "We must let somebody know *quickly!* Oh, but isn't it wonderful news? I'll just get hold of Dick at the office—he'll know who to tell."

She rushed off into the hall.

"If only we'd known about this before," Betty said slowly, "poor Diana needn't have been taken off to Maidstone at all."

"You realise, don't you," I said to her, savouring my triumph, "that we *did* know? And that we told Hugh Gordon and he wouldn't listen to us?"

"You mean—?"

"Of course! John Wickham's mysterious car that drove up at a quarter-past nine and came back a few minutes later! Oh, *won't* I twist Hugh's tail for him about this!"

We left Sheila Henderson still on the telephone, babbling excitedly to her husband. She waved to us across the hall and promised to ring up later in the evening to tell us the latest developments.

Betty and I drove rapidly down the hill to the King's Arms and retrieved Sara, who had just begun to be bored with the goldfish and was inclined to be peevish at having been left so long.

"You were *years*," she complained, "and you *said* you'd only be a few minutes, and you *promised* we could go to Woolworth's."

"I suppose we may as well finish our shopping," Betty said. "Sheila's doing everything that can be done about letting people know and so on. Oh Lee, I'm so excited for Diana—it's the best news I've heard for weeks!"

I agreed, though for a fleeting moment I wondered if it really did let Diana Metcalfe out so completely. There wasn't any actual *proof* that Sir Henry had drunk his hot whisky straight away. Still, things were looking a lot brighter, and now that I had gathered a definite impression from Hugh that the end of the case was in sight, I didn't somehow think he would have spoken in the way he had if it had merely been a tightening of the noose round Diana's neck.

We finished our shopping, including the promised visit to Woolworth's, as rapidly as possible. I was longing to get home to crow over Hugh about the vindication of John Wickham—preferably before he heard about it from any other source—and Betty was equally anxious to spread the glad tidings to Howard. We rushed about feverishly buying toys and odd boxes of handkerchiefs and bottles of bath-salts which would "come in handy for somebody," and it wasn't until we were in the car and half-way back to Staple Green that I remembered that I had still got nothing for Aunt Adelaide who was, as far as I was concerned, the main object of the exercise. However, by that time I was really past caring much—even about Aunt Adelaide. After all, she was Bill's aunt, not mine, and I resolved to send him a telegram in the morning asking him to do something about her on his way through London on Christmas Eve.

I asked Betty to drop me out on the green, and I rushed like a tornado up the steps of the Blue Boar to find out if Hugh had returned. He hadn't; and the look which Mr. Willis gave me was unforgivably arch and knowing. I explained stiffly that I had an important message for Detective-Inspector Gordon, and requested that he should be asked to come straight down to the Tithe Barn the second he came in.

"And supposing he's late, miss?" Mr. Willis insisted. "Do you still want him to come down and see you—whatever the time?"

"Yes, please," I said shortly. "*Whatever* the time. And if everybody's gone to bed by then, I'd be grateful if you'd leave him a note."

I walked off, leaving Hugh's reputation, as well as my own, in shreds.

I found Howard and Betty having tea. They had, it seemed, been backwards and forwards and sideways round this new aspect of the case and were agreed that if at this point Diana wasn't released from Maidstone Gaol without a stain on her character, then British justice was a farce, and you might as well have a Communist government and be done with it.

"And I'll tell you another thing," said Howard. "As well as letting out Diana, it definitely lets out both the Qualtroughs. Didn't you say, Lee, that they were listening to some high-brow concert from quarter-past nine onwards and then playing chess or something until they went to bed?"

"Yes," I said. "They were."

So bang went any idea I might still be harbouring about an earlier excursion up to Oakhurst on the part of either of them—risk or no risk. No, the Qualtroughs were definitely cleared. And just who did this new bit of evidence leave still in the arena?

Of the whole list of possible suspects, we had now eliminated Diana Metcalfe and the two Qualtroughs. Last night, unknown to anyone else, Hugh and I had written off Michael Metcalfe and Sonia Phillips. Who was left?

Betty appeared to be thinking along the same lines.

"It doesn't leave many possibilities," she said frowning. "There's only Michael—and I mean, well, after all!—and Phillips."

It was in her face that she was for the first time seriously considering the fact that she had given a party in her own house in order to introduce her neighbours to a murderess.

Howard put down a plate of scones with a bang.

"The whole thing's crazy," he said flatly. "Of course Michael and John are out of the question—I mean, even if either of them got around to poisoning the old man, which I refuse to believe for a second, they are just about the last two people on this earth who would ever plant evidence to incriminate Diana. They both adore her. And as for Mrs. Phillips—"

The trouble was that he broke down there. It was all very well to say: "And as for Mrs. Phillips—" and let the whole thing trail off into an eloquent exclamation mark of incredulity. But it wasn't proof. Howard shuffled uneasily in his chair, Betty looked at him with faintly raised eyebrows, and I longed to help him out. I knew just as well as he did—in fact, far better—that it *wasn't* Mrs. Phillips. I ached to say so. For an awful moment I nearly broke my promise to Hugh altogether and told them both about the previous evening at her house. After all, what harm could it possibly do? And then I managed to bite it back.

It was just as crazy as Howard said. It was the old Sherlock Holmes one about eliminating the impossible and then whatever remained, however improbable, was the answer.

And the only person who remained was John Wickham.

I was in a very broody mood all through dinner. In fact, we all were. Once the original excitement of Diana's vindication had worn off, it left such a very slender field for speculation. Somehow I couldn't see John Wickham as a murderer. Still less could I see him, as Howard had said, framing Diana. The whole thing was nonsense. It was all *wrong*.

At about half-past ten we were sitting in the drawing-room pretending to listen to the wireless. I had decided it was quite obvious that Hugh wasn't coming. He either hadn't got my message, or else he'd ignored it. In either case I felt I might as well go to bed. I was just gathering up my impedimenta and preparing to say goodnight when he turned up.

He said: "I got your message and came straight down. I take it it was about the letter to Sheila Henderson?"

I was disappointed that he had already heard the great news which I had looked forward to telling him myself, so I admitted rather sullenly that it was. I added that it merely bore out what he would already have known, had he taken the trouble to follow up the information he'd been given, and asked what he proposed to do about it.

"All right," he said. "You win. I never believed in that car. But I did tell Spragg to chase it up in case, and the results of his chasing were completely negative. I realise I shall never live this down. However, you will be glad to know that we shall now be able to put it around that Lady Metcalfe is no longer under suspicion. Therefore, there will presumably be no further strewing of false clues either. All the same—"

I didn't bother to listen to "all the same." It was just Hugh being cautious again. What I really wanted to know was where we went from there. I wanted him to follow up the reasoning of the thing, and to ask him about John Wickham. But, since for some reason he still didn't seem inclined to discuss our evening with Michael Metcalfe and Sonia Phillips, there was nothing much I could do about it. It cramped my style badly.

Howard produced whisky, and Betty and I told Hugh about our day in Tunbridge Wells and my failure to achieve a suitable offering for Aunt Adelaide. He listened politely, but I couldn't really feel that his attention was what you might call gripped.

"Heavens!" Betty said suddenly. "In all the excitement I completely forgot to take those records round to Ann. Oh well, I suppose it doesn't matter tonight. Lee, do remind me in the morning."

"Ann isn't there tonight anyway," Howard put in. "I met old Qualtrough in the village this afternoon and he said Ann was going over to Mayfield on some party. Michael was supposed to be taking her, and then at the last minute he ratted. He lent her Diana's Austin to drive herself over there, but I gather Ann was a shade peevish."

As well she might be, I reflected, considering the most likely reason for Michael's "ratting." It was really rather naughty of Hugh to have forbidden Michael to tell Ann the truth about Sonia Phillips until such time as it was convenient to have the information about her alibi made public. Ann was going to be terribly hurt when she found out, and the longer Michael was compelled to keep up the deception the worse it was going to be for her. I felt suddenly very sorry for Ann, driving forlornly over to a lonely party in Mayfield, in order that Michael might be free to spend the evening with Sonia.

The telephone rang suddenly in the hall.

"I expect that will be Sheila Henderson," Betty remarked. "She said she'd ring up."

She went into the hall, and we heard her say: "Hullo!" She gave a startled gasp. Then she said: "Oh God, how awful! Hold on a minute—I'll get Howard."

She came back with a very white face.

"That was Michael," she said, "speaking from Sonia Phillips' house. He says he rang her up about half-an-hour ago, and got no reply. So he drove over from Oakhurst to see if she was all right—I don't know why he should have been in such a fuss—I couldn't make any sense of that part. But then when he got there, he says he found her lying unconscious on the floor—she's making the most terrible gasping noises, and he thinks she's dying. Howard, will you please go over at once?"

Howard was half-way to the door when Hugh Gordon leapt to his feet.

"I'm coming with you," he said. "We'll go in my car—it's faster. *Hell,* what a fool I am! I ought to have thought of this happening."

The front door slammed and they were gone.

XIX

WE REGRET TO ANNOUNCE THE DEATH

"IT WAS EXACTLY A WEEK AGO TODAY," BETTY SAID AT BREAKfast next morning, "that Howard had been called out late to see Sir Henry and we were sitting here waiting for news. And now we're doing exactly the same thing about Sonia Phillips. Lee, it absolutely gives me the creeps. Somebody in this place must have gone *mad.*"

"I suppose any murderer's mad in a way," I said, gloomily helping myself to marmalade. "Did Howard say it was morphia again?"

"He thinks so. The symptoms were the same. But this time he says there's a much better chance of recovery, because they treated her at once for poisoning—and anyway, if it was morphia, Howard says she's been having regular injections for some time, and that's given her a tolerance. It would take much more to kill her than it would Sir Henry."

"And if it was the same tube of stuff there can't have been many grains left," I reminded her. "What I can't make out is why anybody should *want* to murder Sonia Phillips. She wasn't a public menace like Sir Henry, and—"

Howard came into the dining-room, heavy-eyed from lack of sleep. In silence he helped himself to a kipper from the sideboard and sat down at the end of the table.

"Did you gather," I asked him, "what Hugh Gordon meant

last night when he said he ought to have thought of something happening to Mrs. Phillips?"

"Don't ask me," Howard said, buttering a piece of toast. "He made a number of cryptic remarks, but I was only the poor blasted stooge who rushed the patient to hospital. Nobody tells me anything. I left Gordon there with Michael and a character called Spragg, who turned up on a motor-bike just before the ambulance arrived. Michael wanted to come along to the hospital. He was behaving like a madman. I suppose I'm very much behind the times, but I understood that he was by way of being engaged to Ann Qualtrough; and there he was, moaning away like a hysterical schoolboy, and saying that if Sonia Phillips died he was going to shoot himself and Lord knows what else. Do I take it that it's all off with Ann?"

"If it is, I'm sure Ann doesn't realise it," Betty said. She turned suddenly to me. "Do *you* know anything about this, Lee?" she demanded accusingly. "You went round there with Hugh Gordon the night before last. What *is* all this about Michael?"

There really seemed no point in holding out any longer on this score, since Michael's behaviour had made the whole thing so patently obvious.

"I think Michael's fallen rather heavily for Mrs. Phillips," I mumbled. "But I don't think Ann knows yet, so Hugh said I'd better not mention it."

This was not strictly true, since the object of not mentioning it was that it should not get around that Michael and Sonia had cancelled each other out as suspects for the night of Sir Henry's seizure. However, it seemed to satisfy Betty all right, so I left it rather thankfully at that.

"Well, I must say I call that pretty tough on Ann," was all she said. "What *sort* of cryptic remarks did Hugh Gordon make, Howard? Does he think he knows who did this to Mrs. Phillips?"

"I tell you," Howard snapped, wrestling with the bones of his kipper, "he didn't confide in me at all. In any case I was far too busy with the patient to begin playing games of 'whodunit' with the police. Oh yes, I do remember one thing. There was an empty glass which looked as if it had had milk in it that he and Michael got very excited about."

"Yes," I said. "She always had a glass of milk before she went to bed. She said you'd told her to."

"I believe I did, now you mention it. Well, anyway, the last I saw was the Spragg character picking it up with a handkerchief wrapped round his hand, so I suppose it was about to be carted off as Exhibit 'A'. And let's hope to God this is the last of that damned morph. tart. If this wholesale pogrom goes on much longer I shan't have a single patient left. Half of them will have been hanged for doing in the other half, and Betty and I shall be selling matches in Half Moon Street."

The telephone rang.

"Shall I go?" Betty asked quickly.

"No, don't bother," Howard said, pushing away his kipper. "I'm expecting a call from the hospital."

He was away for several minutes and when he returned he was looking both puzzled and angry.

"Was it from the hospital about Mrs. Phillips?" Betty said. "How is she?"

"It was about Mrs. Phillips," Howard replied deliberately, "but it wasn't from the hospital. It was from Colonel Wilbraham who is sorry to inform me that my patient Mrs. Phillips died early this morning, and that the official verdict is that she committed suicide."

"*What?*" Betty and I shrieked together.

"You may well say 'What?'" Howard agreed. "There's something extremely fishy going on about this case, and I'm not satisfied. That girl was doing well when I left her last night, and in any case why didn't the hospital—"

"Yes, *why* Colonel Wilbraham?" Betty put in. "I mean, surely—"

"He's on his way here now," Howard grunted. "He said he particularly wanted to explain the situation before I went out. I should damn well say it needs explaining. What the hell—"

"But you said she was going to *recover*," Betty protested. "And—surely—suicide?"

Howard put down his coffee cup and rose from the table.

"I'm going to ring the hospital," he said suddenly.

This time he was away even longer. When he came back his face was set in grim lines of disapproval. All he would say was: "I don't want to talk about it now."

We heard a car drive up, and Howard went out to meet the Chief Constable. They remained closeted in the study for close on half an hour.

Betty and I stacked up the breakfast things in depressed silence. I was thinking about Michael Metcalfe and wondering how he would take the news of Sonia's death. Would he really shoot himself? They said people who talked about committing suicide never did it, and I hoped sincerely that they were right. Otherwise the death roll in Staple Green was shortly going to compare unfavourably with Elsinore after the last act of *Hamlet*.

"Howard *said* she would be all right," Betty muttered, gathering up the unused silver. "He never expected her to die. Lee, do you believe she committed suicide? I don't."

Frankly I didn't, but as I had no alternative solution to offer there didn't seem much point in going on about it.

I was up in my bedroom fiddling with a nail file when Howard's voice from the hall below called out: "Lee, can you come down a minute?"

I took the stairs two at a time. Betty was just coming along the passage from the kitchen, and Howard seized her by the arm and hustled us both into the drawing-room in a conspiratorial manner.

"Look," he said abruptly. "I told Wilbraham I insisted on telling you two the truth about this business. I simply couldn't disapprove of the whole thing more—it's unprofessional, and I'm dead against the whole idea. However, he agreed that I'd better tell you in case either of you were asked any questions about Sonia Phillips by anyone in the village, and let it out that I'd told you last night that we expected her to recover."

"Darling, what *is* all this?" Betty said desperately. "Of course you wouldn't have said that unless—"

"Mrs. Phillips isn't dead at all," Howard interrupted. "This, I gather, is some dark plot on the part of Lee's boy-friend Hugh Gordon, to put people off their guards or something. I don't know which people—or what they're to be off their guards about. It all sounds damn silly to me. I told Wilbraham that I refused to be a party to anything so ridiculous, but it was no good. He's all over the idea; and it appears that he's already got round the hospital authorities and is prepared to square any legal consequences which might arise from issuing a false statement. So there's nothing to do but accept his ruling. It's going to be allowed to get round that Mrs. Phillips died last night. And neither of you must let it out to a single solitary soul that the whole thing's a plant."

"But I can't see the *point*—" Betty began.

"We aren't *asked* to see any point," Howard said wearily. "We're just asked to keep up this jolly little deception until such time as Sonia Phillips is fit to make a statement. I shouldn't think that would be before tomorrow. I'm going along to see her after surgery. And in the meanwhile—"

"It's a wicked trick to play on Michael," I said. "He'll be absolutely beside himself if he's told she committed suicide."

"It's a much wickeder trick to play on a poor blasted G.P. with a professional reputation to keep up," Howard said tartly. "I shall tell Hugh Gordon just exactly what I think of this little scheme the next time I see him."

He went out, muttering angrily, and practically slammed the door.

"Well—!" said Betty.

She returned to her huddle with Mrs. Padgett and I continued to sit for some minutes staring blankly out of the window.

Hugh came round about half-past eleven. He was looking smug and pleased with himself; and did not look noticably less so when I had given him Howard's opinion of his behaviour, and added a few crisp comments of my own.

"And now," I concluded crossly, "I suppose you're going to tell me that everything's going simply splendidly and the case is practically over; and when I ask you what on earth you're talking about, you'll tell me to use my intelligence. Well, I haven't *got* any intelligence. I'm completely at sea and quite willing to admit it. Now, have you come round here to torment me with a lot more idiotic conundrums, or are you going to put me out of my misery by telling me what really happened?"

"Not either, actually," Hugh said with his maddening smile. "Though teasing you is the greatest fun I know—you're no idea what heaven you are when you're in a rage! No. What I really came for was to ask Betty if I might use her drawing-room this evening for a little experiment."

"What sort of experiment?" I asked suspiciously.

"I want to test a theory I've got about this case."

"Theories," I replied crushingly, "are all very well for comic little amateurs like me. Scotland Yard officials have to produce *proofs*—and that's exactly what you told me yourself you couldn't do. Is your experiment going to prove anything?"

"I hope so. That's why I want to make it."

"Listen," I said. "Just for one moment you're going to do something *my* way. I'm tired of playing twenty questions with myself and getting all the wrong answers. You told me to use my intelligence and I'm prepared to try—provided you tell me whether I'm working on the correct premises."

"That seems fair enough. What d'you want me to tell you? No leading questions, mind—just plain 'yes' or 'no'."

"Am I right in assuming that both these crimes—Sir Henry and the attempt on Sonia—were committed by the same person?"

"I think so, yes."

"And that you definitely agreed the night before last that Michael and Sonia were out of it?"

"I should be very surprised if it turned out to be either of them."

"I don't call that a plain 'yes' or 'no'. Do you also agree that since Sir Henry was seen alive by this friend of Sheila Henderson's at quarter-past nine that night, therefore anyone who has an unassailable alibi *after* nine o'clock—that is, Diana and the Qualtroughs—are also out of it?"

"I should never attempt to assail the unassailable."

"Don't quibble! Do you agree?"

"Yes, I think that's a reasonable enough assumption."

"Then why on earth," I demanded indignantly, "couldn't you say straight away that it was John Wickham? He's the only person left."

Hugh raised his eyebrows. "Is he?" he asked innocently.

"Oh, good heavens," I exclaimed in exasperation. "No—I suppose it could have been Mrs. Prendergast or Norah Wright. Or—or Mr. Willis from the Blue Boar. Or the Archangel Gabriel with a fiery sword dishing out retribution from Heaven. I think you're perfectly beastly, and I'm going upstairs now to help Robin decorate the nursery. *Good* morning!"

I strode towards the door. As he leaped forward to open it for me, Hugh said: "You will ask Betty if I may do my experiment here, won't you? And, by the way, thank her for the clue she gave me last night. It was most helpful."

"Clue?" I repeated, swinging round and glaring at him. "What clue?"

"Oh, just something she said," Hugh replied airily. "Quite a casual remark. You were there at the time. It made me think of a way I might be able to prove my theory—and so far it's worked out rather promisingly."

I slammed the drawing-room door and went upstairs.

XX

MR. GORDON EXPERIMENTS

I SPENT THE WHOLE AFTERNOON RESTLESSLY FIDGETING ABOUT, unable to concentrate on anything. Hugh's ridiculous experiment was due to take place some time after tea. At a quarter to six he arrived, full of importance, and proceeded to shoo Betty and me out of the drawing-room with a mysterious smile which I found irritating beyond endurance.

"Are you going to move all the furniture about?" Betty asked apprehensively. "Because the leg of that piecrust table isn't very safe. And do be careful of the china cabinet."

"I will be very careful," Hugh promised. "And I don't want to move much furniture."

"Is your experiment going to take very long?" Betty said, hovering by the door. "Mr. Churchill's speaking on the wireless at half-past six, and I don't want to miss him."

"I'll have finished long before that," Hugh assured her. "I'll let you know when I'm ready."

Betty and I went up to the nursery.

"I suppose he knows what he's trying to do," Betty remarked dubiously as we walked up the stairs. "But I can't imagine what he thinks he's going to prove in my drawing-room."

"Hugh loves making childish mysteries," I said. "He really ought to be up here wearing rompers and playing trains with Robin. He's simply never grown up—that's his trouble."

We were in the middle of a game of Beggar-my-Neighbour with Sara, when Hugh's voice from the hall came floating up to us: "You can come down now!"

I had already been beggared, so I left Betty fighting it out with Sara and went downstairs. I entered the drawing-room with a certain amount of foreboding and looked suspiciously round the room to see what Hugh had been up to. Apart from the position of the screen, which had been moved from its usual place behind the sofa and put over on the other side, between the radiogram and the china cabinet, I could see nothing different.

"You can sit down," Hugh said. "No tin-tacks on the chairs, or funny jokes of that kind."

"You surprise me," I said coldly, going over to the sofa.

Hugh glanced at the clock on the mantelpiece.

"Oh, bother," he exclaimed irritably. "I hadn't realised it was so late. We'll have to postpone my experiment for a few minutes if Betty wants to hear Mr. Churchill. It's just on half-past six."

I hadn't realised it was so late, either. I went into the hall and called to Betty to hurry or she would miss the beginning of the speech.

Hugh went over and switched on the wireless, and Betty came running down the stairs just as the clock struck.

"I've turned it on," Hugh said as she came into the room. "It's the Home Service, isn't it?"

Betty glanced at *The Radio Times* on the arm of the chair beside her. "Yes," she said. She added quickly: "I'm sorry to be a nuisance and interfere with whatever it is you're doing in here, but I was rather anxious to hear Winnie. Lee, will you make a long arm to that cupboard and get the drinks out?"

I shuffled off the edge of the sofa.

"Which d'you want?" I asked. "The gin or the sherry?"

"Sssh!" hissed Hugh, as the familiar pungent tones of the Prime Minister suddenly filled the room.

"When I said in the House of Commons the other day," announced the voice trenchantly, "that I thought it improbable that the enemy's air attack in September could be more than three times as great as it was in August—"

"But what on *earth*—?" began Betty, bewildered. "The *enemy's air* attack?"

"You will understand," continued the voice gravely, "that whenever the weather is favourable, waves of German bombers protected by fighters—often three or four hundred at a time—surge over this island—"

"German bombers?" I echoed stupidly. "But that's one of his famous war speeches—I'm sure I remember it! That's what he said at the beginning of the raids in the autumn of 1940. Hugh, has he gone *mad*, or—"

There was a sharp click as Hugh turned off the machine and stepped smiling from behind the screen.

"Calm yourself," he said to me. "And don't worry. Mr. Churchill hasn't gone mad. You're quite right—that was, of course, the beginning of the 'Every Man to His Post' speech which was, as you say, broadcast in September, 1940. It was the only record of his voice I could get in Tunbridge Wells. But if you want to hear what he's going to say tonight you'll have to wait a little longer, because his speech isn't due for another ten minutes."

"But he's speaking at half-past six," I protested. "And now it's twenty-five to seven. Oh, I *see*!"

Betty was still looking extremely puzzled.

"D'you mean you've altered the clock?" she asked Hugh slowly. "But the hall clock's the same. It struck just as I came down. Have you altered both of them? Why? What *is* all this?"

"It's my little experiment," Hugh explained apologetically. "I just wanted to see if the theory I'd formed about this case would stand up to a practical test. And I think it would. This isn't really a fair trial, because you spotted the substitution of the gramophone record at once by the anachronistic mention of enemy air raids and German bombers. You knew you couldn't really be hearing him say that, so there must be a catch somewhere. But suppose instead of talking about the last war, Mr. Churchill had said the sort of thing about the current situation which you were expecting to hear him say tonight? You wouldn't have questioned the voice or the time or anything, would you? And if you'd been asked about it later, you'd be prepared to swear that at half-past six this evening you were sitting in your drawing-room listening to a speech on the wireless, wouldn't you?"

"Yes," Betty agreed after a moment's hesitation. "Yes, I would."

"And if somebody came to you tomorrow and said to you that at six-thirty precisely they'd seen Liane sneaking down the back stairs of the Blue Boar, you'd refuse to believe them, because you'd be able to swear positively that at half-past six she was sitting here in this room with you?"

"Yes," said Betty again.

Hugh walked across the room and lit a cigarette. He threw the match into the fire place with a slight flourish and dropped into the big wing chair.

"Oh, my God!" I exclaimed. "I see what you're getting at."

Hugh nodded grimly.

"It's the only possible way it could have been done," he said. "Picture the same situation that I've created here tonight. Only instead of a political broadcast, substitute a gramophone record of a Mozart violin concerto—a concerto which had been advertised in *The Radio Times* for nine-fifteen. And instead of moving the clocks forward a quarter of an hour as I've just done, move them back an hour while your witness is asleep. And there you've got Ann Qualtrough's unassailable alibi."

Betty made no reply. There was a stunned expression on her face. In her heart she knew Hugh was right, and yet she simply couldn't bring herself to believe it yet.

"I'm just trying to work it out," I said. "The concert Mr. Qualtrough thought he was hearing at nine-fifteen was really a gramophone record put on by Ann at ten-fifteen? You mean that instead of having been asleep for twenty minutes, as he thought, it was really an hour and twenty minutes?"

"Yes. Of course, I don't know to a minute how far Ann altered the clocks. But I should estimate about an hour. She probably reached Oakhurst at about half-past nine by the real time—and altered the clocks in the study and her father's bedroom when she returned. She could have changed them back again any time during the night so that they'd be right in the morning. I've seen their sitting-room. The wireless is in an alcove at the far end, it's practically invisible from the chair Mr. Qualtrough usually sat in. It's an old-fashioned set, run off a battery because they haven't any electric light, and for playing records they use a turn-table with a pick-up. It was obviously impossible to play the whole concerto without giving the show away by the break between the records, so the first movement had to be faded out with the volume control switch and explained as battery failure. That sort of thing had probably happened before. The old man wouldn't question it. And from his chair he couldn't see what Ann was doing with the switch and the turn-table. It's all perfectly simple when you work it out. I ought to have got on to it long ago."

Betty was still looking dazed. She seemed to be trying to take in the implications of what Hugh was saying, but it was clearly a very painful effort.

"But—but—" she stammered, seizing on what struck me even as she spoke as one of the salient weaknesses of Hugh's case: "Even if Ann did what you say—and I find it almost too much to believe that she *could*—even then, how could she possibly rely on her father staying asleep all that time while she went up to Oakhurst? I mean, suppose he'd woken up from his nap a few minutes earlier—suppose he'd looked for her and found she wasn't in the house? It would have ruined her alibi and finished the whole plan."

"Yes," I agreed. "I don't see how she got round that risk, either, Hugh. I think your reconstruction must be right. But Ann did take a tremendous chance in relying on Mr. Qualtrough not waking up until after she'd got back."

"Not such a chance, really," Hugh said. "I think you've forgotten those useful morphia tablets. You may remember that Mr. Qualtrough said he felt very sleepy directly after dinner. He didn't wake up until Ann shook him to know if he wanted another cup of coffee. (That was a clever touch on her part—remembering to heat it up again in case he accepted.) So naturally, he'd *think* he'd only been asleep for a few minutes. Especially when he saw the carriage clock which confirmed it. When he was telling me the story he mentioned the fact that he'd felt sleepy ever since dinner and that was why he went to bed earlier than usual."

"Yes, he told me that, too," I said. "I suppose Ann only gave him quite a small dose—about one tablet."

Betty suddenly burst into uncontrollable tears.

"It's too *horrible*!" she sobbed. "I can't bear to think about it. A girl we've known ever since she was a child. And then—to me this is almost the worst part of it—and *then* to think she tried to put the blame on Diana. *Diana*—who's always been so sweet to her!"

"I'm afraid that was on the principle of trying to kill two birds with one stone," Hugh said. "Lady Metcalfe admitted to me that—although she would never have taken any active steps in the matter because she thought it was none of her business—she wasn't too keen on Michael marrying Ann. She thought Ann wasn't the right person for him. It wasn't any absurd prejudice about the stage, as it was with Sir Henry. It was simply a feeling she had. I think Ann sensed that. And even apart from that aspect, her main object in marrying Michael wasn't just for the sake of his blue eyes. Michael stood to inherit quite a lot of money from his father—and a still greater amount if his step-mother happened to die as well. Ann Qualtrough is a very shrewd young woman. She wanted Michael and Michael's money. Sir Henry stood in the way of that ambition. And then there was another incentive. She had to act quickly before Michael slipped out of her grasp altogether. I'm sure she saw some time ago the way things were going between Michael and Sonia Phillips. I think she must have made up her mind on the night of that cocktail party here, and that was when she stole the morphine tablets out of Howard Sandys' bag. Do you recollect any little incident that night, Liane, which might have indicated to Ann that Michael's interest in her was waning at all?"

As if she were still sitting there, I suddenly saw the expression on Ann's face which I had intercepted, reflected in the looking glass on the wall—her expression while she was watching Michael, whose eyes were fixed on Sonia Phillips. I shivered suddenly.

"Yes," I said. "Michael was taking rather a lot of notice of Mrs. Phillips, and Ann didn't like it."

Hugh nodded slowly.

"I thought so," he said. "Well then, even so, I imagine she still hoped she could get Michael back—and laid her plans accordingly. Michael had told her he was going to London on that Tuesday night. She knew—as everybody in the village knew—that Tuesday was the Metcalfes' staff's night out. That meant the only person she had to get out of the way was Lady Metcalfe. Hence the fake telephone call the night before. Nobody could have made that call more easily than Ann. Little Hodges is on the green—a few yards away from the village call box. She could have watched from the front window until she saw the lights of Lady Metcalfe's car coming down the drive on her way to the Women's Institute meeting, which everyone knew began at eight o'clock, and then slipped out and made the call—"

"But why try to put that on Diana too?"

"I don't know—I can only guess. There was a famous murder trial some years ago called the Wallace case. That hinged on a telephone call just like this one. She may have read about it. Or it may have been quite fortuitous. I can't tell you the answer to that, Liane. But I'm sure it was all part of the plan. Then, after that, all she had to do was to arrange the alibi. It was easy to look up the evening's programme and find something her father would be sure to want to listen to. She slipped up badly there and became careless. She went over to Tunbridge Wells by bus in the morning and bought a record of the first movement of that Mozart concerto. I've checked that at the shop. I suppose at the time she thought it wouldn't matter—that nobody would ever connect it up. She bought a lot of records at that shop, and it was sheer bad luck, really, that anyone put two and two together in that direction."

Hugh expelled a slow cloud of smoke towards the ceiling.

"And then," he went on reflectively, "things started going wrong for her. She must have found out something about Michael's visits to Sonia Phillips. Perhaps she'd always been suspicious. Michael became off-hand with her; he began cutting her dates and making excuses not to see her. It must have been a very bitter moment for Ann when she realised that even when you've taken the powers of life and death into your own hands, you still can't control a small independent organ like somebody else's heart. She'd murdered Michael's father and done her best to get his step-mother hanged. And, after all that, it wasn't any good, because Michael upset everything by falling in love with another woman. I could almost feel sorry for Ann in the moment when she had to face that."

"Was that when she decided to murder Sonia too?"

"Well, I imagine by that time she was desperate. She'd nothing to lose by it, and she'd gone so far by then that there was nothing left but to go on. She still had some of the morphia tablets left—not, as it turned out, enough—but she had to risk that. She knew there wouldn't be a chance to steal any more. Howard kept his bag locked, and Norah Wright was watching the poison cupboard like a lynx. It probably wasn't difficult to get Michael to back out of the party at Mayfield. He would be only too keen to grasp at any excuse not to go—and it would never occur to him that it was Ann who had put the idea into his head. He's probably still feeling guilty about letting her down. Lending her Lady Metcalfe's car to drive herself over would have been a sort of sop to his conscience, I suppose. I don't know what excuse she made for calling on Mrs. Phillips—if Michael had been there, as he well might have been, it would have upset her apple-cart a little. But I think it would only have postponed the attack. She'd made up her mind by that time that Sonia Phillips had to go. So she invented some reason for calling—and there was Sonia alone, and there was the convenient glass of hot milk."

Hugh leaned back in his chair and sighed.

"I haven't yet made enquiries over at Mayfield," he said. "But my guess is that we'll find Ann had engine trouble on the way and arrived very late at that party."

The logs in the fireplace hissed and crackled. The clock on the mantelshelf ticked busily. There was a long silence.

"What was the clue?" I asked. "The one you said Betty had given you?"

"Gramophone records. She mentioned having forgotten to take some across to Ann. That set something working in my brain. I'd been sure for some time that it must be Ann. She was the obvious person. But I still couldn't quite see my way round that cast-iron alibi supplied by her father, who I was certain was perfectly genuine and sincere. Then everything clicked, and I saw how it could have been done. I went over to the shop in Tunbridge Wells this morning—confirmed that Ann had bought that Mozart record last Tuesday week—and at the same time made my own little purchase of Mr. Churchill's speech. D'you remember, Liane, mentioning yesterday that you and Betty wanted to listen to him when he spoke tonight? Well, that gave me the idea—and you saw for yourself how it worked."

I sat there, sorting out my ideas slowly.

"The thing which must have been difficult for Ann," I said, "was to think up a convincing excuse for getting inside Oakhurst at all that night. Sir Henry didn't approve of her—they'd had a row—and I'm very surprised that he let her come in and potter round his study making him hot drinks and everything."

"Well, it's pure guess work on my part," Hugh replied. "But I don't think that need have presented an insuperable difficulty. You remember that Sir Henry's greatest weakness was vanity—and the thing he was vainest about was his china collection. Ann's father was an expert, who had recently mortally offended Sir Henry by suggesting that his precious *famille rose* bowl was nothing but a French reproduction. (Oh, yes—Mr. Qualtrough told me all about that little episode!) If I'd been Ann I think I should have made that the excuse for my visit. I'd have expressed great interest and asked to see the thing—and perhaps implied that my father might have been mistaken, and soothed the old man down that way. He would have trotted off to fetch it, and then I daresay Ann suggested another little whisky for his cold. I should think that's where the hot water jug came in—the morphine would have dissolved more quickly in hot water. You've got to remember that Ann's an actress—and a very clever one. Playing up to an old man's vanity and putting on an 'aren't-you-wonderful' act to get round him must have been one of the least of her worries."

"There was the book, too," I said thoughtfully. "The one on border lilies. She could have pretended she'd come up to borrow that for her father, or something."

Hugh nodded appreciatively.

"Yes, I'd forgotten the book," he said. "I expect that was the original excuse. Then Ann could have got on to the subject of china later. And no doubt it was she who switched on the wireless before she left—probably with some idea of setting the time for shortly after nine when her alibi could be confirmed. She must have spent about half an hour up at Oakhurst, waiting for the old man to doze off. Plenty of time to wipe off fingerprints and then slip upstairs to hide the morphia tube in Diana Metcalfe's bathroom in case—"

Betty sat up resolutely and thrust her handkerchief, now a small damp bundle, back into her bag. She turned to regard Hugh with unwilling respect in her eyes.

"Don't go on," she said miserably. "I'm sure you're right. It all ties up. But—it's so—so *shattering* to think—"

"I suppose," I said rather hurriedly to Hugh, "that you're relying on Sonia Phillips' statement for your evidence? I mean, a reconstruction like this is all very well to satisfy one's own mind, but it could hardly be called *evidence.*"

There was the sound of the front door bursting open.

"As a matter of fact," Hugh said, "we have quite a lot of evidence. Various things like—"

"Who's talking about evidence?" exclaimed a gay voice from the hall. "Darling, can I come in?"

Ann Qualtrough pushed open the drawing-room door and stood framed on the threshold. Her eyes were dancing with excitement, and her cheeks were flushed with colour. Her fair hair gleamed in the reflected light from the hall lamp, and she looked extremely pretty.

She hesitated at the sight of Hugh.

"Oh, I'm so sorry, darling," she apologised to Betty. "I didn't realise you had company! Mr. Gordon—you're just the person I've been aching to get hold of! *Do* tell us the low-down about this riveting sensation of Sonia Phillips having committed suicide. I always *said* she was sinister, didn't I, and how right I was! I suppose it's practically as good as a confession, isn't it? I mean—"

Hugh Gordon regarded her steadily for a moment. Before his unwavering gaze Ann's lashes fluttered down over her eyes. The room was very still.

"I'm afraid you've been misled," he said quietly.

Ann's hand flew to her mouth.

"What—what exactly d'you mean?" she asked uncertainly.

"Mrs. Phillips hasn't committed suicide. She isn't dead. She's in hospital at Tunbridge Wells and she's very much better. We're hoping she'll be fit enough to make a statement tomorrow."

Betty's sherry glass fell from her hand and crashed with a little tinkle of broken glass on to the floor.

And then Ann screamed.

XXI

THE HOLLY AND THE IVY

HOWARD ROSE FROM A CROUCHING POSITION ON THE NURSery floor and straightened his back. Around him was strewn a vast quantity of brown paper and string.

"It's no good," he said flatly. "The thing's impossible."

"You aren't doing it properly," Betty said. "You've got to get that big piece of paper round the saddle and tie it, and *then* wrap another bit round the handlebars. Then the first bit won't slip."

"I can't see that there's any need to wrap it up at all," Howard grumbled. "After all, it isn't a surprise. Sara's known since September that we were giving her a bicycle, so—"

"Of course it must be wrapped up," Betty said inexorably. "Undoing your presents is half the fun. Here, give it to me!"

It was half-past nine on the night before Christmas Eve. The children were in bed and we were all three wrestling with last minute wrapping-up of presents. The nursery was gay with holly and tinsel and paper-chains and a small Christmas tree with crackers and candles stood on the table in front of the window. Bill was coming down in time for lunch the next day, and I was expecting Hugh Gordon to look in some time during the evening to say goodbye. He was going back to London first thing in the morning.

I was glancing at my watch for the twentieth time since dinner when I heard his step in the hall below.

"I'll go down," I said quickly to Betty, who was struggling with the back wheel of Sara's bicycle. "Will you put this cowboy outfit of Robin's in the cupboard with the other parcels?"

"Give Gordon a drink," Howard said, "and say we'll be down in a minute. Why they have to make children's toys these ghastly shapes I don't know. Betty, will you look at this submarine? It doesn't matter *how* I shove the paper round it the conning tower sticks out of the top every time. Next year they're getting nothing but dominoes and jigsaw puzzles in nice flat boxes."

Hugh was standing on the hearth rug in the drawing-room with his back to the fire. He turned and smiled crookedly as I came in.

"You look dead tired," I said. "For heaven's sake sit down. Howard said I was to give you a drink. They're doing up the children's Christmas presents in the nursery and they'll be down in a minute."

"Thanks," Hugh said. "Yes. I could use a drink. I've just been to see Qualtrough."

There was a rather tense pause.

"He tells me," Hugh went on, "that he's known for some time that he's suffering from an inoperable carcinoma. He didn't consult Howard because he didn't want anyone here to know about it. The London specialist gave him till January or February. From the look of him tonight I'd say he won't live to see the New Year in."

"There aren't any words," I said. "You can't say you're 'sorry' for a person like Mr. Qualtrough. I suppose Ann never knew about the carcinoma."

"No—and he won't have her told now. The only other person who knows is Diana Metcalfe. She's taking him up to Oakhurst tomorrow. He's going to spend Christmas with her and Michael—and I should think it's very unlikely he'll ever leave the house again."

"In a way," I said slowly, "I suppose it's just as well. You mean you think he'll die before—before—"

"Yes. He's reserved Atkinson for Ann's defence. If anyone in the world could get her off, Atkinson's the man. But of course the only chance is to plead insanity. Ann went to bits completely in the end, you know. She was warned not to talk, but—well, anyhow, Liane, this isn't a very cheerful conversation for our last evening. What time's Bill arriving tomorrow?"

"Just a minute," I said. "I want to know about this. Did you know that Ann's mother went off her head and committed suicide?"

"No—I didn't. That accounts for a lot. I didn't want to distress you any further, Liane, with grisly details—but I was over at Maidstone this morning, and they say that Ann has gone clean round the bend. They thought it might be just temporary shock and that she'd recover in time for the trial. But in view of what you've just told me, I shouldn't think there could be any other verdict than detention during Her Majesty's pleasure."

I shuddered. Hugh took my hand and patted it gently.

"Try not to think about it too much," he advised. "At any rate, it wasn't Diana Metcalfe. And Michael will be much happier with Sonia Phillips than he ever could have been with Ann. Things do work out, you know, in a macabre sort of way."

I sat down in one of the big chairs and lit a cigarette.

"D'you remember," I said, "when you told me to use my intelligence—"

In spite of my gloom, the expression of concern on Hugh's face nearly made me laugh out loud. He looked really stricken.

"Liane, darling, I've always taken an astringent line with you. Don't you see I *had* to? But for God's sake don't tell me you minded the ridiculous things I said—"

I did laugh then.

"No," I said. "It wasn't that. I mean, no offence was taken. What I meant was that I've only realised in the last two days just how much I *didn't* use my intelligence! I had a clue all the time—something you didn't even know about—and which ought to have told me the truth, or at least given me an inkling, before you ever set foot in Staple Green at all."

"What on earth are you talking about?"

"It was that china bowl," I said. "Sir Henry's famous *famille rose.* He was telling me about it that night at Betty's party a week before the murder. He said he'd bought it a few days before in London, and it hadn't yet arrived. He was full of it, and he invited me up to see it at his house. I never went, though I gather most of the village did. Anyway, the morning after he was taken ill, Ann Qualtrough came in to see Betty and she remarked jokingly that it was a good thing she had an alibi—that she hadn't been inside Oakhurst since the day before Betty's party. That bowl was broken on the night of the murder and the bits were thrown away. Therefore, if Ann was speaking the truth about not having been to Oakhurst for a week, she couldn't ever have seen the thing. *But* when Mr. Qualtrough was talking about it being a Samson copy and the mark on the bottom which showed it, Ann chipped in and agreed that the 'S' mark was very inconspicuous and added that she'd hardly been able to distinguish it herself. So—"

"Well, I'm blowed!" Hugh said. "And you never thought of mentioning that little detail to me! A fine colleague *you* are!"

"I'm sorry," I said humbly. "It came to me in my bath yesterday morning. And by that time it scarcely seemed worth while—"

"The next time we take on a case together," Hugh said, "I'm going to hire a special bathroom for you. And every time Spragg and I are stuck and we can't make any sense of the evidence, I'm going to lock you in that room and wait for you to have an inspiration. I don't know what it is about hot water, but—"

Howard opened the door and tiptoed into the room in a conspiratorial manner. He glanced furtively over his shoulder and then produced from behind his back a charming little green Bristol glass decanter and a piece of holly-sprigged wrapping-paper.

"Quick, Lee," he whispered. "It's Betty's present and I can't make the blasted string stay on. She'll be down in a second—will you hide it in your room and do it up for me some time tomorrow?"

I just had time to thrust it behind the drawing-room curtains before Betty's step sounded on the stairs.

"All this business of Christmas," Howard groaned, mopping his brow and making for the decanter, "is a very great strain. Well, Gordon here's to you! And I hope if you're ever down in this part of the world in the future you'll come and look us up."

"Yes, you must," Betty said warmly. "It would be nice to meet again in—in more cheerful circumstances."

"Thank you," Hugh said. "I should like to do that." He put down his glass and glanced at his watch. "And now I really must push along. Mr. Willis will be getting anxious. He sits up for me in carpet slippers and the most revolting old dressing-gown you ever saw. Goodnight, Betty—goodnight, Sandys. And thank you both very much for all the kind hospitality."

I went with him as far as the front door.

"Give my regards to Bill," Hugh said. "I'm sorry I missed seeing him. Liane, I've got a small Christmas present for you. If I give it to you now, will you promise not to open it before the day after tomorrow?"

"No," I said. "It wouldn't be a bit of good promising because I should only break it. But anyway, Hugh, you shouldn't—"

"Rubbish," Hugh replied briskly. "C.I.D. narks always expect a Christmas box from the boss. Here you are. Goodbye, Liane—happy Christmas—take care of yourself."

He thrust a small packet into my hand and had gone almost before I could open my mouth.

I stood in the hall, turning the little box over and over in my hands, and then I opened it. From a nest of cotton wool I picked out a small old-fashioned brooch. It was made of pearls and garnets, beautifully set in gold, in the shape of a true lovers' knot.

While I stood looking at it, I heard the sound of the Lancia starting up, changing gear, fading away into silence.

I went back slowly to the drawing-room.

"What about an early night?" Betty said. "Personally I'm exhausted with all that wrapping up, and Howard ought to grab the opportunity—"

As she spoke, the telephone in the hall started to ring…

ALSO AVAILABLE

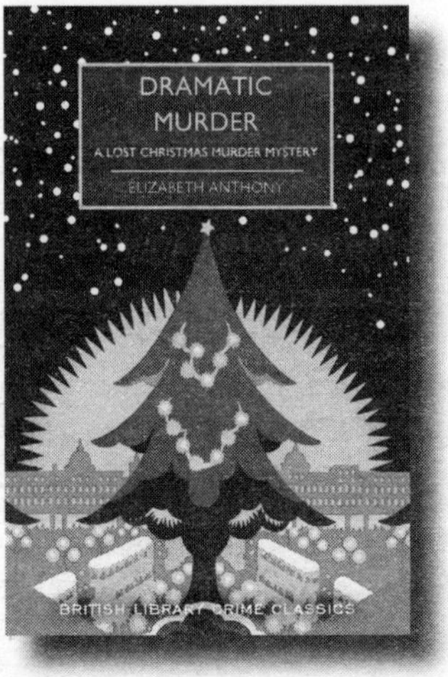

Dimpson McCabe—Dimpsie—has invited all of his closest friends of the theatre world to join him for Christmas at his castle on a private island a few hours' drive from Edinburgh. The festivities have barely had a chance to begin when poor Dimpsie is found draped atop the Christmas tree, electrocuted by the lights with which it is festooned.

The Sheriff's Court yields a verdict of Accidental Death, but in the swirling snow suspicion is dancing among the flakes. Through Dimpsie's cadre of directors, producers, actors, secretaries and agents runs a hot streak of hidden grievances and theatrical scheming, and as the group return to London the dogged Inspector Smith begins to circle, seeking to find the leading man or prima donna responsible for this ghoulish crime.

First published in 1948 and lost for over 75 years, this classic seasonal murder mystery is long overdue its bedazzling return to print.

ALSO AVAILABLE IN THE BRITISH LIBRARY CRIME CLASSICS SERIES

Big Ben Strikes Eleven	DAVID MAGARSHACK
Death of an Author	E. C. R. LORAC
The Black Spectacles	JOHN DICKSON CARR
Death of a Bookseller	BERNARD J. FARMER
The Wheel Spins	ETHEL LINA WHITE
Someone from the Past	MARGOT BENNETT
Who Killed Father Christmas?	ED. MARTIN EDWARDS
Twice Round the Clock	BILLIE HOUSTON
The White Priory Murders	CARTER DICKSON
The Port of London Murders	JOSEPHINE BELL
Murder in the Basement	ANTHONY BERKELEY
Fear Stalks the Village	ETHEL LINA WHITE
The Cornish Coast Murder	JOHN BUDE
Suddenly at His Residence	CHRISTIANNA BRAND
The Edinburgh Mystery	ED. MARTIN EDWARDS
Checkmate to Murder	E. C. R. LORAC
The Spoilt Kill	MARY KELLY
Smallbone Deceased	MICHAEL GILBERT

The Story of Classic Crime in 100 Books	MARTIN EDWARDS
The Pocket Detective: 100+ Puzzles	KATE JACKSON
The Pocket Detective 2: 100+ More Puzzles	KATE JACKSON

Many of our titles are also available
in eBook, large print and audio editions